They Watched the Flames and Talked,

and then Noah kissed her gently, in a way that left her longing for more. With an uncharacteristic boldness, she held his face still so she could return his kiss. Noah froze for an instant, surprised; then his arms tightened as his lips moved over hers.

When she didn't pull away he parted her lips almost imperceptibly until he was able to taste the sweetness of her mouth for the first time. Somehow his sorcery kept her fear at bay, allowing her to feel desire again, to feel like a woman again after so long.

The scars of her past were fading in the shadows cast by the firelight.

LUCY HAMILTON
is happily married and the mother of a young daughter. She writes in her spare time and, she says, she looks forward to "translating a lifelong affection for books into a new career."

Dear Reader:

Romance readers have been enthusiastic about Silhouette Special Editions for years. And that's not by accident: Special Editions were the first of their kind and continue to feature realistic stories with heightened romantic tension.

The longer stories, sophisticated style, greater sensual detail and variety that made Special Editions popular are the same elements that will make you want to read book after book.

We hope that you enjoy this Special Edition today, and will enjoy many more.

The Editors at Silhouette Books

LUCY HAMILTON
The Bitter With the Sweet

Silhouette Special Edition
Published by Silhouette Books New York
America's Publisher of Contemporary Romance

Silhouette Books by Lucy Hamilton

A Woman's Place (SE #18)
All's Fair (SE #92)
Shooting Star (SE #172)
The Bitter with the Sweet (SE #206)

 SILHOUETTE BOOKS, a Division of Simon & Schuster, Inc.
1230 Avenue of the Americas, New York, N.Y. 10020

ISBN: 0-671-53706-7

First Silhouette Books printing December, 1984

10 9 8 7 6 5 4 3 2 1

Map by Ray Lundgren

America's Publisher of Contemporary Romance

Printed in the U.S.A.

BC91

The Bitter
With the Sweet

Chapter One

$\mathscr{T}$he midday sky was a brilliant blue, the air thick and sultry, leaves drooping wearily on the trees as Indiana University simmered in the early-September heat. Walking to lunch on this sweltering Monday, Leigh Michaels fantasized longingly about cool mountain streams and cold ocean breakers, and when she neared the entrance to the Memorial Union her pace quickened in anticipation of the air-conditioned comfort within. The building was usually on the chilly side of comfortable, just what she needed to counteract the muggy heat.

A vast gothic fantasy in white Indiana limestone, the Union was a hub of university activity, stretching for more than two blocks along Bloomington's Seventh Street. It housed, among other things, several restaurants. Leigh crossed the slate-floored lobby and mounted a long flight of marble steps to the mezzanine floor, then followed the maze of hallways that wound its way through the building as she made for the Commons.

A large snack bar-cum-grill, the Commons had a

cafeteria-style serving line and a cheerfully raucous atmosphere. Every available inch of space was crowded with tables and chairs, all filled with students, talking, laughing, eating and even studying amid the furor. Leigh threaded her way through the crush and took her place at the end of the queue, fanning her warm face with her hand as the line moved slowly forward. The stack of trays had dwindled to almost nothing when she reached it, and she stooped awkwardly to pick one up, struggling to retain her grip on both her purse and the large leather artist's portfolio she carried.

"May I get you a tray?"

Leigh made a convulsive grab for her portfolio and straightened, shaking her wayward red-gold curls out of her face. The speaker, a broad, dark-haired, good-looking man, stood behind her in line, smiling at her with warm interest in his eyes.

"Yes," she replied with a cool, polite nod. "Thank you."

"My pleasure." He picked up two trays, but instead of placing one in her hand, he reached around her to slide it onto the tray rack. For a few seconds she was trapped between his bulk and the unyielding bars of the rack, and she shrank back as he leaned over her, his extended arm brushing fleetingly against her breasts before it was withdrawn. She held her breath, cringing uneasily away from that touch, disliking that closeness and unable to relax until the brief contact had ended.

After what seemed like hours he straightened, and she moved quickly away. She *hated* being crowded that way, being touched. All too aware that the man was still close behind her in the line—too close, as far as she was concerned—Leigh pushed her tray quickly along, distractedly selecting a small salad and a cup of iced tea before stopping at the grill.

"What'll it be?"

"A cheeseburger with lettuce, tomato and mayonnaise," Leigh replied, but the cook, a plump woman of sixty or so, leaned over her condiment table, unable to hear above the noise of the lunchtime crowd.

"Cheeseburger with *what?*"

"*Lettuce, tomato and mayonnaise!*" Leigh shouted, and the cook grinned.

"Got it! It'll be just a minute, honey." Leigh nodded and moved her tray farther along, out of the way of the other customers. She leaned a hip against the rack and settled herself to wait.

"Excuse me." The deep voice belonged to her knight-errant of the tray stand, who jostled her slightly as the line of hungry students clogged the serving area. "Is it always this crowded in here?" He was very close to her again, too close, and once again Leigh inched uneasily away from him.

"It's usually crowded at lunch," she told him tersely, then, very deliberately, turned her back on him as she faced the grill again, wishing the cook would hurry with her cheeseburger.

"Shouldn't be much longer," commented the dark-haired man, and Leigh half turned to give him a cool nod.

He didn't quite fit the classic mold of tall, dark and handsome, she noted disinterestedly; he was only an inch or so taller than her five feet nine inches, but he was nevertheless considerably larger than she, with a broad, powerful frame. He was dark, though, and good-looking, with a generous measure of self-confidence added to the mixture. Exactly what she didn't need.

Leigh didn't like handsome, self-confident men, particularly when they seemed to feel they were owed a return on a small favor. She smiled gratefully at the cook as her cheeseburger was placed on the counter, then took it and moved away.

"See you." The comment checked her progress, and the dark man stepped in front of her, blocking her way to the cashier. She looked him up and down, her eyes cold, and thought idly that he resembled a brick wall barring her path. He had the same sort of massive solidity.

"I doubt that," she said curtly and moved around him to pay for her lunch. Some people just don't know how to take a hint, do they? She wondered what it would take to get through to this particular man. A flat statement, something like, "Go away, you bother me," might do it, but she wasn't too sure. Men like this seldom paid any attention to anyone's wishes but their own, as she knew all too well. A bitter little smile twisting her lips, she took her change and carried her tray into the melee of the Commons.

Whatever his faults, the pushy stranger had been absolutely right about one thing: The Commons was even more crowded than usual. As she looked around she could at first see no unoccupied tables. She worked her way through the mob until she spotted an empty table in the corner behind the jukebox and pounced on it triumphantly, dropping her portfolio and tray onto the scarred wood of the tabletop and sagging into a hard chair with a sigh of relief.

She had only her lunch hour to prepare for her 1:30 class, and she fished in her portfolio with one hand as she took the first bite of her cheeseburger. After a moment's rummaging she produced a sheaf of lecture notes to review while she ate, insuring that she would present a coherent class. With the ease of long practice she tuned out the hubbub all around and focused her attention on her notes.

"May I join you?"

Whenever the Commons was crowded, one expected to share a table with a stranger, but Leigh had not expected the request to come from the pushy stranger, and her dismay was obvious when she looked up and recognized him.

He saw her dismay, and something like regret flickered across his face. "I don't mean to bother you," he went on with a hint of diffidence, "but I honestly don't see anywhere else to sit." He looked around the crowded room, then back to her with an apologetic shrug.

"All right," she sighed, and moved her portfolio off the table so he could put his tray down. She had looked around the room, too, and she knew that what he said was true, but it was the diffidence, that hint of shyness, that disarmed her.

"I appreciate this," he told her as he squeezed mustard from a plastic packet onto a ham sandwich. "I was afraid I'd have to eat standing up."

"Mm-hm," was Leigh's uncooperative reply. She hadn't really looked at him in the line, only noted his size and solidity, but while he was occupied with his sandwich, she studied him with her clinically appraising artist's eye and saw an unusually attractive man. He was, as she had noted, something under six feet tall, perhaps five ten or so, and strongly built, with broad shoulders and muscular limbs. She would be taller than he with heels on, Leigh thought with a hidden smile, but he was twice her size, nonetheless.

He looked to be in his mid-thirties, ten years older than she, and certainly older than most of the students who patronized the Commons. He was better dressed, too, in a well-tailored, summer-weight suit. His face was strong-boned, too angular to be classically handsome, but very attractive in a hard, masculine way. His cheekbones were high, his eyes deep-set beneath level brows, his jaw square and cleanly carved, and his lips were firm, with a deep crease at either side. His hair was wavy and thick and cut fairly short, and shone jet-black beneath the glaringly bright lights, but his eyes, unexpectedly, were blue. His skin tone matched his hair rather than his eyes; it was darkly tanned, with olive undertones, and at the open neck of his shirt she could see the beginnings of thick chest hair.

With detached objectivity Leigh decided that he was one of the most striking men she had ever seen, and wondered with a touch of amusement if he had ever considered working as an artist's model. He didn't look as if he needed the paltry money it paid, but her friend Kate Holland would kill, she thought with some amusement, to have him model for her life-drawing class.

She was half-smiling at the thought when he looked up from his sandwich and caught her staring at him. Her study of him had been thorough, and he watched her flush, his expression a mixture of amusement at her discomfiture and puzzlement at her smile.

"I'm sorry I was staring," she apologized a bit defensive-ly. "I'm an artist, and I tend to study faces."

"That's perfectly all right." He smiled, amused by her embarrassment. "I imagine I should be flattered that I have an interesting face. Are you a painter?"

"No." Leigh shook her head briefly.

"A sculptor?"

"No."

"What *do* you do?"

"Fiber art." He raised an inquiring eyebrow at her terse reply, and she sighed, then elaborated. "Weaving, quilting, appliqué, embroidery, fabric painting and dyeing, knitting, crochet—anything to do with fibers and textiles." She looked down at her plate, ready to end the conversation at that, but he refused to take the hint.

"Are you a student?"

"No."

"Then you're on the faculty?" he persisted, and she answered with a brief nod. "In that case we're colleagues. I'm here as Visiting Professor of International Law this year. I'm Noah Burke." He extended his hand. "And you are . . . ?"

"Leigh Michaels."

Leigh was watching his face as she spoke her name, and she saw a flash of surprise, as if he were startled to learn who she was. That was nonsense, of course; there was nothing surprising about her name, but she thought she saw a moment's hesitation, as well, before he moved his ex-tended hand an inch closer.

Reluctantly she reached out to him. This was going farther than a case of two strangers sharing a table, and she wanted to put a stop to it for the simple reason that she had no interest in this or any other man. The sooner Mr. Noah Burke, Visiting Professor of International Law, realized that, the happier she would be. She withdrew her hand after the briefest of contacts and dropped her gaze to her plate, once again signaling the end of the conversation. Once again her companion declined to take the hint.

"Michaels," he repeated thoughtfully, and Leigh looked up again, exasperated, waiting for some new variant on the old don't-I-know-you-from-somewhere line. All he said, though, was, "You look very young to be a faculty member. What do you teach?" Sighing in frustration, Leigh met his smile with a look of blank indifference.

"Woven and Constructed Textile Design," she quoted from the course listing. "I'm a lecturer in the Fine Arts Department." This time she knew she was not mistaken. For the briefest instant his face had held frank surprise, followed almost immediately by a slight narrowing of his eyes. Leigh was having none of it. She didn't know or care why he should be surprised at what she taught, but Mr. Law Professor Burke could just turn his curiosity elsewhere. "Look, I don't mean to be rude, Mr. Burke, but I have a class to give this afternoon, and I need to review my lecture notes." She indicated the stack of papers beside her tray. "Will you excuse me?"

His eyes flicked to the notes, then back to her face, penetrating, searching. After a moment he nodded. "Of course," he replied equably, his curiosity apparently under control. "I have some reading of my own to do." He opened the folder he had brought with him, and with a sigh of relief Leigh devoted herself to her cheeseburger and her lecture. At last he seemed to have gotten the message.

For some time they ate in silence, Leigh ignoring her table partner, assuming he was as absorbed in his work as she was in hers. She was unpleasantly surprised, therefore, to glance up momentarily and discover him staring at her. He didn't drop his gaze when she caught him at it, either, only smiled slightly and continued to watch her.

As unnerved as though *she* had been caught staring again, Leigh looked hastily back down at her notes and tried to continue with her review. She was definitely not imagining things; the man was studying her like a bug under a magnifying glass! Though she tried to concentrate on her lecture, with his gaze on her, practically boring through her, she was unable to make sense of the notes. She shifted her shoulders uneasily, read the same sentence for the third time and realized to her disgust that she still had no idea what it said. When she risked another glance and found that he was still watching her with that same unabashed interest, she gave up.

"I have to go to class," she excused herself curtly. "Good-bye, Mr. Burke." Ignoring her half-eaten cheese-burger and nearly full iced tea, she gathered her belongings, said something inane and conventional when he rose courte-ously to bid her good-bye and made her escape.

Escape was no doubt too melodramatic a word, Leigh told herself as she left the crowded Commons. Still, some-thing about the way he'd been looking at her made her uneasy, even more uneasy than his pushiness in line. Which was really pretty silly, she reminded herself sternly, since she had been staring at him first. Her staring, though, had been an artist's impersonal appraisal, while there had been something uncomfortably personal about the way he had looked at her, something almost predatory, and it had begun when he learned her name.

Her name. Why should her name be of any interest to a total stranger? And why should he be so surprised to learn what course she taught? None of it made any sense to Leigh, but she shivered a little as she hurried along the hall.

She welcomed the sun on her skin when she walked outside, the golden heat easing the tension in her, but something, a prickling between her shoulder blades, kept her from relaxing totally. She glanced back at the building she had just left. The white limestone gleamed in the sunlight; in contrast the doorway gaped darkly, and framed in that darkness stood Noah Burke, watching her with an intent, unwavering gaze.

Leigh stared back at him for a moment, then turned to walk quickly away, suddenly, irrationally, frightened.

Noah gazed after the hurrying woman for a minute, then turned away, wondering if he'd lost his touch. Somehow he had managed to frighten her, and he had deliberately tried to avoid that once he realized just who she was. He was certain it was not his name that had set off her internal alarms, for he had been watching her face when he told her who he was and he'd seen no flicker of reaction. No, she didn't know who he was—yet.

It was too bad he had scared her. If he had been able to draw her out, to get her to talk about herself, he could have learned a great deal, all in the guise of lunchtime chat. He was good at drawing out information people had no idea they were giving him, it was an innate talent that served him well as a lawyer, and he was disappointed that he'd missed the opportunity to use it on Miss Leigh Michaels. The little he had learned about her had only whetted his appetite for more.

He tried to concentrate as he walked outside. God, it was hot! The thick, heavy air engulfed him, making a mockery of the autumnal date. He didn't understand how Leigh Michaels had managed to look so cool. That was one thing he'd learned about her, anyway. She managed to look cool and fresh even in this weather. He had learned that she was not interested in lunch-line pickups, that she was somewhat prickly, that she became afraid more easily than he would have expected and, of course, that she was beautiful.

Noah knew many beautiful women, models, actresses and dancers he dated at home in New York, but this woman was truly lovely, and he could still form an astonishingly vivid image of her in his mind. Tall and slender, nearly as tall as he, in fact, she had hair of a shade somewhere between red and gold, loosely curly and cut in feathery layers to frame her face and fall casually to her shoulders. Her eyes were large and green and slanted like a cat's in a heart-shaped face with delicately classic bones. There was a sprinkling of freckles across her small, straight nose, and her mouth was pink and soft and curved at the corners as if she was just waiting to smile. There was a sadness in her eyes that belied that smiling mouth, though, and Noah wondered what could have put it there; she looked too young to have seen the dark side of life.

She didn't look like an agitator either, of course, but if he was losing his touch, he might also be losing his ability to read his opponents. She would be an interesting adversary, though, he mused as he ran up the steps of the Law School, a very interesting adversary.

"It was really kind of weird, Kate," Leigh said as she closed the classroom door and walked with Kate Holland down the hall. "First, he kept trying to pick me up in the line, even though I made it *very* clear that I wasn't interested, and then he came to my table!"

"To have lunch with you?"

"I'm not sure. Not like a date or anything. You know how it is when the Commons is crowded; if you have an empty seat at your table, someone will ask if they can sit there."

"Mm-hm, I know. Did he just sit, or did he try to get friendly?"

"He *talked*. I kept trying to get it through to him that I didn't want to sit and chat, but he just kept on asking me questions. He seemed to be pretty thick-skinned, not to mention nosy."

"Thick-skinned or just interested?" Kate asked with a knowing glint in her eye, and Leigh scowled.

"A hide like a rhinoceros," she said firmly. "He asked what kind of artist I was, and then if I was a student, and then he generously passed along the information that he's a visiting law professor."

"Very impressive," Kate interjected with a little moue of appreciation.

Leigh's scowl deepened. "It doesn't take much to impress you, does it? I don't know why Ken puts up with you."

"Just because I'm married, as the saying goes, it doesn't mean I'm dead. Anyway, Ken knows he's my man. Now, tell me what this mystery man of yours said."

"He's not *my* mystery man! That's all he said, anyway.

He's a visiting law professor, and his name is Burke, and he asked my name and what I teach."

"Did you talk about anything else?"

"No, thank goodness, but he looked surprised when he heard my name. I thought I was imagining things, but I wasn't, Kate, really. I saw his face, and he was surprised, even though he hid it right away."

"Why on earth should he be surprised by your name? It's not *that* unusual, after all."

"If I knew why, it wouldn't bother me."

"It shouldn't bother you anyway. Maybe he's just interested in you. What happened next?"

"I told him I had to go over my notes for class, and he finally took the hint that I didn't want to talk. And don't start telling me," she added, as Kate opened her mouth to protest, "that I should have flirted with him. You know how I feel about that!"

"I just want you to be happy. What you need is a good man and a good relationship—"

"Kate, I know you mean well, but you have got to stop this matchmaking propaganda!"

"Okay, I'll be quiet . . . for now." Leigh shot her friend a fulminating glance, but Kate was unrepentant and undeterred. "Just tell me what he did that was so weird . . . besides looking surprised at your name."

"Well, I wasn't paying any attention to him while I was reading my notes, but when I looked up he was staring at me, really staring, studying me, like a psychotic killer in a movie, or something, and when I caught him at it, he didn't look away, or look embarrassed; he just kept watching me. It's creepy to have someone stare at you like that, so I left. I didn't even wait to finish my lunch, and when I got outside the Union I looked back, and he was standing in the doorway, still staring at me. It was *creepy!*"

"It doesn't sound creepy to me." Kate unlocked the door of the office they shared. "It sounds to me like you have an overactive imagination. 'Psychotic killer!' " she snorted.

"Honestly, Leigh, you've been watching too many late-late movies! He just sounds to me like a man who's interested in getting to know you better."

"Oh, please!" Leigh dumped her purse and portfolio on her desk. "I made it as clear as I could that I didn't want anything to do with him. In fact, I was just plain rude to the man. Why should he want to get to know me better?"

Kate grinned. "He looked at you, didn't he?"

"What if he did? I certainly didn't want him to," Leigh said tartly, and Kate laughed again.

"If you don't want 'em to look, Leigh, you'll have to wear an overcoat and dark glasses. I wish I were four inches taller, with that gorgeous hair, and—"

"You're just fine the way you are," Leigh interrupted as Kate began a familiar refrain. "And you have a husband who adores you, so don't complain." Ken Holland thought his wife was the most beautiful woman he had ever seen, and told her so frequently.

Kate grinned as she dropped into her desk chair. "So you were nasty and rude to this mysterious stranger, and he was immediately enslaved by your beauty—"

"Kate . . ." Leigh interrupted on a note of warning, but Kate grinned broadly and ignored her.

"—*and* your charming personality. What does he look like?"

"Oh, I don't know." Leigh shrugged. "Big, but not tall, not much taller than I am, in fact. Dark hair and blue eyes, like Ken has, but a different sort of face than Ken's, not as nice."

"You can do better than that. Here." Kate flipped a sketch pad and pencil onto Leigh's desk. "Draw him."

Leigh felt an odd reluctance to attempt a likeness of Noah Burke, but Kate could be very persuasive, and very persistent, when she wished. The portrait that emerged from beneath Leigh's quick-moving pencil was a good likeness, the economical strokes and subtle shading reproducing his physical characteristics and hinting at the strength, the arrogance and the touch of humor she had seen.

Leigh passed the sketch pad back, and Kate studied it for several minutes before looking up, wide-eyed. "He's gorgeous," she breathed, not joking at all. "What's his name again?"

"Noah Burke."

"His *name* is even gorgeous!" The teasing note was back, and Leigh rolled her eyes at the ceiling in mock disgust.

"He has his parents to thank for the name *and* for the face," she pointed out. "Anyway, gorgeous or not, I still think the way he was staring at me was strange, and I didn't like it."

"Don't be paranoid. You've lived like a nun long enough, and you should be glad you've had the good luck to run into a man who is obviously interested in you."

"I don't think it's so obvious," Leigh countered doggedly, "and I think he finally got the message that *I'm* not interested. I'll probably never even see him again." She finished on a defiant note. Happily married Kate felt that the one thing Leigh needed was a man in her life, while Leigh had her own reasons for wishing to avoid any sort of romantic entanglement.

She ripped the sketch of Noah Burke from the pad and glanced at it briefly, then crumpled it and tossed the wad of paper in the wastebasket. With a vague sense of relief she repeated, "I'll never see him again. And now can we get down to some important business, like the afternoon mail?"

"Ah, the afternoon mail," Kate drawled. "*Such* a fascinating topic, the mail. Let me see . . ." Kate searched the chaos atop her desk for a moment, then produced Leigh's mail with a little grunt of triumph. "Here you are, my sweet." She presented it with a flourish. "Your mail."

"Thank you, my dear." Leigh smiled saccharine-sweetly and took the stack of envelopes, sifting through them as she returned to her desk. There were a few moments of silence, broken only by the tearing of envelopes as Leigh opened them and scanned the contents, then, "What!" she sputtered, staring at one letter. "They can't be serious about this!"

"Can't be serious about what? And who can't be? I mean, what *is* that, Leigh?"

"This?" She waved it angrily in the air. "This is an outrage, that's what this is! I can't even believe this! I can't believe they mean this!"

"Can't believe *who* means *what?*" Kate yelled in frustration and snatched the letter from Leigh's hand. She scanned it quickly, muttering under her breath as she read, then slapped the pages back onto Leigh's desk, as irate as Leigh. "They must be kidding!"

Leigh lifted the letter again, regarding it with distaste. "I have the distinct impression that they're not."

"Swell. The pro-strikers are going to have a field day with this little jewel, aren't they?"

"They sure are, and I only hope we can talk them out of voting on it, because they could probably get a strike vote out of this."

"When's the next meeting?"

"Thursday night, so I'll have to see if I can talk to the administration people before then, just so I have something to tell everyone. I don't know what I can say, though, after reading this. The administration has 'no plans to restrict class size at this time,' and they have 'retained legal counsel,' and they 'hope this matter can be resolved expeditiously and with results satisfactory to both parties involved.' No kidding, they've retained legal counsel; it would take another lawyer to make sense of all this mumbo jumbo!" Leigh leaned back in her chair and sighed wearily. "This is what I get for agreeing to chair the committee, isn't it?"

"'Fraid so, kid. We need you, though. It was your complaint about class size that got this all started, and it's your voice we need to speak for us."

"That's very flattering, Kate, but I never expected anything like this. I thought we'd form a committee in favor of reasonable class enrollment, get some petitions signed, the administration would agree to limits on class sizes, and that would be that. I never expected to be involved in meetings with 'legal counsel,' and talk of strike votes by the teaching assistants and junior faculty, and I certainly never saw myself as a crusader. This whole thing has gotten out of hand!"

"It's certainly gotten involved," Kate admitted, "but at least it hasn't been terribly public so far. It's really just been you and the administration people arguing about budget versus quality of education."

"Not for long," Leigh predicted gloomily. "This kind of flat refusal, along with the 'legal counsel' business, means there may be a strike after all, and the papers aren't going to ignore that, or even the hint that it might be a possibility. We're all going to be famous before this is over, and this isn't the kind of fame I want."

"I know. I'm not crazy about it either, and I don't want a strike any more than you do, Leigh, but it's too late to back out now. You know we have a strong case to make, and like it or not, you are our spokesperson."

"The trouble is, your spokesperson can see the other side of the issue, too. The university doesn't have a lot of extra money to throw around, and smaller classes mean more teaching assistants and junior faculty to teach the introductory classes, and that means spending more money. Somehow we have to work out a compromise."

"If we can."

"Well, I'm going to try every means at my disposal to see that we can, starting with a little chat with Dean Anderson and the dreaded 'legal counsel.' I'll have to insist that they see me before that meeting on Thursday, or I can't promise there will be anyone to teach classes next week."

She reached for the phone on her desk, and as she lifted the receiver, Kate murmured, "Good luck, Leigh."

"I'll need it," was the dry reply.

Chapter Two

 $\mathcal{T}$ he meeting was finally scheduled for late Wednesday afternoon. Both the Dean of Fiscal Administration and Planning and the highly vaunted legal counsel had extremely full schedules, and Leigh hung up the phone with the impression that she was expected to be grateful for being allowed to meet with them at all. That didn't sit well with her, and she was in no mood to be conciliatory as she hurried toward the meeting room at 4:45 on Wednesday. Personally she thought the possibility of a strike, however remote, warranted some rearrangement of schedules, but apparently the opposition didn't regard the issue as seriously as she did.

The opposition. Leigh sighed at her own choice of term. She was becoming as confrontation oriented as the most hotheaded members of the committee, and that was something she wished to avoid. Someone had to remain cool, to speak with the voice of reason, if a strike was to be avoided, and that someone had to be she. For that reason, she had declined to bring her own "legal counsel" along, though the graduate law student who served in that capacity had offered to come. She would no doubt be grateful for his assistance at a future date, but she didn't want to give the impression that she was spoiling for a fight, so she was heading into this meeting as she had to so many others, on her own, a bit edgy, but not afraid.

She was just on time as she knocked softly and then opened the door of the meeting room in response to a low "Come in" from inside.

The door blocked her view of most of the small room, but she was facing the dean, who rose from the conference table as she entered. A small, dapper, ruddy-faced man in his fifties, he had been her administration contact since the issue was first raised, and she had had frequent dealings with him. She couldn't quite make herself like him; though he was always polite and seemingly cordial, he gave away almost nothing, and negotiating with him was a frustrating experience.

"Miss Michaels, come in," he invited. "I'm happy to see you again, though I must admit I'd prefer different circumstances."

"So would I, Dean Anderson, but I'm afraid we have a problem to deal with first."

"I suppose we do," he said with faint regret, then ushered her into the cramped room, "but I hope we can resolve it quickly. You haven't met our legal adviser yet, have you?"

"No, I—" Leigh broke off as she moved past the door and saw the other occupant of the room, who was also rising politely to greet her. The dreaded "legal counsel" was not a stranger to her, after all; the dreaded "legal counsel" was Noah Burke, the same pushy stranger who had so unnerved her in the Commons on Monday! Her face went very still for a moment.

She barely heard the dean's introduction, and when she spoke, her eyes and her voice were chilly. "Actually, Dean Anderson, we have met, but Mr. Burke didn't see fit at the time to make me aware of just whom I was meeting. Good afternoon, Mr. Burke." She gave him a cool nod, but made no offer to shake his hand before she took the chair Dean Anderson held for her.

Leigh said nothing else; she deliberately kept her face expressionless, but beneath her unruffled exterior, she was seething. Damn the man for his sneaky, unethical conduct! She hadn't been imagining his unusual interest in her after all; he'd known who she was as soon as she told him her name, and he'd known that she was unaware of just who *he* was, so he had taken advantage of her ignorance to pump her for information!

"Miss Michaels?" Dean Anderson cleared his throat and called her wandering attention back to the business at hand.

"I'm sorry, what were you saying?" Leigh forced herself to concentrate. This was neither the time nor the place to deal with Mr. Underhanded Noah Burke.

Two hours later she was tired, hungry, frustrated and wondering if she could deal with anything at all. She had made all her points about class size and excellence in education, she had argued and explained and done everything but plead, but she had still gotten nowhere. Arguing with Dean Anderson was like punching a marshmallow; she hit him with her best arguments, and he just took the blows and bounced back again with the same bland refusal to compromise.

Noah Burke had, to her surprise, stayed out of the discussion, speaking only when Dean Anderson asked him to clarify a legal point, but his presence had done nothing to smooth Leigh's ruffled feathers. She almost wished he *had* argued with her; she'd have loved the excuse to lash out at him verbally, and was frustrated anew at being unable to do so. Frustrated, too, by the lack of results the meeting had produced.

"Then you will keep this issue open and let me take it back to the committee?" she asked, pressing the dean for a clear reply.

"You drive a hard bargain, my dear, but yes, the issue will remain open, for now, at least."

"I haven't driven a bargain of any kind yet," she told him with a small, tired smile. "If I may speak plainly, though, and confidentially . . . ?" He glanced at Noah Burke, then nodded. Leigh breathed deeply and took the plunge. "I am not making a threat, sir, but speaking realistically, there will have to be some sort of compromise on this issue, or I will not be able to prevent a strike."

"The situation could go that far?"

"It could, and I don't want to see that happen any more than I want to see the quality of education compromised by parsimonious budgeting." Leigh's soft voice delayed the impact of her words, and it was a split second before the dean's eyes narrowed as her meaning sank in. She had known that Noah Burke had been watching her throughout this meeting, evaluating and assessing, and she had an idea that he was less surprised by her bluntness than the dean was.

"I will keep that in mind, Miss Michaels," Dean Anderson said after a moment, his tone no longer indulgent. "When do you meet with your committee?"

"Tomorrow night."

"Then shall we have another meeting here, on Friday, perhaps?"

"I think that would be a good idea," Leigh replied with a coolness equal to his.

He nodded. "Very well, Friday at five, if that is agreeable to you both. Now, you must excuse me, it's gotten quite late. Good evening." With a little bow to Leigh and a nod to Noah Burke, he left them.

"So the gloves are off at last."

Leigh had been slipping papers back into her briefcase, but she looked up at Noah Burke then with a brief, cold glance. "If you want to put it that way. I just thought Dean Anderson should know what sort of situation he's dealing with."

"How well can you control your committee members?"

"I don't *control* them, Mr. Burke. This is a democracy.

We have a serious grievance, and we will vote on the course of action to take. I hope a strike does not become necessary."

"So do I. Strikes rarely improve a situation, though they may resolve it."

Leigh looked across the table at him, skepticism in her eyes. "An admirable sentiment, from someone like yourself."

" 'Someone like myself'?" He wasn't taking her seriously. In fact, he was actually enjoying this sparring match; it showed in his eyes, and somehow that was just too much for Leigh to take.

" 'Someone like yourself,' Mr. Burke," she repeated with frosty emphasis. "Someone who isn't overburdened with ethics. Someone who tries to pry information out of an opponent without making himself known. Someone a little bit sneaky, a little bit underhanded."

His small smile broadened. "The gloves *are* off, aren't they?"

"Yes, they are, and don't tell me you're surprised. That stunt you pulled in the Commons was unfair, and you know it."

"Yes, it was unfair." Leigh was brought up short by the admission. "I apologize. I didn't know who you were when I sat at your table, but when you told me your name I should have identified myself."

"You didn't know who I was?"

"No, I didn't."

Leigh couldn't quite buy that one. "You didn't know who I was when you tried to pick me up in the line?"

"You are blunt, aren't you?" His smile widened, and he shook his head. "No, I didn't know when I tried to pick you up. Am I that obvious?"

"Painfully," she drawled. "And just to set the record straight, Mr. Burke, I am not a pickup."

He shrugged ruefully. "I know that—now. I apologize if I offended you."

"Accepted," she replied tersely. Leigh zipped her brief-case and picked up her purse. "Good evening, Mr. Burke."

"Just a moment." She paused and looked at him, impatient to be off and making no effort to hide it. "Where are you going?"

Her eyebrows rose. "To eat." The clearly understood, though unspoken, addendum was: not that it's any business of yours. She glanced at the slim digital watch on her wrist. "It is seven-fourteen."

"May I take you to dinner? We can discuss this problem further."

Leigh could feel herself going cold. She just stared at him for a moment while her face visibly paled; then she shook her head, quickly and emphatically. "No, thank you, Mr. Burke."

"May I know why not?"

"I don't think so." Leigh moved toward the door, stumbling against a chair in her agitation, almost desperate to get away from this man. She couldn't go to dinner with him, she couldn't; it was out of the question. With clumsy hands she righted the chair, but she couldn't leave the room, because he stood between her and the door, his rock-solid bulk blocking her escape. "L-look," she stammered, "I've got to go. I—I've got to—"

He ignored her plea, his own face giving nothing away. "Tell me," he said in a voice of quiet command, "why you can't have dinner with me. Are you married?"

To Noah's astonishment she gave a little spurt of half-hysterical laughter, then shook her head. "No," she said, in a quiet, bitter voice. "No, I'm not married."

"Engaged?"

She shook her head.

"Pinned? Going steady? Involved?" To each, her reply was a silent headshake. "Then what's the problem?"

Leigh shook her head again, searching for an answer to give him, because, of course, she couldn't tell him the truth. "I—I told you before," she said at last. "I'm not a pickup."

"This isn't a pickup!" he barked, exasperated. "It's late, and I know we're both hungry, and I don't feel like eating alone."

"Well, I can't imagine why you'd want to eat with me," she told him tartly. "I certainly don't want to eat with you."

He winced at that. "Look, Miss Michaels . . . Leigh, I'm sorry we got off on the wrong foot, and I sincerely apologize for failing to inform you of who I was when we met. Believe me, I never meant to take advantage of you. I would like you to have dinner with me tonight partly in reparation for that, and partly to discuss your perspective on this possible strike, and last of all because I simply don't want to eat alone. I told you I'm a visiting professor, and in the two weeks I've been here I've eaten alone far too many times. Will you take pity on me, even if you don't like me?"

There was something in this very big, very male man that suddenly reminded Leigh of a lonely little boy, and she felt herself weakening in spite of her determination to remain firm. "What did you have in mind?"

"Just something to eat." He spread his hands, palms up. "No ulterior motive. All I'm asking you for is a little of your time. No strings."

"I—" She paused and thought for a moment, then let her breath out on a long sigh. "I'll go with you, or rather, you can come with me. I'm having supper in the Commons because I have another errand to run. And we *will* discuss the committee and the possibility of this strike?"

"That's fine with me." He smiled, and the smile transformed him; a charm she could almost feel reached out to Leigh. "Anything is better than eating alone. Shall we go?"

They went. The charm had done it, somehow circumventing all Leigh's carefully crafted defenses. She couldn't really believe she was doing this, that she was having dinner with a man, but she was, and she had to deal with it, in spite of her misgivings and the fear she was feeling as she walked beside him through the early-evening quiet of the campus.

Though she had a few friends, acquaintances, really, who were men, she hadn't been out to dinner with a man in years—not since she was nineteen, in fact—and all her old terrors were returning to haunt her. She had met a handsome, charming man then, too. Tony Brown had been thirty and had seemed excitingly sophisticated to a naive nineteen-year-old. He had swept little Leigh Michaels off her feet. A few weeks after they met, over her parents' vehement protests, she had married him.

At nineteen she had been aware of the existence of "battered wives" only as a chapter in a sociology book, but she had learned, very quickly, some hard and bitter lessons. Only six weeks after their wedding she had run from Tony, driving away in her car while he, drunk, pursued her. He had rammed her car repeatedly, trying to force her off the road, and had finally sent her into a ditch. She had been badly injured in the crash, had in fact been lucky to survive, but Tony had lost control of his own car, hit a bridge abutment and been killed instantly.

Leigh had spent several weeks in the hospital, but her physical injuries had healed more easily than the psychic wounds. According to her psychiatrists she showed great resilience and strength of personality; she had emerged from her ordeal able to pick up her education where she had left off, and had established a career. She had become, to all appearances, a confident, independent woman. Even the loss of her elderly parents a year later had not broken her, but in one area the image she projected was misleading.

In one area the psychiatrists had been unable to help her, and she had finally terminated therapy. She had not had a romantic relationship in seven years, not since her love and trust had been so cruelly destroyed. She had been wildly in love with Tony, had given herself to him body and soul, and had been drawn into a nightmare of pain and terror and betrayal. In all the years that followed the memory of that betrayal had kept her from allowing anyone inside the protective wall she'd erected around herself.

She needed that protection, that wall, and despite the inauspicious beginning of their relationship, it seemed that Noah Burke was uncomfortably close to breaching it already. That made her afraid, and her fear was beginning to show. She had seen the puzzled look on his face when she moved hastily away rather than let him take her arm. He must have noticed that she was so tense that she found it difficult to make conversation as they walked, and he had no way of understanding the reason. Leigh was trying, but she knew she was unable to completely conceal her feelings with a man so near, with *him* so near.

Apparently he read the signs; although he was impeccably courteous, he made no further attempt to touch her, and he talked easily of inconsequential things, covering her stiff silence. The Commons was nearly deserted at that hour, in quiet contrast to the daytime uproar, and the table they took, in an isolated corner of the large room, gave an illusion of privacy.

"Why did you get involved in it?" he asked when they had begun to eat. "This committee and the strike business."

Leigh studied him for a moment before replying, noting the deep intelligence in his eyes, the honest interest as he waited to hear her reply. She was beginning to have trouble keeping him in his place as the villain of the piece. She didn't want him to be complicated, to be interested, to be human. She didn't want to be interested in him. Shoving the thought aside, she sipped her coffee and framed her answer.

"I never thought it would end up like this. At first it was no more than an expression of concern. Classes have to be small enough to allow effective teaching, and I thought we could get some petitions signed, point out the growing problem of class size to the administration and the policies would be changed. I never thought I would end up chairing a committee considering a strike vote, and I never wanted that. All I ever wanted was a reasonable limit on class size."

"But the situation took on a life of its own, and now you have something else entirely to deal with, don't you?"

"Exactly." Leigh sighed heavily. "I have a responsibility to see it through, but sometimes it's a lot to deal with."

"I don't suppose it helps that you're negotiating with Martin, does it?"

"Dean Anderson?" Leigh shook her head. "He's mind-boggling! I've talked and talked and talked to him, and I haven't gone anywhere but around in circles."

"He's a tough negotiator, all right," Noah agreed with a chuckle, "but I think you'll come to an agreement eventually."

Leigh shook her head, smiling wryly, then sobered. "I sincerely hope so, and I hope it happens before a strike vote is taken."

"So do I."

They ate in silence for a few moments, then Leigh pushed her empty plate away. "It's been surprisingly pleasant having dinner with you, Mr. Burke, but I have some more work to do tonight."

"What other work could you have to do at this time of night?"

"It's only eight-thirty," she pointed out, "and I have to go over to the gallery to look over an exhibit that's opening Sunday."

"Why do you have to see it?"

"I'm responsible for it. It's fiber and textile work, and a lot of the pieces are by my students."

"The students in your classes? The classes that are too large?"

"Mm-hm."

"May I go with you? To see what you're teaching, what your classes are getting too large for?"

Leigh considered it for a moment, then shrugged. "I don't see why not. I have work to do, but if you want to come along it's all right with me."

"Thank you. I'll appreciate having an expert guide." He smiled and rose with her. He had the tact not to take her arm as they walked half a block to the handsome I. M. Pei gallery, and he asked her about the exhibit with genuine interest.

"I don't really know anything about textile art, or fiber art, or even if the two are the same," he admitted. "In the long-ago days of my undergraduate education I did take a class in art appreciation, but all I can remember are Roman statuary and eighteenth-century landscapes."

"This will definitely be a change from the landscapes!" Leigh smiled, but she said no more about the exhibit, only advising him to "Wait and see."

Several of the pieces on exhibit were her students', and several more were her own, but she didn't intend to let Noah know that just yet. She was finding, to her intense surprise, that she enjoyed talking with him, and she was anticipating enjoying a little joke on him, as well. Carefully concealing her amusement, she allowed herself only a tiny smile as they entered the gallery. He walked through the exhibit at her side, watching her make notes or straighten a slightly crooked hanging, and listened to her knowledgeable comments on the rugs, flat wall pieces, three-dimensional fabric sculpture, and even garments labeled "Wearable Art."

Noah's was a quick and agile mind; he listened and absorbed her explanations of the various weaving and dyeing techniques, seeing, even before she pointed it out, where the same technique had been used to create different effects. He wandered off through the exhibit while she was discussing the lighting with a gallery employee, and some minutes later she found him in front of a wall hanging of hers. He listened attentively to her explanation of the ikat process—dyeing a pattern into the yarn itself before it was placed on the loom and woven—and how the subtle shades of green and blue had been created by dyes made from such substances as huckleberries, peony flowers and beets.

"Beets?" He was incredulous. "Wouldn't you get a dark red from beets, instead of that bright green?"

"It depends on the chemicals used to make the dye and treat the yarn. With beets you can also get a lovely peach shade and a dusty olive-green." She took a step back to look up at the large hanging whose wavelike pattern of blues and greens gave an undersea effect of fluidity and movement. Noah looked up at it with her for a moment, then turned to look sharply at her.

"How do you know so much about this one?" he asked slowly, suspicion dawning in his face; then he took a step forward to examine the small label. "'Seascape,'" he read, "'warp-ikat in wool and cotton. Artist: L. Michaels.'" He turned accusing eyes on her. "'L. Michaels?'"

Leigh struggled to keep a straight face, but her twitching lips betrayed her. "You finally figured it out!" she laughed. "I wanted to see just how long it took the big-deal lawyer to realize whose piece he was looking at!"

"Well, it took me long enough, didn't it?" he said in dry disgust. "I assume there are more pieces of yours around?" She nodded, still smiling. "Then let me see if I can pick them out." He moved purposefully off through the exhibit again, exclaiming softly in triumph each time he correctly identified an item as a creation of Leigh's. Finally he took one last look around him and turned back to her.

"Have I found them all?" She shook her head. "Damn!" he muttered. "Well, how many did I miss?"

"Just one. It's the—"

"No, don't tell me." He was scowling in frustration at the works all around him. "I'll find it if I have to stay here all night."

"There's no need for that, you know. You only came here to see my students' work, after all."

"I didn't know I'd have the opportunity to see yours as well. Now that I'm here I want to see it all."

"You're very determined, aren't you, Mr. Burke?"

"I suppose so." He shrugged. "And I think we can make it Noah now, don't you?"

"I—I guess so . . . Noah. I'm almost done here, though, so I'll give you five minutes, and then I'll show you which one it is, whether you like it or not."

"Okay." He accepted her unintentional challenge and moved off on his purposeful prowl again, leaving Leigh to look after him and reflect on the personality trait she had inadvertently discovered. He was determined and competitive, and those were dangerous characteristics in an opponent. The allotted five minutes were nearly up when he suddenly turned to her with a questioning look that became a triumphant grin when she nodded. "I'm not surprised I missed it at first; it's very unusual, isn't it?"

"When all you've seen of my work are a few woven pieces, yes, it's unusual." Leigh stood beside him, looking at the jacket, labeled "Fan Coat—Purple," displayed in the area devoted to wearable art. The loosely fitted jacket was composed entirely of pieced and appliquéd fans in a multitude of purple-hued and -patterned fabrics. The sleeves turned back into cuffs displaying a pale lavender lining, and there were no buttons or other ornamentation to distract from the richness of the design.

"It's beautiful," Noah said. "Has it been sold?"

"Not this one. I've sold one in red and white, and one in blue, but I think I'll keep this one."

"I'm glad," he said softly. Leigh looked sharply around at him, alarmed by a new note in his voice. "I'd like to see you wearing it." His deep, velvety voice was a caress, his eyes warm and knowing. "You must look very beautiful in it."

Leigh stared at him in dismay while the familiar icy fear crept along her veins. The easy atmosphere had been shattered by the look in his eyes, by the tone of his voice, and the fear she had fought so hard to control held her prisoner again. He was too big and too male and much too near, and slowly, stiffly, she edged away from him, her smile set, her eyes enormous in her pale face.

"Leigh?" He was watching her with a puzzled frown. "Are you all right?"

"Y-yes." Her voice was strained and shaky, and she cleared her throat to try again. "Yes, I'm all right. I'm just . . . tired. I'd like to go now." The frightened trembling of her voice robbed the request of any rudeness, and after only a brief pause and a searching look at her set face, Noah nodded.

"Of course."

"That—that's okay. You can stay if you want to," she said weakly. "I just—I just have to go. I have to—" She turned toward the door, only to be brought up short by a call from somewhere in the shadowy depths of the gallery behind her.

"Leigh! I thought that was you." Kate was hurrying toward her from another room. "How's your exhibit? Is it all set for Sunday?"

"Oh, hi, Kate. Yes, it's all ready. The only problem was with the lighting, but I think we have that all straightened out now."

"Well, good. I'm glad I have another whole month to get my still lifes hung. I'm a nervous wreck already. How did you ever—oh!" She looked past Leigh, and her eyes widened as she saw Noah. "I didn't know you had a guest, Leigh. Will you introduce us?"

Leigh had to suppress a groan at the quick flare of interest in Kate's eyes, but she did her best. "This isn't precisely a guest, Kate; this is Noah Burke, the administration's 'legal counsel.' He's here to see some of my students' work so maybe he'll understand why we need smaller classes and more individual instruction. Noah, this is Kate Holland, a colleague of mine and a good friend."

There was no need for Leigh to say more. Kate cheerfully took over the conversation, and Leigh could only listen in disbelief as she told Noah Burke about her life-drawing and still-life classes, and even asked him if he'd be interested in modeling. Nude. Leigh discarded the idea of leaving without him; she couldn't possibly abandon him to Kate's tender mercies when he didn't know what outrages to expect. Kate managed to perpetrate several before Leigh dragged him away, but in spite of his rather bemused expression, she thought the worst of the damage Kate might have inflicted had been avoided.

Leigh put up a token argument when Noah suggested walking her home, but gave in with what she would later consider appalling ease. She rationalized her capitulation with the thought that the streets weren't really all that safe after dark, but in truth it was his charm that had effected her surrender. He charmed her into agreeing, just as he had charmed her into having supper with him and then taking him to the gallery. That charm, she mused, was another potent weapon, and one she would have to be wary of when they began negotiating in earnest, for she had no doubt he would use it to good effect.

Even his charm had little effect on her as they neared her house, though; the old fears were driving out any other thoughts. He was walking her home, just like a date, and he would expect a good-night kiss, just like a date, and she couldn't do that. It was impossible. She could feel nausea rising in her throat, choking off her voice so she spoke in stiff monosyllables, leaving her unable even to feign calm. Aware that he glanced sidelong at her as they walked, his confusion evident, she was nevertheless helpless to do anything about it. She was struggling just to control her panic.

She was alone in the night with a man, a man she scarcely knew. He could be a mugger, a murderer, he could be anything at all, yet he was walking her to her house, to her home, to the one place where she had thought she was safe. She had thought she was safe, but she had never taken a man to her house before. Would he expect to come in? Would he expect her to make coffee? It was impossible, she knew; in fact, this whole situation was insane, yet it was happening.

"This is it." Her voice trembled as she paused at the foot of her sidewalk, and in the glare of the streetlight she could see Noah frown. "I had—I had a nice time." She started to move away, but he came with her.

"I'll make sure you get inside," he said firmly, then walked with her up the sidewalk and the steps to the front porch. They paused in the yellow glow of the porch light Leigh had left on to welcome her home, and she fumbled with shaking hands to fit her key into the lock. It stuck, and she jiggled the knob for a frantic moment until the heavy door swung free. With her hand on the knob she turned back to find him standing just behind her, leaning toward her, very big and very close, and so much stronger than she. . . .

She shrank back against the oak panels, her eyes wide and fearful in spite of herself. Noah Burke stood very still, examining her face in the glow of the porch light, then straightened and moved slightly away from her. "Good night, Leigh Michaels," he said. There was a touch of irony in his deep voice. "I've enjoyed this evening. It's been most instructive."

"I—I'm glad you think so," she stammered stupidly. "Thank you. I—it was nice." She backed a half step farther into the secure haven of her house, and Noah's mouth twisted in a wry smile.

"Good night, Leigh."

"Good night."

He lifted his hand in a brief wave, then swung around and ran lightly down the porch steps as she slipped inside and closed the door. Standing in the dark entry hall, listening to him leave, she fought to control her panic, knowing it was irrational but unable to banish it. The nightmare memories of raised, angry voices, of pain and fear and the death of love, were crowding her, hammering at her, and she took deep, gulping breaths, clenching her hands together to stop their shaking, and feeling her heart thundering in her breast.

"No," she muttered. "I won't panic. I won't let myself panic! It's okay. He's gone. He's gone now." Whispering encouragement to herself, she moved through the house, turning on lights in every room before making a pot of coffee and carrying it to the living room. She switched on the television without checking the channel; all she wanted was the sound of human voices to drown out the voices in her mind, electronic companionship during the hours before she would dare to sleep.

Chapter Three

*Y*ou look awful!"

"Thanks a million," Leigh replied sarcastically as Kate breezed into the office. "You, on the other hand, look wonderful, as always. And, by the way," she said, turning in her chair to fix Kate with an icy stare, "I want to have a word with you about last night."

"A word? About what?" Kate's face was angelically innocent, but Leigh was unimpressed.

"Your performance, my sweet, as well you know! Asking a man I'm going to be negotiating with if he's interested in doing nude modeling for your class!"

"The pay's not bad," Kate pointed out sincerely, then giggled. "Anyway, the look on his face was priceless!"

Leigh had trouble stifling a giggle of her own, because Noah Burke had certainly been taken aback by the offer, but she wasn't ready to let Kate off the hook just yet. She swallowed the giggles and directed a severe schoolmarm look at the other woman. "Somehow," she said, very dryly, "I don't think Mr. Burke really needs the three dollars and fifty cents an hour he'd earn modeling."

"Apparently not, since he politely declined, but *I* think he was flattered."

"I think he was stunned, not flattered."

"Spoilsport. Did he say anything about it?"

"No." Leigh shook her head.

"Well, what did he say? And how did you happen to be out with the administration's legal counsel, anyway?"

"I wasn't out with him, Kate. The meeting with Dean Anderson ran late, and Noah asked if he could eat with me afterward. And before you ask, we ate at the Commons, and I paid for my own meal."

"So what were you doing at the gallery?"

"I had to check the exhibit. You know that."

"Don't be dense, Leigh; you know what I mean!"

Leigh relented. "He was with me because I mentioned where I had to go, and he asked to come along and see what I'm teaching my students, and why it can't be taught in a huge class. I think it was probably a mistake to take him there, though, and I *know* it was a mistake to let him walk me home."

"You let him walk you home?" Kate burst out in astonishment. "Really? That's wonderful!" Kate had known Leigh long enough to know of her aversion to men, and something of the reason behind it.

"It was far from wonderful," Leigh corrected flatly. "I probably shouldn't have gone anywhere with him anyway— isn't that like conflict of interest or something? And I wasn't comfortable with him, he couldn't help but notice that, and when we got to my house I nearly got hysterical just because I was afraid he might expect to come in for coffee or something. He probably thinks he's going to be negotiating with a raving paranoid or something!"

"Oh, Leigh, I'm sorry," Kate said softly. "You didn't really get hysterical, did you?"

"No, I didn't scream or anything like that. He saw how scared I was, though, and he didn't have any idea why, naturally; he undoubtedly thinks I'm a nut."

"I can't believe it's that bad. After all, you wouldn't be expected to be that friendly to someone in the enemy camp, anyway."

"I hate to have to think of it as the 'enemy camp.'" Leigh shook her head. "I have a feeling that's what the committee is going to call them, though, after I report what happened last night."

"What did happen?"

"Nothing. That's the problem. Dean Anderson smiled and nodded and refused to budge, just like he's been doing all along. The only time he showed any honest emotion was when I told him a strike is a very real possibility. That shook him."

"I'll bet it did," Kate replied with grim satisfaction. "Do you think a strike threat will get him to move?"

"I don't know. We can only hope, I guess."

"Well, what about the legal eagle? Did he say anything?"

"Nope. He only spoke up when Dean Anderson asked him a direct question. He's going to be a tough one to deal with, Kate; he's very good. He sat there and listened to me and the dean and never said a word he wasn't asked for, but you know he was picking up everything, both what was said and what wasn't."

"He may not be so tough, you know." Kate grinned slyly.

"Oh? And why not?"

"Because he's smitten. How can he be tough with you when he's got a thing for you?"

"Did anyone ever tell you you have an overactive imagination, Kate?" Kate shook her head. "Well, you do. The man sees me as an opponent in this class-size business, *and* he no doubt thinks I'm more than a little flaky after the way I acted. He's probably sitting in his office right now, planning ways to bulldoze me in negotiations."

Kate shook her head. "Maybe you're wrong, Leigh. I'll bet he's planning to meet you for lunch again today, just so he can feast his eyes on your beauty."

"And maybe pigs can fly?" Leigh grinned, picking up her

purse and a folder of notes. "Don't overtax that imagination, Kate; you might blow a fuse in your brain. I'm going to see if I can put together something to tell the committee while I have lunch—alone."

Absently Leigh pushed her tray through the serving line, collected a sandwich and an apple, paid for them and carried her tray to the quietest corner of the room. She didn't even look around her, just took a bite of her sandwich and flipped open the folder to scan the pitifully few notes she had. She really had nothing at all to tell the committee. Leigh frowned in frustration. The way things were going, this problem was going to drag on all winter, and she just didn't know if her persuasive powers were equal to the task of preventing a strike or some other group action. Concentrating, she ignored the people all around her until someone spoke.

"May I join you?"

Her head flew up, her wide, startled eyes widening even more as she stared at Noah Burke. Good Lord, she thought, Kate was right! After a moment she shrugged and moved her purse and notes aside. He sat down, spread mustard on his sandwich, tore open a bag of corn chips, took a bite, chewed for a minute and finally broke the lengthening silence.

"You didn't expect to see me, did you?"

Leigh regarded him levelly for a moment, then told him the truth. "No, I didn't."

"Didn't want to either, I'll bet." Leigh let that one go unanswered. He knew how she felt. After a moment he nodded. "You were uncomfortable last night." It was a statement, not a question. "Was there a problem of some sort?"

Leigh looked down at her plate for a moment, then took the easy way out. "It occurs to me that we're going to be on opposite sides of what could become a very tense issue. Isn't this going to give the appearance of conflict of interest?"

He blinked, startled, then began to smile. "I don't think

we're in a situation that warrants worry about that, Leigh Michaels. I'm only acting as adviser to the administration so far. If they ask me to formally represent them, I probably will, but I can always decline if I feel I'd be compromised. You, on the other hand, would have no problem with conflict, because this is your cause."

"There's another thing," she said. Noah looked at her inquiringly, and she scowled, suddenly irritated. "You know, I wish you'd take this seriously!" she snapped. "This may be just some sort of college-life joke to you, but to me and a lot of other people it's an important issue!"

"I'm sorry," he said, sobering. "You're right; this isn't a humorous issue. What was the other thing you mentioned?"

Leigh swallowed. "Last night was for business, except that it wasn't really all that businesslike, but I can't think of any reason for us to eat together today, except that you want to know more about me so you'll know who you're negotiating with, know what my weaknesses might be."

"So that I'd—" He bit off the words, and Leigh met his angry eyes with a level stare. "Why would you think that?"

"You did it before," she pointed out with irrefutable logic, and he had the grace to look uncomfortable.

"I deserve that, don't I?"

"Yes, you do. I don't like being spied on, and I don't like being tricked, and I think you did both when you didn't tell me who you were the first time we met. I don't like that, Mr. Burke, and I'm not so sure I like you either."

"Ouch!" He winced. "I thought we'd agreed on Noah, instead of Mr. Burke. Look, Leigh, I freely admit that I was wrong to do that, and I do apologize. I promise you it won't happen again."

"It won't happen again because I won't let it," Leigh said dryly. "But I accept your apology. I still don't know why you're here though."

"Don't you?" he asked quizzically, and Leigh shook her head. He sighed. "I would like to get to know you, Leigh, that's all, and maybe even to become your friend. I haven't been in Bloomington long, so I don't know too many people, but I would like to get to know you." He extended his hand to her, and for a moment Leigh just looked at it, hesitating. He sighed again, heavily. "As a friend, Leigh, no strings. This isn't a proposition."

"But why me? I don't see—"

"Good grief, is it that hard to understand?" he demanded, frustrated. "You're bright and you're interesting. I like talking to you, and I'd like to talk to you some more. That's all!"

He finished on a clearly irritated note, and somehow that very irritation was what finally convinced her that he was sincere. Leigh had been weakening before, but now she realized that she was going to accept his offer.

Slowly she reached out, and her hand was engulfed in his grip. Warmth seemed to flow from his fingers so that even after the brief handshake was over, she could feel the tingling imprint of his touch. She dropped her hands into her lap for a moment, looking down at them in confusion, then raised her eyes to find Noah watching her.

"You know," she said, a little breathless, "I'm still the chairperson of the committee, and you're still the legal counsel for the administration. We're still going to be enemies."

Noah grinned. "At least we can be friendly enemies."

Leigh didn't take the remark too seriously, but apparently Noah did. Over the next three weeks he met her for lunch each day, sometimes discussing the committee and the ever-present possibility of a strike, but more often simply talking to her about life in general. Leigh found to her surprise that having lunch with a man wasn't as traumatic as she had feared. She was able to relax with Noah as she grew more accustomed to his company, and was even able to enjoy the time they spent together.

She also noticed, though, that their acquaintance had no softening effect on his performance as a negotiator. In their more heated moments of argument she sometimes wished she really could influence him, but more often she felt an unwilling respect for his apparent incorruptibility. The biggest concession she and her legal adviser had managed to wring from Noah and Dean Anderson was a mutual agreement to postpone action for thirty days while the availability of extra funds in the university budget was researched.

"I think it's wonderful!" Kate said on a golden, early-October afternoon.

"It's wonderful that no one is going to do anything for thirty days. I can't decide if it's progress or just another of Dean Anderson's stalling tactics."

"Not that! *I* think it's wonderful that you and Noah are seeing so much of each other."

"Kate, you think everything is wonderful," Leigh sighed. "It's no big deal. I just share a table with him while we eat lunch and we talk."

"For anybody else that would be no big thing," Kate said quietly, "but for you, it's a big step. I'm glad to see you taking it."

"Don't build this up into more than it is," Leigh warned her friend. "It's not that kind of friendship, and anyway, it's not friendship that I can't handle."

"I only know what I see, Leigh, and I see a man who's interested in you."

"Kate, you're incorrigible!"

"It's part of my charm."

Noah only realized that the sun had set that evening when it grew too dim for him to read his mail. He frowned, squinting at the letter in his hand, then looked up to find his living room shadowy and the last traces of sunset staining the western sky. He shook his head at his own lack of awareness and switched on a lamp, wondering, now that his concentration had been broken, what Leigh was doing.

She could be eating dinner, or reading her mail as he was, or working, or taking a bath and relaxing. An image formed in his mind of Leigh luxuriating in a tub full of scented bubbles, her red-gold hair curling in the steam, her fair, creamy skin gleaming wet, flushed and rosy. He dwelt on the image voluptuously for a moment before banishing it reluctantly.

It was obvious to him that she would have no part of anything but a platonic relationship. Noah was much too aware of her as a woman to abandon all other ideas, but he was willing to put them in abeyance until she conquered her fear, whatever it was. It wasn't difficult to determine that someone or something had hurt her badly in the past, leaving deep psychic scars, but Noah was convinced that in time she could come to trust him, and their friendship could grow in new directions. For the present he would content himself with the relationship she seemed willing to accept, because he was fascinated by this quiet, beautiful, intriguingly fey artist.

With an effort of will he forced his attention back to the letter in his hand. A similar fat missive arrived each week, keeping him apprised of current happenings at his law firm, a prestigious New York-based group handling international cases. Noah led a hectic, high-pressured life there, flying at a moment's notice anywhere around the world and returning to an equally hectic social life.

His initial reaction to the offer of a position as visiting professor had been to dismiss it out of hand as absurd. Three exhausting weeks shuttling between New York and Frankfurt, trying to negotiate an import agreement between people who behaved on the approximate level of vindictive three-year-olds, had persuaded him to rethink his decision, and he had found himself an academic.

His first week in Bloomington had presented a stark contrast to New York, but he was beginning to find a niche for himself, to adjust to the slower pace of life and to find that it had its own unique appeal. His New York cases seemed less important now, his involvement with the problem of class size as important in its own way as the contracts and trade agreements he had been negotiating, and he scanned the rest of the letter quickly before tossing it aside to pick up the next item.

The handwriting was his sister's, and he smiled in anticipation as he slit the envelope and extracted several closely written pages. Marcia was forty, three years his senior. She happily managed a raucous household of a husband and four teenagers, and sent infrequent, entertaining letters. This one detailed the latest goings-on of her brood, then went on to describe the autumn splendor of the Connecticut hills around her. Noah had heard a bit about southern Indiana's fall spectacular, and an idea occurred to him as he read.

He flipped through his pocket address book, punched out a number on the telephone dial and leaned back in his armchair. He was about to hang up when the receiver at the other end was lifted.

"Hello?" Leigh's voice was breathless and abstracted.

"Hello, Leigh, this is Noah Burke."

"Oh. Hello!" She sounded surprised, and Noah smiled to himself.

"I hope I didn't interrupt anything," he apologized, thinking of that bath. "Did I catch you at a bad time?"

"Oh, no. I was weaving, and it takes a minute to get to the phone. Is anything wrong?"

"Not at all, but I have a favor to ask of you."

"What's that?" He could hear the grin in her voice as she relaxed, and his own smile widened.

"Well, it's an awfully big favor, but I wonder if I might persuade you to take me for a walk in the woods this weekend."

"A walk in the woods? That's a big favor?"

"To me it is. I've heard a lot about how beautiful the hills around here are in the fall, and you're the only person I know of who might be able to guide me. If you'd be willing to come, I'll provide a picnic for us. Will you?"

"Of course I will." The smile was still in Leigh's voice. "I know just the place to go, too." Pleased, and a little surprised by her ready agreement, Noah arranged to pick her up on Saturday morning, promising to supply plenty of food for the picnic and warning Leigh not to be too hard on him in her choice of a hiking trail, since he was a city boy.

Leigh agreed, laughing at his protestations of weakness, and said good-night. Noah carefully replaced the receiver in its rest. Whatever the reasons for Leigh's avoidance of a romantic relationship, at least she was willing to continue to see him, and for that he was grateful. She was entrancing. At times quiet and introspective, she also had a quick wit and a quirky sense of humor that delighted him. He had no intention of letting her out of his life, not for a long, long time. He leaned back against the soft leather of his chair and let his mind wander, unsurprised at the channel it chose to follow.

Leigh was awake early on Saturday morning, happy to see that the day had dawned clear, cool and bright, perfect for a hike. She was dressed and ready well before Noah was due to collect her, a little nervous about his imminent arrival, though she knew she had no reason to be edgy. It still felt odd to invite a man into her home, even for a short time; it still felt a little bit dangerous, and she found herself walking through the familiar rooms, unable to settle down.

Irrelevantly she wondered what he would think of her home, what he would learn about her from seeing it. It was white clapboard with gingerbread trim that she had painted in shades of red and gray, and had five rather high steps leading from the sidewalk up to a front porch large enough for a swing, and tall, narrow windows with leaded panels of stained glass at the tops. Inside there were two small bedrooms and a turn-of-the-century bath, complete with claw-footed tub, as well as a big, charmingly old-fashioned kitchen where she ate, a large living room with a fireplace and a madly ornate Victorian hearth and mantelpiece, and through an archway, facing the street, a front parlor, which was her studio.

The studio, the biggest room in the house, had a bay window and was crammed with bookshelves, cabinets, a desk, her sewing table and two sewing machines, one of them a heavy-duty industrial model, and a fabric chest. A large floor loom occupied the center of the room, while a quilting frame was propped against a wall, and another loom, disassembled, resided behind a storage chest. Heaven knew what he would make of that semiorganized chaos.

Maybe the rest of the house would make up for the workmanlike jumble in the studio. She'd furnished the place gradually, with pieces that fit the fin de siècle mood, until it was a warm and charming home, but that warmth and charm did nothing to ease her restless tension now as she paced nervously from room to room.

She told herself firmly to calm down, but when the doorbell sounded she started violently, one hand going to her throat in a classic gesture of distress. Swallowing hard, heart pounding, she forced her legs to carry her to the door, forced her shaking hand to open it, and then sagged against the doorframe in relief when she saw who waited on the porch.

"It's a zucchini alert!" her neighbor, Marge Greene, informed her, grinning at her over an armload of dark-green, torpedo-shaped squash. "I've got 'em, and I hope you want 'em. My garden is still producing like mad, though this is probably the last hurrah. You *do* want them, don't you?" She peered hopefully at Leigh.

"Of course I do! Just bring them in and pile them on the kitchen table. I'll get to them later."

Marge dumped her squash on the table and glanced around, searching for Leigh's cat, a huge, jet-black gourmand named Leon. "Where's Leon?"

"In the living room, I think," Leigh told her. "Thanks for the zucchini, Marge. You know how I love them."

"I'm glad you do, because I certainly grew more than I needed this year." Marge looked at Leigh's tote bag waiting on a chair. "Leigh, if you're getting ready to go out, I'll leave."

"It's okay, Marge, I'm waiting for someone, and he's not due for a little bit. I'd be glad if you'd stay and talk to me, actually; I'm kind of nervous."

"The someone is a man?"

"Mm-hm. But, you know, it's the first time a man has come for me . . ."

"Since your husband died?"

"Mm-hm."

"It's a big step, I know."

"It shouldn't be. I mean, other people go out with men all the time . . ."

". . . but those other people aren't you. There's nothing wrong with being a little bit nervous, Leigh, but you'll be fine; you'll see."

"Thanks for the encouragement, Marge. I know it won't be like it was . . . then, but I'm still nervous, scared. It's comforting to know someone understands."

And Marge really did understand her fears as much as anyone ever could. Though she was by profession a clinical psychologist, her understanding was firsthand. She and Leigh had never discussed it in detail, but Leigh knew that Marge's marriage, and her divorce ten years ago, had been as painful and traumatic as Leigh's disastrous marriage had been. It was deeply comforting to know she was not alone with her problem.

They sat in companionable silence for a few minutes until Leigh heard the sound of a car pulling up in front of her house. "Oh, God," she breathed faintly.

Marge patted her hand. "It'll be all right, Leigh. Just take it as it comes. Have fun!" She left by the back door, and when the bell rang Leigh stood shakily and went to answer it.

"Good morning." She managed a smile as she opened the door. "Ready for a hike?"

"Good morning, yourself. I'm ready if you are." Noah looked her over with a smile. She wore a navy sweater with multicolored flowers embroidered at the neck, a blue oxford shirt, well-worn jeans and two-tone cowboy boots.

Leigh was making a discreet appraisal of him as well, and she decided that hiking clothes suited him as well as the conservative suits he wore every day. A plaid flannel shirt stretched across his shoulders, the sleeves turned back over powerful forearms, and faded jeans outlined the long muscles of his thighs. He wore battered running shoes over white athletic socks.

"Come in," she invited, moving away from the door. "I have to get my jacket and tote bag. Would you like coffee or anything?" Somehow it was easier to make that offer at 10 A.M. than at 10 P.M.

"No, thanks. I've had—good God, what is that?" He was staring at Leon, who sat in the center of the living-room rug, fixing Noah with a basilisk stare.

"That's Leon," Leigh replied with a shaky giggle. "My cat."

"Is he part panther?" Noah stooped and held out a hand to the cat, who looked consummately bored.

"Not that I know of, but nothing would surprise me. You can introduce yourself while I get my stuff." Noah grunted assent, and when she returned to the living room Leigh was amused to see him still crouched beside Leon, deep in conversation.

He looked up as she reentered the room. "I think he likes me. At least he hasn't bitten me yet."

"He won't bite, but you should feel flattered. He's pretty picky about people, and if he didn't like you, he'd just disappear."

"I'll consider myself honored then." He rubbed Leon's ears for a moment, and the cat stretched luxuriously, a throaty purr rumbling in his chest. "I still can't believe how big he is." Noah gave the cat a final pat and rose, looking down at him in wonder. "Do you know how much he weighs?"

"Twenty-three pounds at his last visit to the vet." Leigh grinned. "I'm ready if you are."

"All set." He led her to his car, a Porsche, and as Leigh got in she noticed a knapsack in the back.

She glanced at it, then back at Noah. "What did you bring for lunch? I warned you that walking in the woods makes me hungry."

"You'll be fed." His teeth flashed white against his tan. "You can wait till we get there to find out what it is though."

"Spoilsport! Did you cook it yourself?"

"I'll never tell." He grinned and sat back in his seat to drive. Leigh relaxed into the plush comfort of the leather upholstery to watch the brilliant hills they passed. The hiking trail she eventually directed him to was steep and winding, and once out of the car they followed it as it climbed high into the hills. Dotted with towns and patchwork fields nestling in small valleys, the landscape was splashed with the orange and yellow and scarlet of October.

Leigh looked around her, smiling at the sheer beauty of the day, tasting the clean, crisp air, cool with the hint of winter to come, though the sky was a deep azure blue, and the sun, when they emerged from the dappled shade, was warm on their shoulders.

As they neared the crest of one knob-shaped hill Leigh turned off the trail to push through a cluster of bushes and slither down the hill, with Noah following gamely in her wake. She knew he must be wondering where on earth she was taking him, but he kept his counsel until Leigh forced her way through a last patch of thick, scarlet-leaved bushes and emerged into a small, perfect, sunlit glade.

Bounded on three sides by a colorful wall of foliage and on the fourth by a crystalline, chattering stream, it was carpeted with fresh green grass and flooded with sunlight, so that the colors of leaves and grass glowed with jewellike intensity. She walked to the center of the clearing, dropped her tote and turned to watch Noah's face, a wide, happy smile on her lips as he looked slowly around him in pleased surprise.

"This is beautiful!" he said when he had turned full circle and faced her again.

"Isn't it? It looks like a setting for a medieval romance. I found it by accident when I was out here last year."

"Well, it's a treasure. Is there anyplace in particular you'd like to eat?"

"Right in the middle, where it's sunny and warm."

Noah took a waterproof groundsheet from his knapsack and shook it out, topped it with a light blanket, and together they set out the picnic. It made quite an array, and Leigh sat back on her heels to admire it for a moment before fixing a plate for herself.

"Chicken and rolls and salads and fruit, and even wine! You make a terrific caterer," she told him. "If you ever get tired of law, you have a second career all lined up."

"Why, thank you, ma'am," he drawled, handing her a paper cup of crisp white wine. "You, on the other hand, make a pretty good wilderness guide."

"It's a pretty civilized wilderness," was her dry rejoinder. "But thanks for the compliment. Cheers."

"Cheers." They drank the toast and attacked their picnic with appetites sharpened by exertion and fresh air, and for a time the conversation was limited to the "More chicken?" "Yes, please" variety of remark. Finally Leigh dropped an apple core on her plate and leaned back on her elbows, replete.

"That was wonderful," she said. "And I ate entirely too much, and I don't care." She closed her eyes for a moment, lifting her face to the sun, then abruptly abandoned her indolent pose and rolled to her feet in a lithe, graceful movement. "I don't want to go to sleep yet though."

"Why not?" mumbled Noah, stretched out on the grass with one arm thrown over his eyes to shield them from the sun.

"Don't be lazy. For one thing, we need to clean this up." She began gathering the remnants of their meal, and Noah sat up again to help. When all the scraps were bundled together to be carried back with them, Leigh rinsed the cutlery and washed her hands in the icy stream, then rummaged in her tote bag and produced a pocketknife and ball of twine. Noah had washed his hands and stood drying them on a handkerchief as he watched her, puzzled.

"Are you planning to tie me up?"

"Nope. I'm going to cut some bittersweet and tie that up."

"What?"

"Bittersweet." She gestured toward the eastern side of the clearing. "Over there." A mass of the plant, something between a vine and a bush, thick with brilliant orange berries sitting atop cups formed by the four lobes of the rust-red hulls, was growing around the trunk of a tall maple tree. "You must have seen it before."

"I suppose so." Noah watched as she began cutting pieces from the enormous plant. "But I never gave a lot of thought to where it came from."

Leigh laughed. "Spoken like a true city boy. Here, you can hold this for me." She began to pile bittersweet into his arms, stopping only when he could hold no more. "I guess that's enough," she said with a wistful glance at what remained.

"Enough for what?" Noah chuckled. "You've got tons of it here!"

"Maybe so, but I have a big vase in the entry hall, and a copper teakettle in the kitchen, and a vase on my desk, and I like to hang a bunch of it on my loom, and—"

"I get the idea!" he laughed. "And it is pretty stuff, isn't it?"

"It's pretty, but mostly it's a part of fall for me, like the smell of leaf smoke and the crisp air." She slid the last bundle of bittersweet branches into her tote and sat back on her heels. "There. Now I'm ready for fall."

"Why is this stuff a part of fall for you, besides the fact that you're picking it in the fall?"

"Mainly that, I guess, but it's warm and glowing when everything else is beginning to fade into the gray of winter." She lay back on the blanket and squinted up at the sunlit leaves high above her. "That must be where the name comes from," she mused. "It belongs to the season that's a bridge between the sweet warmth of summer and the bitter cold of winter."

"A lot of things are like that," Noah commented, lying back on the groundsheet beside her, close, but not so close that his nearness made her uneasy. "A lot of things are a mixture of bitter and sweet. Life, for instance."

Leigh pondered that for a moment, thinking of her brief marriage and its tragic end, and her mouth twisted in a tight little smile which held no trace of joy. "Yes, life is a mix of the two," she agreed in a flat, cold voice that contrasted sharply with her earlier warmth. "It's the proportions that are important though. How much bitter do you have to take with the sweet?"

From the corner of her eye she could see Noah's sharp movement as he turned to look at her, and she knew he was going to question her. Already regretting her ill-considered words, she continued quickly, before he could begin an interrogation.

"I'm going to enjoy some of the sweet now and have a nap in the sun," she told him, and rolled over to lie facedown. "You don't mind, do you?"

"Not at all. Sleep well."

"Mm-hm." She pillowed her cheek on her crossed arms and closed her eyes. Aware that Noah was watching her, aware that he was pondering her bitter words and the reason for them, she lay stiffly, listening to the sounds of the leaves rustling above them, the gurgling of the stream as it tumbled over mossy stones, the shriek and twitter of birds in the trees. Gradually the outdoor music and the soothing warmth of the sun worked their spell, and she relaxed, slipping into sleep.

A growing chill woke her. The sun had swung into the western sky, touching the treetops with gold and leaving the little glade in shadow. She lay curled on her side, a bit stiff from the hard ground, shivering as she surfaced from the depths of slumber, then opened her eyes and blinked in confusion.

She was looking into a pair of dark-blue eyes. Close to hers, very close, they were regarding her with unblinking steadiness, and she could only watch, still disoriented by sleep, as they came closer, as a warm whisper of breath touched her cheek, and then lips touched her own.

In that limbo between sleep and waking, where dreams and reality blurred together, Leigh wasn't conscious of where she was or whom she was with. She knew only that she was being held, being kissed, and she had been without affection for so long, had been starved for a kiss, a touch, for closeness, denied them by her own fear. Now, in this dream, she could respond instinctively, her lips softening, her body moving into her dream lover's embrace with the confidence and trust that had once been hers.

As she began to respond his lips firmed on hers, becoming insistent, trying to force hers apart, and a spasm of blind panic shot through Leigh, bringing her violently awake and into her private terror. In an instant the warm, responsive woman Noah held had vanished, replaced by a terrified girl who twisted her face away from his and hit at his shoulders, fighting to be free.

His arms loosened automatically, and she rolled quickly away and got to her feet, walking a few steps to the edge of the clearing. She stood stiffly with her back to Noah, shoulders hunched and arms crossed protectively over her breasts.

Noah got slowly to his feet, staring at her slender back, conscious of how vulnerable she looked, how afraid. "Leigh," he said quietly, from a few steps behind her, "I didn't mean to frighten you."

She shrugged. "I know you didn't mean to." She rubbed a hand over her mouth, scrubbing away the kiss.

"Look at me, Leigh." There was a note of command in his quiet voice, and reluctantly she turned to him. She met his gaze bravely, unable to read anything in his face and hoping he could read nothing in hers. "I'm sorry I frightened you," he repeated, "but I'm not sorry I kissed you."

She looked down at the grass beneath her feet. "You shouldn't have done it," she muttered to the green blades. "We're supposed to be friends, that's all."

"Is there a law against kissing your friends?" He stepped a pace closer to her. "I care about you, Leigh. Don't deny me the opportunity to express that. I'm not going to force anything on you; all I ask is that you give yourself the chance to relax and enjoy it. Can you do that?"

He reached out to tip her face up to his. His eyes were dark and bottomless, and she gazed into them, trying to read his thoughts, wanting to trust him, yet afraid to take the first step.

For a long moment they stood motionless, gazes locked; then, very slowly, Leigh nodded. Still holding her eyes with hypnotic purpose, Noah leaned close and kissed her lightly on the lips.

Chapter Four

*H*ours later, long after Noah had brought her home, Leigh could still feel that kiss tingling on her lips, the kiss she had assented to. It was far more significant than the first kiss, the one he had given her when she was still half-asleep. It was a kiss she had allowed, and that surprised—no, it astounded her.

She hadn't let a man kiss her for a very long time, hadn't expected ever to let a man kiss her again. Yet just that afternoon, on that sun-washed hillside, it had happened. It was an indication of how important Noah had become to her, how much she trusted him after the short time she had known him. She had no idea when, or how, it had happened, but over the last weeks he had become a part of her life, a part, she realized to her surprise, that she didn't want to lose.

She sat curled in the corner of her sofa, lost in thought, staring blindly ahead of her while a forgotten cup of tea cooled on the table beside her. The situation was becoming very complicated, not only because she was at last lowering the barriers that had kept men out of her life for so long, but because the man who was entering her life was the man across the table from her at those increasingly acrimonious negotiations. Leigh wanted to do the best she could for her side, and she knew from hard experience that Noah would do his best, kisses or no kisses, but he seemed to have less trouble than she in separating the personal and professional parts of his life.

It wasn't so easy for Leigh. When she looked at him across that bargaining table she saw Noah the man, as well as Noah the lawyer, and when she had lunch with him the day after a particularly stormy session she had difficulty concealing her feelings. She sighed heavily. Her life had been well ordered and peaceful such a short time before, before the committee and before Noah, but she wondered if it would ever be that way again.

Another realization came to her, something she admitted only reluctantly to herself. The kiss, *his* kiss, had not been unpleasant, and that was perhaps the most surprising thing of all. It upset all her preconceptions. She could still feel his lips, warm and firm on hers for that brief moment, and she was still astonished to realize that she hadn't disliked the feeling.

And yet why should she? Leigh thought, annoyed with herself. Other women enjoyed kissing men; why shouldn't she? And anyway, she told herself firmly, as Noah had said, there was no law against kissing a friend.

Despite those brave thoughts she awoke the next morning with the feeling that she had taken the first step onto unknown and potentially treacherous ground. She was oddly nervous about the prospect of seeing Noah again, unsure how either of them would behave when they met. And that was just plain silly, she thought, staring moodily into the inky depths of her breakfast coffee. Why was she wasting a gorgeous autumn Sunday brooding about what might happen tomorrow?

What was important today was a one o'clock meeting of the executive council of the committee. She hoped it wouldn't be a difficult meeting, but she was afraid that might be a vain hope; the pro-strike faction was growing impatient once again. By 4 o'clock that afternoon she realized just how vain that hope had been.

"It's time to show them we mean business!" Jonas Petersen shouted. "And a strike is the way to make our point!"

"A strike isn't going to prove anything at this point except that we don't keep our word," Leigh replied, exasperated. "We've been through all this before, Jonas. We agreed to give them thirty days to explore budget loopholes, and the thirty days aren't up yet. No strike."

"That's easy for you to say, but what about all the rest of us?" Jonas glared across the table at her, his thin, bearded face red with frustration, as the six others there shifted uneasily in their seats.

"What *about* the 'rest of *us*'?" Leigh repeated, deliberately including herself in the "us" she referred to. "The rest of us voted, Jonas, and we voted *not* to strike. We're going to stick to that decision, and we're going to give the administration the thirty days they wanted." Without giving him a chance to argue further, she changed the subject. "What did you find out about the state budget allotments for education, Mike?"

"Good news and bad news," replied Mike Morris, the graduate law student who was acting as the committee's legal adviser. "The budget isn't frozen from one year to the next. Extra money can be appropriated, but it takes time, and it has to pass the state legislature. If we go that route we'll be fighting the university and the budget-cut people in the legislature, and we'll probably have to send someone to testify before the budget committee. In short, it can be done, but it won't be easy."

"None of this has been easy," Kate Holland pointed out from the end of the table. "But if we push, we might have the extra money by next semester, and the university would have no reason not to mandate reduced class size."

"We '*might*' have the money by next semester?" Jonas

scoffed. "Be serious, Kate! The only thing that will get the administration off their duffs is a show of force!"

"Oh, grow up, Jonas! A strike won't produce anything but bad publicity for us! Haven't you heard anything Leigh's said? She's working with Dean Anderson and the lawyer to solve this without resorting to something like a strike." Leigh sent Kate a grateful smile, which froze on her lips an instant later.

"She's working with that lawyer, all right," Jonas sneered, "but I doubt if solving this is what they're working on!"

Leigh's face went white, and she turned to meet Jonas's scowl. "Why don't you say what you mean?" she invited coldly.

"I mean I've seen you having lunch with Burke, and it didn't look to me like you were discussing business!"

"If you feel I'm not doing my job for the committee, feel free to call for another election." Leigh held his gaze until he looked away, then turned to the others. "I think we've done all we can for today. I'll investigate the possibility of taking this to the legislature, and I'll see you on Wednesday. Thank you."

There was a brief hubbub as the others left, then Kate and Leigh gathered their things and followed. Kate was still fuming.

"Where that little twerp gets the nerve, I don't know! I could just about slap him when he starts that strike-or-nothing nonsense, but to make insinuations like that about you and Noah! That's too much, Leigh; it really is."

"I don't like him either, but you know, Kate, he does have a point."

"What?" Kate demanded loyally.

"I do eat with Noah a lot, and people do see us, and considering the positions we're in, it's bound to look a little bit fishy. I said something to Noah about it once, and he brushed it off, but if Jonas is saying something about it to my face, you know he's been talking about it behind my back for ages. There are probably other people wondering what's going on, too."

"So let 'em wonder. You know you're not doing anything wrong."

"Yes, but the appearance of something fishy can be just as harmful as the reality. I think maybe I should stop seeing Noah before things get any worse."

"Leigh, *no!* If Jonas wants to vote on Wednesday for a new chairperson, that's his business, but don't you let him tell you how to conduct your personal life! If he calls for an election you'll be reelected hands down, anyway!"

"You're a dreamer, Kate, but you're good for my ego." Leigh laughed.

"I'm not trying to be good for your ego, silly. I'm telling you the truth!" Kate paused as they reached the corner where their paths home diverged. After they exchanged good-byes, Kate walked off with a cheerful wave, and Leigh continued on her way home, deliberately choosing a circuitous route through the oldest part of the campus. She didn't make a conscious decision, but after a few minutes she realized that she was no longer making for home but simply wandering through the campus, enjoying the late-afternoon beauty of it and trying to think, to work things out.

Her efforts were not outstandingly successful, and she finally stopped walking when she reached an ancient domed observatory. It was no longer used by the astronomers; a newer, larger observatory had replaced it some time ago, but it still sat in its small clearing, surrounded by smooth green lawn, with a conveniently placed park bench waiting for the weary stroller. Leigh dropped onto the green-painted slats to sit, head back, face turned to the last of the sunlight, and let her mind wander.

"Well, hello! What are you doing over here?"

Her head snapped up as someone spoke from behind her, and Leigh turned sharply to see Noah approaching along a path she recognized as leading from the Law School. She straightened and lifted one hand in a little wave. She had been nervous about seeing him again, but meeting him by chance like this, with no warning, she had no opportunity to be tense. She smiled as he walked across the grass to her bench.

"I'm just sitting," she told him, "and trying to get my thoughts together."

"That a tough job today?" He dropped onto the bench beside her.

She nodded, frowning. "Unfortunately it is. We had a meeting of the executive council this afternoon."

He nodded as if that said it all. "Things didn't go well?"

"You could put it that way."

"Care to tell me about it?"

"I'd better, since it concerns you." He looked around sharply at that, and Leigh nodded. "I was attacked again, by the worst of the hotheads, but that's nothing new. He's always accusing me of being too wishy-washy, too accommodating. What *was* new was that he brought up the 'shocking' fact that you and I have been seen eating together in the Commons, and we haven't been acting like enemies."

Noah muttered something rude under his breath. "I hope you told him what he could do with his scandal mongering."

"I told him if he wanted a vote on the chairmanship on Wednesday night he was free to call one."

"Do you think he'll call your bluff?"

"I don't know." Leigh shrugged. "He might be angry enough to try it. I would like to see this thing through, now that I've gone so far with it, and I'd hate to be voted out of the chair at this point, but I'd survive. What I really don't like is the appearance of compromise. If he'd bring this up to my face, he's been talking about it behind my back. I don't know how much credibility I have right now."

"I'm sorry about that." Noah reached over to cover her hand with his, then clasped her chilly fingers to warm them. "Good grief, you're freezing! Come on, let's walk a little bit and get your circulation going." He pulled her to her feet and set off through the shadowy woods. "I'm really sorry you've been questioned because of me. I didn't think that would happen."

"It's not the end of the world, Noah, really. Jonas doesn't have a lot of credibility himself, and my reaction will carry some weight, too. I just don't like all the uproar, especially when it interferes with getting things done." She walked in silence for several moments. "Are we getting things done, Noah? Is the administration going to move a little bit, or is this thirty days just another of Dean Anderson's stalling tactics?"

From the corner of her eye Leigh saw Noah glance quickly at her, but it was too dark, she thought, for him to read anything in her face.

"You know I can't answer that," he said after a moment.

"I know you can't," she sighed. "I wonder, though, how much you learn from me, and how you use it. I wonder if I really am compromising the committee's position."

There was a moment of silence, then he said coldly, "I'm not using you, Leigh."

"I'm not trying to make you angry, Noah," she said, not apologizing, just explaining. "But I do wonder sometimes, and the wondering makes me uncomfortable."

"Mm-hm." They walked on, absorbed in their own thoughts. Darkness was falling rapidly. Leigh heard something rustle in the fallen leaves and looked in the direction of the sound when she stumbled on the uneven paving and fell against Noah.

"I'm sorry!" she gasped as he caught her with an arm around her shoulders. "I should look where I'm going and—"

"Don't worry about it." His voice was warm again, with a soft burr of laughter underneath. He dropped his arm to her waist, holding her beside him when she would have pulled away. "I won't let you fall." Walking on, he took her with him, his arm still at her waist, and with the giddy, reckless feeling of someone sitting atop the first, steep drop of a roller coaster, Leigh let him hold her.

It was fully dark when they reached her house, a fat, golden harvest moon illuminating the street and casting inky shadows beneath the trees. They walked in silence up her front steps, then paused in the darkness of the porch, an undercurrent of subdued expectancy running between them.

"Thank you," Leigh said softly, "for walking me home. It was nice."

"I was glad to do it." He brushed her hair back from her forehead. "You don't have to thank me."

"But I—"

"Don't." The single soft word silenced her, and Noah looked gravely into her eyes for a moment. "I wanted to walk with you, and now I want to kiss you, Leigh."

She froze for an instant, too surprised to react. She should have been frightened, repulsed, she should have reacted with horror to the very suggestion, and yet he had kissed her the day before and she had survived. She was a little frightened, but it was more a nervous anticipation of what was to come than the choking terror that was so familiar to her. There was none of the revulsion, the horror she had grown so accustomed to. On the contrary, she was startled to realize that a part of her wanted him to kiss her. She wanted to experience again his closeness and his touch.

She tipped her face up in silent acquiescence, expecting a brief caress like the one he had given her on the sunlit hillside, but he reached out to draw her to him, closing his arms gently but securely around her.

"Come to me, Leigh," he murmured as she held herself stiffly against the strong, solid warmth of him. She wore flat running shoes, and he seemed somehow taller when she was so close, taller and broad and powerful and very, very male. A tremor ran through her, and Noah must have felt it, because he coached her through the kiss in a way that seemed to vanquish her fear.

"Put your arms around me." He guided her arms around his waist, so that her palms lay on the muscles along his spine, while his own arms held her close to him, her softer contours molded to the hard lines of his body.

Her fear dissolved as he bent slightly to touch his lips to hers. This was not the perfunctory salute she'd expected, but a real kiss, warm and firm and tender and seeking, and it touched something deep inside Leigh that had lain dormant and unacknowledged for a long, long time. Gradually, tentatively, she began to relax, to accept the kiss, and as Noah felt her resistance ebb, he tried to part her lips.

The fear shot through Leigh instantly, and this time Noah could not soothe it away. She jerked her mouth from his, pushing to be free of his arms as well. Noah let her lever her body away from him, though he kept his hands loosely on her shoulders, looking at her with a spark of puzzled interest in his eyes and a tiny smile on his lips.

"You see," he said softly, "I won't push you, Leigh. You can stop me any time. I won't do anything you don't want me to." He stepped back, releasing her, leaned over to brush his lips lightly across hers, and was gone.

"How do you feel about it?"

"I'm scared."

"Do you think there's something wrong with feeling that way?"

"Oh, Marge, don't be a psychologist with me, okay? I get all the well-reasoned, logical advice I can take from Kate, but you understand how I *feel*."

"I know." Marge shrugged. "And I'll quit playing therapist with you, I promise. I think it's an occupational hazard, or something."

They laughed together, and Leigh pulled her jacket more closely around her as the crisp autumn afternoon slid into a chilly autumn evening. Her shiver was not entirely due to the temperature, though, and Marge noticed it.

"What is it that you're frightened of, Leigh?"

Leigh considered the question for a moment. "Myself, I think, and what's happening to me, even though he—he tempts me." Marge looked at her inquiringly, and Leigh tried to explain. "It's not just that he kissed me yesterday when he brought me home, although that's amazing enough. It's that when he walked up while I was sitting on that bench I was glad to see him. I wanted to walk with him, and when he asked if he could kiss me, I wanted that, too."

"It seems to me that's a good sign, not something to be frightened of."

"In a way it is, I guess. At any rate, Noah's doing more for my fear of men than the psychiatrists ever could, but it isn't enough."

"It isn't enough for what? I don't see how you can quantify that."

"It isn't enough for the future, for any future. I did want him to kiss me, but at the same time I was afraid of it. At first it was okay, but then he wanted more of a kiss, and I panicked, just like always. I can't escape that fear. I can't be what a man would want me to be."

"What does Noah say he wants?"

"A friend."

"Well, then, where's the problem?"

"I just can't see that there's any future in it. He's weaving himself into my life the way I'd weave a thread into a tapestry. It's easy to weave it in, but if it has to be removed later, the only way to take it out is to cut the fabric up. Or tear it apart," she added slowly. "And I don't want my life torn apart when Noah finally understands there's no future for us."

"Aren't you jumping the gun a bit?" Marge asked with a grin.

"How's that?"

"The man says he wants to be your friend, but you're acting like he's asked you to marry him."

"Oh." Leigh flushed.

"You're being too pessimistic. You can't assume that he's going to tear up your life just because he happens to be a man, and there's no point in worrying about a future you can't predict. Just enjoy his company and take things a day at a time. The future can take care of itself, you know."

"I suppose so." Leigh thought about that for a moment. "Is that what you're doing—taking it a day at a time?"

"How?"

"With Joe." Joe Russell was a detective with the local police, in love with Marge and frankly eager to marry her, but though she cared for him, Marge couldn't bring herself to reenter the bonds that once had been a trap for her.

"I guess that is what I'm doing. It seems silly that even after ten years I'm still so afraid of marriage. I know Joe is a good man, and I do love him, but I can't stop remembering the way it was."

"I know," Leigh said softly, sadly. "I remember, too." Suddenly she laughed at herself, at both of them. "And aren't we a swell pair, sitting out here in the cold, brooding about what's past and done with!" She rose and reached down to pull Marge to her feet as well. "Come on, *Ms.* Greene, let's go in and have a cup of coffee before we freeze solid out here!"

"You got it! *Ms.* Michaels!"

Leaving the future to take care of itself sounded like a formidable task, but Leigh found that to accept each day as it came wasn't so difficult after all. The busy days slid past, she and Noah continued to see each other, yet Leigh never felt she had to make a conscious decision about their relationship, it just grew and matured without any interference from her.

She had other things to occupy her thoughts, of course, including the power struggle in the committee. She wasn't really surprised when Jonas pressed for another vote, but she wasn't made happy by it. When the vote was called she turned the gavel over to the vice-chairperson, Mike Morris, and took a seat next to Kate to await the results.

"Don't worry, Leigh. You have it in the bag." Kate patted her hand.

Leigh shrugged. "I don't know if I even want to win it, to

tell you the truth. Sometimes it seems like more trouble than it's worth."

"Don't say that!" Kate snapped. "We need you."

It was to be a voice vote. Mike asked for a yea vote for Jonas; the assembled crowd responded with a chorus of yeas. Then he asked for votes for Leigh, and to her amazement the room erupted with a thunderous roar of shouting, cheering and applause, which went on until Mike called Leigh back to the podium and she signaled for quiet again.

"Thank you!" She held a hand up for quiet, and the uproar began to abate. "Thank you! Please, that's enough! Thank you! I appreciate your vote of confidence. I'll do my best to see that I deserve it." The room grew noisy, and Leigh had to wait for quiet once more. "Thank you. I'm meeting with Dean Anderson and the administration's legal counsel tomorrow to discuss the possibility of taking this issue to the state legislature. If any of you has knowledge of, or experience with the legislature, I'd appreciate volunteers to help plan strategy. That's all for tonight, and I'll see you again next week. Thank you."

She sat down to renewed applause, but what caught her eye was Jonas's glowering face in the front row. It would be just like him to nurse a grudge, to try to undercut Leigh's position and end up jeopardizing the committee's cause. She sighed, wishing there were some way to persuade Jonas that she had no wish to see him publicly embarrassed.

"Terrific, Leigh! Didn't I tell you you had nothing to worry about?" Kate squeezed her arm, smiling gleefully. "See you tomorrow, Madame Chairman!"

"Thanks, Kate. I'll see you."

Kate walked away, smiling triumphantly, and Leigh gathered her papers together, shoving them into her briefcase carelessly, eager to leave. The room was clearing when she left the dais in front, and she thought she saw, in the back row, a familiar profile. He turned, and she realized she was right; Noah was sitting back there, watching as she followed the crowd to the exit, spying on the meeting!

Furious, she averted her head, ignoring him as she left the building. He followed her, but she was a block from the building, walking fast, when he caught up with her. She glanced at him, scowling, and walked faster.

"That was an incredibly stupid thing to do, you know!"

"I thought it was very instructive," Noah replied calmly, and Leigh stopped short, livid.

"You had no business there! That was a meeting of the committee, and spies are *not* welcome!"

Noah's smile vanished. "Is that what you think I was doing? Spying?"

"What else?" she snapped. "You're legal adviser for the administration, and I saw you sitting in the back row at one of *our* meetings. What was I supposed to think?" She turned on her heel and strode off toward home, Noah beside her. "Noah, you said you weren't using me!" she cried after a moment, and he grabbed her arm to yank her to an abrupt halt.

"I'm *not* using you!" he barked. "I knew you'd be at the meeting until late, and I thought I'd walk you home."

"So why were you sitting in the back, listening to everything that went on?" Leigh demanded, too angry to be easily mollified.

"Because I got there early!" he snapped. "I didn't see any reason to stand outside in the cold until God knows when, waiting for the meeting to break up, so I slipped in and sat in back. Is that a capital offense? So I heard some of the debate; I didn't exactly hear any state secrets!" He glared at her, his eyes cold, and Leigh felt a little prick of anxiety break through her anger. "Look, lady," he snarled, releasing her arm and giving her an ungentle shove along the sidewalk, "I came to walk you home, and I'm going to, so get moving."

"I didn't ask you to walk me—"

"Just get moving," he ordered her in a low tone. "I don't want to waste the evening arguing about it."

Leigh moved. Lord, he was furious. She had been furious when she saw him in the back row, but her anger was nothing to the cold rage she'd felt in him since she'd accused him of spying. He had a right to be angry, of course, but Leigh had never been able to entirely quell the nagging suspicion that Noah might be learning things from her that he could use; hadn't he misled her the first time they met? She didn't want to believe that, she wanted to believe that he was her friend, but the doubts had stayed with her, right or wrong, and now, because *she* was angry, she had blurted them out to Noah.

And because she had blurted out those furtive, half-formed doubts, she had broken their growing friendship into a million pathetic fragments. He marched her to her front steps, stopped at the bottom and said, "I'll wait until you're inside."

"Noah, look," Leigh began, "I didn't mean—"

"I know what you meant," he interrupted coldly. "Good night, Leigh."

She looked up at his face, hard and implacable in the blue-vapor glare of the streetlight. "Good night, Noah."

She turned and ran up the steps, fleeing into the house. When she looked out the window of her studio he was already striding away into the darkness. Suddenly cold, Leigh dropped the curtain back over the window and rubbed her arms. She'd said, "Good night," but she had an idea that "Good-bye" might have been more appropriate.

Leigh waited ten long days before she decided what to do, ten days during which she felt more lonely than she would ever have thought possible, ten days during which her sense of guilt grew until it threatened to overwhelm her. As her own anger died she began to accept Noah's right to be angry and her own responsibility for it. Yes, he had deceived her the first time they had met, but he'd admitted it was wrong and apologized. He had never lied to her, and Leigh knew of no instance when he had used anything she'd told him against her.

She thought of herself as his friend, and as his friend she should have trusted him, should have listened to his explanation and not unfairly taken her temper out on him. She was far from proud of herself and came to the realization that she would have to be the one to apologize.

She had seen Noah only once in those ten days at a short meeting between the committee's executive council, Dean Anderson, Noah and the comptroller. It had been an acrimonious meeting. Leigh had come very near to losing her temper and had announced her intention of seeking redress through the state legislature, a move that angered Dean Anderson. No one had been in a very good mood when that meeting adjourned, and Leigh hadn't even dared to speak to Noah, who'd listened stonily to everything she said without ever once meeting her eyes.

On Halloween she finally plucked up her courage, and without giving herself time to think and probably chicken out she left the Fine Arts Building a little earlier than usual, walking quickly toward the Law School. Noah's office was squirreled away on the third floor, and she hurried along the corridors, afraid of losing her nerve if she hesitated.

His door stood ajar, and she could hear his voice as she approached, aware from the cadence of the conversation that he was speaking on the phone. ". . . Okay, I'll pass that along, but you know I have reservations about it. It's not my decision to make, after all. . . . Right. Bye."

Leigh heard a ping as the receiver settled back on its rest, then moved forward again, breathing deeply to steady her shaking hand as she reached out to tap on the door. Noah grunted a "Come in." He was writing, his head down, and he looked up only after several seconds. His eyes widened, then narrowed.

"May I sit down?" she asked, feeling that she was speaking to a stranger.

"By all means." He nodded to a chair opposite him. "But are you sure this doesn't constitute consorting with the enemy?"

Leigh flushed, but she wasn't going to be chased away by sarcasm. She closed the door carefully behind her and perched uneasily on the edge of the hard chair. "I—" Her voice cracked humiliatingly, and she had to clear her throat and try again. "Noah, I want to apologize. I realize you wouldn't use me to spy on the committee, and I should never have accused you of that. I should have trusted you, and I'm sorry."

There was a moment of taut silence, while Leigh stared down at her hands. She was aware of the little sounds in the room, the tick of a clock on the desk, the hiss of steam in the radiator, the creak of Noah's chair as he shifted his weight. She jumped when he finally spoke.

"Is that all?" She looked up to see that his eyes were hard and opaque, giving nothing of his feelings away.

"Yes," she said softly. "I needed to apologize to you."

"And now you have."

"Yes." So this was how it was to be. She had failed to trust, and their friendship was over, almost before it had begun. Leigh stood, pulling her coat around her again. "Thank you for hearing me out, Noah. Good-bye." His only reply was a nod, and as Leigh walked out of the office she heard him dialing the telephone again.

Though Leigh was hardly in a festive mood it was still Halloween, and she stopped on her way home to purchase candy for trick or treaters and a pumpkin to carve. She managed to get the candy into a big bowl by the front door and the pumpkin carved and onto the porch with a candle flickering inside before it was fully dark.

Her nonfestive mood notwithstanding, she was grateful for the diversion provided by little superheroes and ghouls, and she regretted the tapering off of visitors that occurred after 9 P.M. She was on her way to peek through the curtains when the doorbell rang. She hurried to answer it.

It was no tiny monster who stood in the glare of the porch light, though, and Leigh gasped as she opened the door. "N-Noah?" she said, not quite believing he was there, and he nodded.

"Should I say 'trick or treat'?" His mouth curved with wry humor.

"I—ah—sure, if you want to," Leigh replied weakly,

cursing her stupid, stammering tongue. "Won't—won't you come in?"

"Thank you." Noah certainly had more presence of mind than she did. He smiled and walked inside, pausing in the living room to wait for her. "Could I possibly have a cup of coffee as my treat?"

"Oh! Yes, of course." Leigh hurried to the kitchen to pour it. Why was he here? When she left his office she'd had the impression that their friendship was over, so why was he here? Her hand shook as she poured coffee, and she muttered under her breath. She had to calm down or Noah would think she was certifiable, but *why was he here?*

When she carried the coffee in he was seated on the couch, scratching Leon under the chin while the cat lay beside him, eyes slitted in ecstasy. "Here you are." She handed Noah the cup, and he took it with a murmur of thanks.

He drank, then set the cup on the low cocktail table and looked across at Leigh in her armchair. "I want to apologize," he said without preamble, startling Leigh.

"But why? I'm the one who—"

"I was very angry about what you accused me of, and I overreacted. I was ungracious in my office today. I want to apologize for both of those."

Leigh met his level gaze for a moment, then nodded. "I don't think you have anything to apologize for, but I accept."

"Thank you." He looked at her rug for a moment, seeming oddly ill at ease. "Leigh?"

"Hmm?"

"Do you think . . . Can we be friends again?"

"I—" She looked at his face and felt a warm flush of pleasure run into her cheeks. "Yes, Noah, we can be friends."

"Great!" He leaned back, smiling freely now, relaxing, and Leigh wondered that he should be so openly pleased by her acquiescence. Surely it didn't matter so much to him?

"Now, since we're friends again, will you come over here?" He patted the couch beside him, and Leigh moved to join him, settling back trustingly into the curve of his arm.

This was right, this was the way it should be. It felt like coming home, and Leigh was too happy to wonder at that, too content to explore the depth and the meaning of her feelings. She knew only that she was where she wanted to be, that now, with Noah there, all was right with her world.

Chapter Five

$\mathscr{I}$t was so right for her to be together with Noah, and Leigh found that as the amount of time they spent together increased, so did her need to be with him. And almost imperceptibly the tenor of their chaste lovemaking was heightened. When Noah kissed her and held her, Leigh found she was becoming less fearful, not quite relaxed, but no longer afraid of any affectionate gesture. There was still that core of remembered fear, though, and Noah drew back whenever he felt it in her, apparently content with the friendship they maintained.

"So when do you testify?" It was the middle of November, and Noah was walking Leigh home through a gray and drizzly evening.

"Not until after New Year's. Apparently the legislature doesn't want anything to interfere with their holiday," Leigh replied dryly. "This is all so frustrating! I thought it would be settled by the end of this semester, and now it looks as though we'll be lucky to resolve anything before the end of the school year!"

"'The wheels of justice,' as they say, 'grind slowly.'"

"Yeah, well sometimes I wonder if these are grinding at all." She kicked a clump of sodden leaves off the sidewalk.

"I got a letter from my sister today."

Leigh glanced over at him, considering the deliberate change of subject, then decided it was probably better than arguing about "the wheels of justice." "Did you? What did she say?"

"She and the family are going to her in-laws' for the Thanksgiving weekend. They have a huge bash every year."

"That's nice. It sounds like fun." Leigh didn't really know where this conversation was going, but she was game.

"They'll enjoy it." They walked in silence for a minute. "What are you doing for Thanksgiving?"

"Me? Nothing much."

"Not going to relatives', having dinner with your neighbors, anything like that?"

"No. Nothing like that."

"Then will you have Thanksgiving dinner with me?"

"I . . ." Leigh's instant of hesitation was born of surprise rather than reluctance; then she nodded, smiling. "Yes, I'd like that."

"Good," Noah said with a satisfied smile of his own. "Is there any particular restaurant you'd like to have dinner at, or shall I—"

"Dinner at a restaurant? You mean have *Thanksgiving dinner* at a restaurant?" Leigh was frankly horrified.

"I thought so, yes. Where else?"

"Home, of course."

"You mean, cook a turkey?" He was as taken aback as she had been, and Leigh laughed aloud.

"Of course, cook a turkey, and all the other stuff, too." Noah was still unconvinced, and Leigh poked him in the ribs with her elbow. "Don't be such a party pooper! It'll be fun; you'll see."

Thanksgiving Day dawned cold and crisp, with a gray sky and a few snow flurries for atmosphere. Leigh had a light breakfast of toast and coffee ready when Noah arrived, bringing with him a bottle of red wine for dinner, the newspaper and a portable color television.

He came in and leaned forward, arms full, to kiss Leigh lightly on the mouth. His skin was cold, his lips warm, and even after he had stepped away she was tingling at his touch. She covered her moment of confusion by helping him slip out of his fleece-lined, leather bomber jacket and unwind the scarf around his neck, and while she hung his coat in the closet, Noah carried everything else into the kitchen.

When Leigh joined him, he was busily setting everything up. The wine went onto a shelf to wait for dinner, the newspaper was set aside to be read when the cooking was done and the television was plugged in, placed in the middle of the table and tuned to the Thanksgiving Day parades.

"There, now we're ready." He was rolling up his shirt-sleeves as he spoke. "What do you want me to do first?"

Leigh had to laugh. "I am impressed!" She looked from Noah to the television and back, chuckling. "I've never seen anyone so thoroughly *prepared* to fix a dinner."

"It's Thanksgiving!" he protested, wounded. "We can't miss the parades, can we?"

"No, of course we can't." Leigh might have been soothing a child, and when the humor struck them both at the same instant, they erupted into laughter.

"Come on, Mom." Noah draped an arm around her shoulders and steered her toward the counter, where a heap of vegetables waited. "Show me what to do."

"You got it." Leigh handed him a cutting board, a knife and a pile of onions and celery. "The onions need to be peeled, the celery washed and then it all needs to be chopped for the stuffing."

"Gotcha." Noah set to with enthusiasm, cutting and chopping as Leigh prepared the turkey for stuffing and seasoned a large bowl of bread cubes; then he watched in amazement as she poured boiling broth and melted butter over it all and tossed it together. *"That's* stuffing?" He was incredulous.

"That's it." The large bowl steamed gently as she set the roasting pan beside it and produced the turkey from a pan in the sink. The bird was big, cold, slippery and pale, not the least bit appetizing.

"*That's* the turkey?" He simply could not believe that anything that looked that awful could be transformed into Thanksgiving dinner.

"This is it." Leigh upended the bird so she could spoon stuffing inside, and Noah shuddered. "You wait," she admonished him. "You're going to love this."

"If you say so." Noah watched, skeptical, as the turkey was stuffed, trussed, brushed with melted butter and deposited in the oven. "It doesn't look like any turkey I've ever seen, though."

"That's because you've only seen them cooked, silly!" she retorted, exasperated. "Have a little faith in me, okay? I promise I won't ask you to eat raw poultry."

"I'll hold you to that," he muttered, and dragged his eyes away from the oven door. "What do we do now?"

"Now we have a cup of coffee." Leigh dropped into a chair and poured herself a cup.

"And after that?" Noah passed her the sugar.

"You really are a glutton for punishment, aren't you?" She grinned at him over the rim of her cup, and he shrugged, trying to hide a smile.

"I only want to learn," he replied piously. "And you offered to teach me how to do all this, after all."

"You're a nut!" Leigh reached out to tap his cheek with her fingertip, laughing into his eyes. "But if you want to you'll learn."

"I want to." Noah captured her hand and pulled her to him, then kissed her quickly, first the tip of her nose, then her lips. "And I may be a nut, but you're cute in an apron, so teach me to cook, Ms. Michaels."

"Okay, Mr. Burke." Leigh mimicked his pedantic tone, her cheeks very pink, her eyes bright. "We have to make rolls, and pumpkin pie, and sweet potatoes, and salad, and vegetables and finally gravy, when the turkey's done."

Noah's eyes had been getting wider and wider as she reeled off the list, and he leaned back in his chair with a low whistle. "That's some menu! Are you sure we can eat all that?"

"It's Thanksgiving!" she reminded him. "Now, let's see how good you are at kneading bread dough."

"Bread dough?"

"For the rolls."

"Oh."

Before long he was busily kneading dough while the table and its environs gradually turned white beneath a powdering of flour. At the other side of the kitchen Leigh stood at the sink cleaning cranberries and broccoli, and preparing a casserole of yams and orange slices. The kitchen was warm and inviting, with the scents of sage and turkey drifting from the oven while the two of them worked in harmony, as if they had done this before, Leigh thought, as if they would do it again, would prepare many holiday dinners together.

The longing was startlingly strong, and so sudden that it took her by surprise. She wanted this to be just one of many Thanksgivings she spent with Noah, one of a long line of them stretching into the future, a future they would share. She could feel her face pale, then flush, and turned hastily back to the sink. She was being ridiculous!

She knew perfectly well that there was no future for them, she had said as much to Marge, and yet here she was, fantasizing like a dreamy adolescent. She glanced over at Noah, a frilly apron incongruously decorating his middle while flour covered his hands and forearms and dusted the expensive charcoal flannel of his trouser legs. He looked very large, and utterly male, and as if he were enjoying himself immensely as he worked the dough. That enjoyment hardly fit the image of a high-powered international lawyer, but as Leigh had been learning since she met him, there were many facets to Noah Burke.

He turned to smile at her then, catching her off guard, her face gentle and a little sad. He hesitated, searching her eyes with his; then he grinned and the moment passed.

"Here." He held out the bowl full of dough. "It's not sticky anymore, like you said. Now what do I do with it?"

"Cover it"—Leigh draped a clean cloth over the bowl— "and put it over here where it's warm." She set the bowl on the countertop next to the stove. "And let it rise while we make a pie."

"I like the sound of that!" He rubbed his floury hands together in anticipation and joined her.

They worked side by side, Leigh more conscious of Noah than ever as they cooked and talked and laughed, aware of a poignant wish that this day would never end. It was a bittersweet longing. The day would end, just as Noah's year in Bloomington would end, just as their friendship would, inevitably, end. The minutes rushed past, and though she wanted to catch them, to hold back time, she let none of that show. She laughed and smiled and dutifully admired the marching bands and the Rockettes, and knew she would always remember these hours, the warmth and the caring and Noah's presence mingling with the rich aromas of turkey and spices and the music of brass bands.

"Why?" Noah groaned and lay back on the sofa, legs extended, a cup of coffee in his hand. "Why did I eat *two* pieces of pie?"

"Because you rolled the crust out with your own little hands and it was wonderful," Leigh, similarly situated at the other end of the sofa, answered without opening her eyes. "You can't just blame the pie, though. I saw an awful lot of turkey go your way, not to mention the rolls and the potatoes and cranberry sauce and—"

"Please! No more! I don't think I can take a discussion of food in my weakened condition." He gestured with his cup at the center of the living-room rug, where Leon sprawled like a beached whale, stuporous from turkey, gravy and, to Noah's amazement, cranberry sauce. "Even Leon's suc-cumbed to an overdose of food. In his case, though, it's probably the cranberry sauce. There's something unnatural about a cat eating cranberries."

As if aware that he was under discussion, Leon rolled over, stretched hugely and favored them with a monstrous yawn.

"You can't apply the ordinary rules to Leon." Leigh watched the cat subside into sleep again. "He's a law unto himself."

"He's big enough to enforce it, too." Noah slid lower on the sofa and tried to stifle a yawn almost as wide as Leon's. "Sorry. I think I may be as zonked as he is if I don't do something about it."

"Such as?"

He considered for a moment. "How about a walk?" He sat up. "A nice, brisk walk around campus in the nice, cold air. How about it?"

"You must be nuts." Leigh's eyes stayed closed. "It's acting an awful lot like winter out there."

"Just what you need." Noah seized her hand and hauled her to her feet. "A little cold air will put the roses in your cheeks, and it may even whet your appetite for turkey sandwiches later!"

"No! Anything but that! I'll go with you, but only if you promise not to mention food."

"I'll talk about football, all right?"

"Even football talk is better than food talk." Leigh let herself be dragged to the entry hall, stuffed into her down jacket, knit hat and mittens and led out into the cold.

Noah was right, of course; a long walk in the afternoon cold was just what they both needed to overcome the effects of too much dinner. They returned to the house in the early evening, red-cheeked from the cold, breathless from the exertion of a walk that had covered nearly every corner of the sprawling campus and laughing together at nothing in particular or anything at all. Leigh didn't know when she'd been so happy and relaxed with anyone, and she knew she'd never felt this way with a man, but with Noah she could be herself; with Noah she could be at ease.

"Whew!" She closed the door behind them, shutting out the wind, which was unusually cold for southern Indiana in

November. "It's *cold* out there! It feels more like New Year's than Thanksgiving!"

"It's not usually this cold?"

"Not in November. We're far enough south here that we don't usually get the real cold until after Christmas, but it feels like winter today." She pulled off her hat and fluffed her red-gold curls absently as she shrugged out of her jacket. "Coffee, tea, cocoa or chicken soup?"

"Hmm?"

"Which would you like? I think it's definitely time for a hot drink, don't you?"

"Oh, yeah. And I think I'd like coffee right now. As a matter of fact, I think I'd like a little something with my coffee. Maybe a little turkey sandwich and just a bite of pie, and—"

"You *can't* be serious!" Leigh followed him to the kitchen. "Not after that enormous dinner."

"That was hours ago." He pointed to the wall clock in the kitchen. "See? It's almost seven already, and I seem to have worked up an appetite." He opened the refrigerator and began foraging through the leftovers.

"Well"—Leigh took the plates and bowls as he passed them to her—"I guess it has been a while since dinner. How about turkey and cranberry sauce sandwiches?"

"Turkey and *what?*" Noah paused with a plastic bag full of rolls in one hand and a dish of yams in the other.

"Turkey and cranberry sauce." Leigh relieved him of the rolls. "We use these rolls and fill them with lettuce and turkey and cranberry sauce." She glanced up to see open disbelief on Noah's face and shook her head at him. "Still don't trust me on the food issue, eh? Well, take my word for it, it's great. You'll love it."

"Okay, I'll take your word for it—this time." He was dubious, but game, and they quickly assembled a light supper of sandwiches and yams for themselves. Noah approached his sandwich cautiously, clearly uncertain about the combination. He took a careful bite, chewed thoughtfully, and then looked across the table at Leigh with dawning surprise in his face.

"You know, that's not bad," he said slowly, and took another bite. "Actually, it's good!"

"I told you so!" she replied. "Maybe you'll believe me next time, huh?"

"Madam, henceforth, you will receive my utmost confidence in culinary matters! As strange as this sounds, it's really good."

Leigh looked up with a grin, which faded as she met his eyes, deep and dark and smoky. She couldn't look away; she was drowning in the dark-blue depths of his eyes. There was a message there that warmed her cheeks and made her heartbeat accelerate, and there was something magical about the evening, about the two of them sitting there in her kitchen, alone together in the cozy haven while a rising wind whined around the eaves outside.

The magic was still with them as they carried coffee into the living room, where a fire leapt and crackled in the hearth. The sofa was drawn up to the fire, and it seemed perfectly natural for Leigh to curl into the curve of Noah's arm, her legs stretched along the cushions and her head on his shoulder as they watched the flames and talked of nothing.

The conversation faded into a contented silence, and when Noah leaned down to kiss her it was only a continuation of the magic. Warm and relaxed and drowsy, Leigh lifted her face, half smiling into his eyes before her lids fluttered down and she felt his lips, firm and sweet on hers.

He kissed her gently, brushing his lips over hers in a way that left her languorous and longing for more. With an uncharacteristic boldness she laid one hand along his jaw, stilling his face so she could return his kiss. Noah froze for a startled instant, surprised by her unprecedented daring; then his arms tightened, his hands warm on her back as his lips moved over hers.

When she didn't pull away he gently, carefully, slid the tip of his tongue along her lips, parting them almost imperceptibly until, still without frightening her, he was able to deepen the kiss, to taste the sweetness of her mouth for the first time. Leigh responded to him more freely than she ever had been able to, though even while she allowed the kiss to continue, she was but a passive recipient. Made eager by her new acceptance, Noah gently eased her into love play.

As he held her mouth captive his hands moved over her, gently sliding up and down her back, along the length of her slim arms, up to cradle her skull between his palms and then down again to ease beneath the hem of her bulky sweater. The whisper-light touch of his fingers along the skin of her waist burned like fire, the slight roughness of his hands igniting a flame in her that she had thought long dead.

Somehow his sorcery kept her fear at bay, allowing her to feel desire again, to feel like a woman again after so long. She shivered as his hands skimmed the lines of her body, evoking a response she was helpless to deny. Something of that helplessness must have communicated itself to him, because this time Noah did not draw back from her as his own desire mounted.

Without being aware of just how it had happened, Leigh found herself stretched out on the sofa with Noah, wrapped in his embrace as his lips hardened and his body shifted to cover hers. Her awareness of his desire was unavoidable, and with that awareness came her fear, growing as his kisses and caresses grew more demanding.

His hand slipped further under her sweater, seeking her breast, and she wriggled, trying to avoid the caress, then pushed ineffectually at his hands as, in a quick, smooth movement which took her completely by surprise, he peeled her sweater over her head and tossed it aside. Her sheer lace bra was no barrier to either his eyes or his hands, and Leigh could feel herself flushing hotly as she strove to push him away.

This time, though, he did not withdraw when she resisted him, but shifted his body to hold her captive beneath him. "Don't push me away again," he muttered into her hair.

"Not this time. I've waited so long, and I've been patient, but you're so beautiful. . . ." He found her mouth again, kissing her with hot insistence as panic shot through her and she tried to twist away. "I've waited so long. . . ."

His weight pinned her to the sofa; she was helpless against his greater strength, though she struggled in earnest, her fear a bitter taste in the back of her throat. It was all happening just as it had before, and Leigh could feel herself sinking deeper and deeper into a black whirlpool of remembered pain and terror, her own puny strength useless against a man's passion and power.

"No," she whimpered. "Please, no . . ." But the hands on her tightened; the body pinning hers grew harder, heavier; the lips forced her mouth. Lost in her private nightmare, Leigh fought frantically, no longer conscious of who she was fighting, knowing only that she had to fight, that she was threatened. Kicking and squirming, she finally freed one hand and hit him, hard, on the cheekbone.

"Damn it, Leigh!" Noah jerked his head back, wondering what she was playing at and angered by her fighting; he knew he hadn't hurt her. Seizing her hand before she could hit him again, he pulled it above her head and pinned it there, rendering her helpless. She went suddenly still beneath him, and he lowered his head toward her again.

"No . . ." She moaned again, a low, feral sound, as his head blotted out the firelight, throwing her face in shadow. "No. Please, no . . ."

"Leigh . . ." he began, intending to reason with her, but she answered with a wordless moan. "Leigh, come on—"

"No," she moaned again, then cried, "no! No, Tony! Please, Tony, no!" She finished on a high, thin wail, and Noah froze in furious shock at the sound of another man's name.

"Who the hell is Tony?" he snarled. Leigh didn't reply, and his anger grew, fed by frustrated desire and a surge of jealousy of Tony, whoever he was. He reached above her head to snap on the lamp.

What he saw in the sudden blaze of light drained the

anger and the passion from him in a heartbeat, leaving him cold with shock and horror. Her eyes were wide and dilated and blind, seeing only something in her memory, and her face was a frozen mask of terror.

"Dear God," he gasped, and rolled away to kneel beside the sofa. As soon as his imprisoning weight was gone Leigh curled into a tight ball, her hands shielding her face from some threat Noah could only guess at. She looked, he realized in staggered comprehension, as if she were going to be beaten. "Oh, my God!" he whispered again.

Sick with remorse, he was swept by a wave of hatred so powerful that it left him shaking, hatred of the man who had done this to her, and hatred of himself for the almost criminal insensitivity he had shown. He snatched an afghan from the back of the sofa and folded it around her shivering form, then tried to pull her into his arms again.

He meant only to hold and comfort her, but she flinched sharply away from his touch, still lost in terror, and he drew back. He had to calm her; somehow he had to calm her. She looked as though she might literally die of fright, and he couldn't stand to see her suffer this way. He *had* to pull her back from the nightmare and hysteria, and if he couldn't use his hands, then he'd have to use his voice.

"Leigh, it's Noah," he began in a low, level tone, fighting his own emotion as well as her panic. "Leigh, Leigh, honey, it's Noah. I won't hurt you, Leigh; you're safe now. I won't hurt you." He kept speaking soothingly, not daring to touch her, exerting an almost desperate control over himself in order to calm her, and finally she pulled her hands slowly, fearfully away from her face.

"Tony?" she said in a voice that, eerily, was hers, and yet not the voice he was accustomed to. It sounded high and thin and very young, hesitant and afraid.

"Tony isn't here," he told her as calmly as he could. "I'm here, Leigh, and you're safe now. Nothing will hurt you now. Tony isn't here."

"Tony's gone," she said in that thin voice that so dis-

turbed him. "Tony's dead." Her face crumpled, and she
burst into tears.

This time she let him cradle her in his arms. Deep, tearing
sobs racked her body while he stroked her hair and murmured soothing nonsense and prayed that she'd be all right.
When the sobs died away at last, he spoke very gently to
her.

"Leigh? Are you all right now?"

"Yes. I-I'm okay." She was hoarse from tears, but she
was in control of herself once more, and her voice was her
own. Noah felt himself go limp with relief.

"I'm going to help you put your sweater on, okay?" he
said gently, and she nodded passively.

"Okay."

Carefully he pulled the sweater over her head and
threaded her arms through the sleeves, then bundled the
afghan warmly around her again. "Leigh?"

"Mmm?"

"I'm going to get you something to drink. I'll be right
here, so you don't need to be afraid." She didn't look up as
he moved across the room to splash brandy into a glass, and
when he returned to kneel by the sofa she was still staring
into the fire, her eyes wide and haunted. "Drink this,
Leigh."

She reached obediently for the glass, but her hands were
shaking so badly that Noah had to help her hold it while she
sipped, choked a little, then sipped again. He made her
drink most of it before he judged that she could be left alone
for the few minutes it would take him to make coffee.

"I'm going out to the kitchen to make coffee, Leigh. Will
you wait here for me?" She nodded indifferently. He
brewed the coffee as quickly as he could, looking repeatedly
into the living room to make certain she was all right. To his
growing dismay she continued to stare apathetically at the
fire, showing no interest in anything around her. She drank
the hot, sweet coffee when he gave it to her, but she was still
deathly pale, her eyes dark and haunted despite her surface

calm. Noah sat watching her in silence for a time, but the question was burning inside him, and it had to be asked.

"Leigh?"

"Hmm?"

"Who is Tony?"

If she were upset by the question, she gave no sign of it; her gaze never left the flames. "He was my husband."

Noah started in surprise. Whatever he had expected, it wasn't this. Watching her face closely, he asked, "Was?"

"He's dead." She said the words with no noticeable emotion, and after a moment she continued in a flat, toneless voice. "I was married when I was nineteen. My parents didn't approve. He was over thirty, and he didn't have a 'regular' job; he called himself an entrepreneur and played the stock market. I was—I was certain that I was in love. I wouldn't let him make love to me before the wedding—I wanted to wear white—and he seemed to find that amusing. I did wear white, though, a long white dress, in a big church wedding."

She paused, then drew a deep, shaky breath before continuing. "I suppose I knew that there was such a thing as battered wives, but of course I didn't know anything about that, except that it only happened to other people. I—I learned how wrong I was. At first I thought it was my fault, that I must have done something to make him angry; then I began to see that it wasn't me, that there was nothing I could do to change him. And that hurt," she said softly. "That hurt so much, because I had loved him and trusted him, and the man that I had loved and trusted didn't even exist. He was only a mirage, an image projected to hide the ugliness underneath. Everything I had based my love and my hopes on was a mirage; it was like trying to stand on quicksand."

"You don't have to talk about it, Leigh, if you don't want—"

"It doesn't matter. You should know." Her voice was calm, but she hunched forward, hands clenched together, staring blindly at the flames. "I gave up on a night when he came home late. He'd been drinking, and he was angry, and he—he wanted me. I wouldn't . . . I couldn't, and that made him even angrier." Her voice shook, but she steadied it and went on. "When he was—when it was over, and I got free, I ran to my car and drove away, but he drove after me. He tried to force me off the road. My car went into a ditch, but he lost control and crashed, too. He hit a bridge abutment. The police said he died instantly. We had been married for six weeks."

"And you?" Noah asked in a carefully controlled voice. "Were you hurt?"

She shrugged. "I was in the hospital for several weeks."

"My God," he whispered, and bent forward, covering his face with his hands. "My God," he repeated, muffled. "I'm so sorry, Leigh."

"What for?" Her tone was artificially bright. "You did nothing—"

"But I did!" he exploded, turning to look at her. "I frightened you, and hurt you! My God, if I'd known—This explains so much; this explains why—"

"Oh, it explains, but it doesn't change anything, does it?" There was a trace of sarcasm in the words, and the first animation she had shown. "It's still the same; I'm still afraid—"

"But there must be help for you, therapy of some kind."

Leigh smiled bitterly. "I spent months seeing psychiatrists. I'd still be seeing them if I thought it would do any good. They helped me return to 'normal,' or at least as normal as I can ever be. I came back to school about a year after I was married, and I was able to get my degree and my Master's. I work and I study and I teach, but they weren't able to help me with the other problem."

"But, you've kissed me, many times now."

Leigh looked at Noah, startled. "Yes," she agreed after a moment, "I have."

"Leigh, listen to me," he said urgently, leaning toward her and frowning when she edged away, her uneasiness evident. "Leigh, I won't hurt you. I won't! You must know that you can trust me." He was watching her face intently, and something must have shown there, suspicion or skepticism, despite her efforts to appear calm. "Leigh, you have to know that I'd never hurt you!"

"I don't think that's what matters." She shrugged. "No one ever said this was a rational problem, after all. Look, Noah, you've spent a lot of time with me, and I appreciate that, I really do. I appreciate your patience, but you must see that there's no future in it. I can't give you what you want, what any man would want—that should be painfully obvious. I've enjoyed knowing you—you'll never know how much it's meant to me—but you don't need to feel obligated to waste any more time on me."

"Stop it!" Noah's incensed roar made her jump. "Stop it right now! You're not going to shove me out of your life this way; I won't let you!" He leaned over her again, the fury in his face daring her to flinch away. Somehow she managed to hold her ground. "I want a lot of things," he went on, his voice dangerously quiet. "I'd like a Rolls-Royce and a million dollars, but that doesn't mean I can't live without them. It's not just sex that I want from you, or from any woman. If it were you'd have every right to be offended, and to tell you the truth I resent the fact that you would think that of me."

Leigh flushed, ashamed that she'd never even considered the fact that she might be doing Noah an injustice in her judgment of him. He spoke more gently then, his eyes on her face.

"It's not just sex I want from you, Leigh, it's much more. I want your company, your conversation, your time. I want to *be* with you, to share with you. I want your friendship."

Leigh looked at him for a moment, disturbed by the idea, unable to understand, her eyes very wide in her white face. "I don't see why," she said at last. "And you want more than that, too, don't you? Why should you settle for any less?"

"If you don't get it, I'm not sure there's anything I can do to make you understand right now. You'll just have to take my word for it that there's far more than sex involved in a relationship, and that it's only a small part of what's involved here. I want your friendship and your companionship, Leigh, believe that."

"But it's so—"

"Don't worry about it!" He cut off her protest sharply, then frowned as she winced at the annoyance in his voice. "Just agree to be my friend, Leigh. That's all I ask." She hesitated. "Will you do that, Leigh?"

"I—I don't—"

"Will you do that?" he pressed. "Please?"

Leigh looked at him for a long time, at the hard, dark face, the deep indigo eyes, trying to read his thoughts. She was half-hopeful, half-afraid. She looked into his eyes again, and something there compelled her answer. She nodded slowly, and he sighed heavily.

"Thank you," he said, so softly that she might have imagined it, and sat back to gaze silently at the fire. It might have been five minutes, or thirty, that they sat there, lost in their thoughts. When Noah spoke again, Leigh jumped, startled. "Leigh, I think you . . . I'm sorry. I didn't mean to scare you, but I think you should go to bed. You look worn out. And I'm sorry for that, too," he added heavily. "I seem to have a lot to be sorry for this evening."

"Noah, don't." Leigh laid her hand on his arm, the first time she had touched him since her fears had blown up in her face. Noah looked startled. "Noah, none of this was your fault. You didn't know—"

"Maybe not, and yes, you should have said something to me, but it happened, and I'm sorry, and I think you should go to bed. You look terrible."

"Oh."

"I didn't mean it like that, you know. Come on, you're exhausted." He took her hand and clasped it warmly, then rose and pulled her to her feet beside him. He led her to her bedroom, and Leigh, too tired to think for herself, trailed meekly along.

Noah had never been in her room, and he looked around

appreciatively as he switched on lamps and pushed Leigh into the comfortable chintz wing chair by the window.

Numb, practically drooping with exhaustion, Leigh slumped in the chair, watching as Noah searched quickly in her tiny closet, then turned to the chifforobe and produced a long-sleeved, high-necked, ankle-length nightgown in pink flowered flannel. He nodded in satisfaction as he brought it to her.

"Go brush your teeth and get into this," he said as he handed it to her. "I'll make you something hot to drink, okay?"

"Okay." When Leigh hesitated Noah pulled her out of the chair and headed her toward the bathroom.

"Go on."

She went. When she returned the bed was turned down invitingly, one lamp cast a subdued glow, and Noah waited with two mugs of cocoa on a tray. Leigh was a bit embarrassed, but Noah, matter-of-fact and brisk, gave her no reason to be uncomfortable.

"Get in, before you get cold." She slid between the smooth sheets, and he tucked her in warmly, then handed her a mug of steaming chocolate with a marshmallow melting on top.

She sipped her cocoa and licked sticky-sweet melted marshmallow from her upper lip. "Mmm, this is good, but I feel like a little kid."

"Everybody needs to be taken care of now and then." Noah had watched her tongue tip clean her lip, and when he spoke his voice was brusque, his eyes opaque and expressionless for a moment before they warmed again. "Do you think you can sleep now?"

"Mm-hm, I think so." She handed him the empty mug. "Thank you, Noah."

"Don't thank me." He sat silently for a moment. "Leigh?"

"Yes?"

"Have you ever had nightmares?"

"Yes, but how did you . . . ?" She fell silent as she understood, then said carefully, "Why do you ask?"

"Because I don't think you should be alone tonight."

"Noah, please, it's all right. You've taken care of me, now go home and get some sleep yourself."

"No, I'll stay here." His tone didn't allow for question or argument. "You have another bedroom, don't you?"

"The room opposite the bathroom, but—"

"Is the bed made up?"

"Well, yes, it is, but—"

"Good, I'll stay in there." Whatever Leigh might have had to say was obviously of no interest to Noah. One corner of her mind realized that she ought to be annoyed at the high-handed way he was taking over, but the rest of her brain was too numb with fatigue and stress to care. She gave in without a struggle.

"There's an extra blanket in the cedar chest in there," she told him, and lay back on the pillows, her eyes falling closed. Her face was nearly as white as the bleached muslin, and Noah felt another spasm of remorse.

"I'll find it. Do you want me to leave the light on?"

"What?" She blinked sleepily up at him. "Oh, no, I don't need a light." She snuggled under the comforter. "I gave up on night-lights when I was about four, Noah. I'll be fine."

"Yes, you will." He brushed a hand across her forehead, smoothing back an errant curl. "Good night, Leigh. Sleep well."

"G'night, Noah," she mumbled, turning to bury her face in her pillow, and he flicked off the light and went to find his bed.

He came awake with a start in the small hours, roused by soft sounds of distress from across the hall. In seconds he had rolled out of bed, dragged on his slacks and crossed quickly to Leigh's room. She twisted in agitation beneath the tumbled covers, muttering and whimpering, and he knew she was struggling and crying out for help in her dreams. He desperately wanted to help her, but he was afraid to touch her, afraid she would mistake him for her dead husband and become even more terrified.

Hating his own uselessness, he hesitated for a moment, then switched on the bedside lamp. What he saw gave him no comfort. Leigh's face was white, frightened, wet with tears, her eyes squeezed tight against whatever terrors she saw in her mind.

"Leigh." He leaned close, speaking as calmly as he could. "Leigh, you're having a nightmare. *Leigh.*" He fought the urge to take her into his arms. "It's all right; it's only a dream. Wake up, Leigh, darling. *Wake up.*"

She did, starting up in bed, her eyes wide, still looking inward at the memories. He kept speaking, and gradually her eyes cleared and focused on him. She stared for a second; then recognition dawned and her face began to crumple.

"Oh, Noah . . ." Her voice was a thin whisper, and then the tears came. This time he did hold her, her face pressed into the warm flesh of his shoulder as she sobbed out the night's terrors. It took a long time, but at last she was calm again.

"Here, sweetheart." Noah raised her face and dried her cheeks with a corner of the sheet, hurting for her, hurting at the sight of her white, strained face, the vestiges of fear lingering in her eyes. She seemed so frail, vulnerable, her bones fine and fragile under his hands. He wanted to protect her, to take away the pain she had suffered, and his helplessness was a cruel punishment. "Do you want a drink of water? Or some more cocoa, maybe?"

She shook her head. "No, that's okay. I don't need anything." She slid out of his arms and lay back on the pillows. "Thank you for—for putting up with me. I'm sorry I woke you up."

"Don't worry about it." He studied her for a moment. "Can you sleep now?"

"Yes. But, Noah . . . ?"

"Hmm?"

"Would you—would you mind leaving the light on?" It tore at his heart to hear her ask; she was so obviously ashamed of her need. She wanted to be strong and independent and self-reliant, when she needed more than anything else to be cared for, protected. He wondered how many times she had awakened from a similar nightmare, alone in the darkness with no one to cling to.

"I'll leave the light on," he assured her, "and I'll sit in here with you until you go to sleep." She peered at him uncertainly for a moment. "Go to sleep, Leigh."

"Okay." She lay back, exhausted. "Good night, Noah."

"Good night, Leigh. Sleep well." He got a blanket from his bed and wrapped it around his naked shoulders, then settled himself comfortably in the armchair, watching as she relaxed and slid into sleep, her breathing deep and regular. Her sleep seemed peaceful this time; somehow he had been able to ease her terror. He just wished someone could ease his guilt and calm his anger.

He couldn't imagine the kind of sick, twisted man who could take a bright, beautiful girl and do that to her. She was tall and graceful and strong, but when he'd held her in his arms as she shook with fear he'd been aware only of how fragile she was, how easily hurt.

She could be easily hurt physically as well as emotionally, and yet someone had hurt her, some sick, pathetic man had beaten her, not once, but many times—had raped her and in his final act of savagery had nearly killed her. Noah was filled with a cold, murderous rage at the unknown, dead Tony.

How could anyone do that? In what he recognized as a completely irrational moment Noah almost wished that that bastard were still alive, so he could have the pleasure of murdering him himself. Somehow it seemed that Tony had gotten off too easily, that he deserved more punishment for the damage that had been done to Leigh. As the hours passed, Noah was not surprised to find sleep elusive.

Chapter Six

Leigh woke to a brilliantly sunny morning, bitter cold but
bright, with at least six inches of new snow blanketing
everything outdoors. She blinked up at the ceiling for a
moment; then memory returned in a rush and she felt
herself flush hotly. Oh, Lord, now she remembered! She
had made a complete fool of herself; and Noah had put her
to bed, and then, to top it off, she'd had the nightmare
again, waking Noah up, and he'd insisted on sitting up with
her.

How humiliating! He had come in to awaken her from the
nightmare, and then she'd cried. She had let him hold her in
his arms, her face buried in his bare shoulder, while she
cried her eyes out. He had dried her face, she remembered,
but she didn't know whether he'd ever dried his shoulder.

She remembered lots of things, now that she was waking
up and her mind was clearing, things like how warm his
shoulder had been, the smooth skin and crisp hair on his
chest where her cheek had rested, the scent of him, warm
from sleep and clean and male. She remembered how strong

his arms had been, how warm his hands had been, sliding over her back in a comforting caress. She remembered all those things, and she remembered, to her astonishment, how right they had all felt. It was astounding, but she had wanted him to hold her; she had drawn courage and strength from him, and it had felt utterly right.

That was something she would have to think about later, when she was alone. Now she had to get up. The chair Noah had occupied was empty, but the seductive scents of coffee and bacon provided a clue to his whereabouts. Leigh slid out of bed, then wrapped a deep violet velour robe around herself and padded out to the bathroom.

Her first look in the mirror was not reassuring. The night's upheaval and tears had left her with bruised circles beneath swollen eyes, wildly tangled hair, and a pale, drawn face. She quickly made what repairs she could, then took a deep breath and went to meet Noah.

He was deeply absorbed in cooking breakfast and didn't immediately notice her in the doorway, so she took advantage of the opportunity to study him. He had redonned his gray flannel slacks and pale-blue oxford shirt, wearing socks but not shoes, with his shirttail out and sleeves rolled up. His face was scrubbed and alert, his hair roughly combed, but he hadn't shaved, and the dark shadowing of stubble on his jaw added a raffish air.

She was a bit nervous of meeting him this morning anyway, not certain whether she were more grateful he had been there to help her or humiliated that he had seen her at her weakest. Seeing him like this, vibrantly masculine, seeming to fill her kitchen with his presence, did nothing to ease her tension. It was odd, she thought idly, but Noah always seemed taller than he really was, as though his natural air of command added inches to his height.

He took down a plate and began forking crisp bacon from the skillet, the movements stretching his shirt across the breadth of his back, and Leigh was reminded anew of just how strong he was. He was solidly massive, utterly male, and yet he was the first man in all these years with whom she was not afraid to be alone. He covered the plate and set it aside, and Leigh followed the motion, unable to pull her eyes away. He turned and caught her watching him.

"Good morning. How do you feel about pancakes?"

Whatever she had expected his first words to be, she hadn't anticipated this, but perhaps such a mundane topic was precisely what she needed. "Pancakes?" she repeated, considering. "Love 'em." She showed him where to find what he needed, then asked, "Can I help?"

"Not with the pancakes." Noah broke an egg into the bowl and reached for the milk and a measuring cup. "But if you want to mix up a can of orange juice, that would be great."

"Right away." She made the juice while Noah made the pancakes, and by the time they sat down to eat she was relaxed and even hungry. They ate heartily, and in near-silence, until they finished.

"Mmm, that was wonderful!" Leigh sat back and sipped her coffee. "Where did you learn to make pancakes like that? I always cheat and use pancake mix."

"Pancake mix? That's sacrilege! They taught us to make the real thing in the boy scouts."

"You're kidding! Really?" He nodded. "Well, the boy scouts have my vote as the pancake champs, then. Those were terrific."

"They weren't bad, but actually they're better when you cook them over an open fire, out in the woods. I kind of missed the challenge of burning the first six or eight before I figured out the right temperature." Noah ate his last bite, savoring it like a connoisseur. "Mm-hm. Not a bad batch at all." He lifted his own cup, and for a few minutes neither of them spoke. When he turned back to her, though, his face was sober, and Leigh felt her heart lurch at what she saw in his eyes. She waited almost fearfully for him to speak, but when he did, his question surprised her.

"What do you want out of life, Leigh?"

Had she replied immediately, Leigh might have given him a flippant, joking answer, but she hesitated, because it was clear that Noah had asked the question seriously. She wasn't sure what to answer; she wasn't sure what she really did want out of life.

"I haven't given it a lot of thought," she admitted at last. "Success in my career, I suppose, health, happiness."

"How about a family? Do you want a husband? Children?"

Irritated by the assumptions she read into the question, Leigh scowled. "I've already had a husband, remember? That's not an experience I'm eager to repeat, and the question of children has been taken out of my hands. Anyway," she added sharply, "is that what I *should* want? Am I supposed to want those things just because I'm a woman?"

"Not because you're a woman," Noah patiently corrected her, "but because you're human. Most people, women *and* men, want a family eventually."

"Do you?"

"Yes," he said after a pause, "I do. It's taken me too long to come to that realization, but I do."

"Tired of the international jet-set playboy life, are we?" Leigh asked pertly, and he grimaced into his coffee cup.

"That's almost too close to the truth to be funny. I'm not particularly proud of my private life recently, but I seem to be growing up at last, gaining a maturity that's long overdue. The difference for me, or for any man, is that I don't have a biological clock ticking away inside me, marking the end of the time when I'm able to have a family."

"And I do?" Leigh's voice was barely more than a whisper.

"As any woman does."

She leaned back in her chair, closing her eyes tiredly against the brilliant glare of sun and snow outside the window. "I'm only twenty-six. There's plenty of time."

"But if there weren't?" Noah pressed. "If you were ten years older, thirty-six instead of twenty-six, and there were no longer 'plenty of time,' what then?"

"I don't know!" she cried angrily, wheeling around to glare at him. "I don't know, okay? I guess I'd just be alone then, wouldn't I?"

"That's an awfully bleak prospect," he commented. "Not one I'd relish. If you don't take some steps to change the direction you're going, though, you will be alone and lonely for the rest of your life. I want you to think about it, Leigh. Think about what your emotional isolation means. Not all men are like your husband was—very few are, in fact—and you have to recognize that if you're ever to learn to love again."

"How can I?" She scowled at the tablecloth. "How can you expect me to do that? I loved Tony, and look what happened. Can I risk that again? Can I even *try* to love another man and put myself in that helpless position again? I can't—no, that's not right—I don't want to love, to trust, like that again."

"You trust me, don't you?" The question caught her off guard, and she considered for a moment before she nodded.

"Yes, I trust you, in some ways, but it isn't the same. You and I aren't . . ." She blushed, stumbling over the words. "We're not . . ."

"No, we're not lovers," Noah finished for her. "We're friends, and that can be a more intimate relationship in many ways. You know me better than you know most men, right?"

Better than I've ever known any man, Leigh thought, but she just nodded.

"You know me, and you trust me, despite the fact that I'm a man." His voice grew more urgent. "Sweetheart, you're only half alive right now, and if you're honest with yourself, you'll realize it. Life's too short to spend it hiding from the risk of hurt, afraid of what might happen. If you can learn to trust me, maybe you can escape that trap, break down that wall of isolation you've built around yourself. I can help you, Leigh, if you'll let me."

She studied him in silence for a long time, trying to work out his motives and failing miserably. It didn't make sense to her, and finally she asked, "Why should you help me? Why should you bother with me at all, when you could be with any number of other women, women who aren't emotionally damaged, who could give you all that you want?"

"What I want is you." Noah reached out to capture her hand, and his strength seemed to flow into her. "I want you, Leigh, not those other women. I want your companionship, your friendship, your humor which always surprises me, and yes, I want your kisses, if you can give them to me. I think that wall around you can be made to crumble, and I want to be here when it does, and you begin to live again."

"But what if that doesn't happen? What if nothing ever changes? Won't you regret having wasted so much time and energy on me?"

"I won't regret anything."

"So how was your Thanksgiving?" Kate looked up as Leigh entered the office on Monday morning, her cheeks pink from the cold.

"Snowy," was the dry reply. "But I wish it had stayed snow, instead of turning into slush."

"Don't avoid the issue. How was your Thanksgiving? Did you and Noah have a lovely dinner?"

"I cooked it." Leigh grinned. "Naturally it was great. How was yours?"

"Crazy, as always. Big families are wonderful, but they can be kind of overwhelming in large doses. Now, how was your weekend with Noah?" she asked for a third time, and Leigh sighed heavily.

"You're not going to leave me alone until you pry it out of me, are you?"

"Nope." Kate sat back and waited.

"Well, it wasn't quite what I expected, that's for sure."

"What went wrong?" Kate asked, watching Leigh's face, and Leigh shrugged.

"I flipped out." She gave Kate a heavily edited version of Thursday's events. "I told Noah about Tony," she concluded, and heard Kate's sharply indrawn breath, "but I'm not sure it was the right thing to do."

"I don't know," Kate said slowly. "It might have been the best thing you could have done. You know, Leigh, Noah could be just the man to bring you out of your shell."

Leigh was beginning to feel annoyed at all this determination to improve her. "I'm not all that sure I want to be brought 'out of my shell,' thank you very much!" she said tartly. "My shell and I have gotten along just fine for years. Anyway, I'm also not sure it's fair of me to go on seeing Noah at all."

"Why on earth not?"

"Because I may never be what he wants. I may just be a waste of his time and energy. It's as if he wants me to use him, but I don't want to be a user."

Kate choked on a swallow of coffee. "You, a user?" She shook her head in dismissal. "Noah's a big boy, Leigh. Why don't you let him make his own decisions? I'm sure if he feels you're taking unfair advantage of him, he'll let you know. Now"—she pulled a folder from her briefcase— "here's what my representative thinks about funding for higher education, and our chances of changing anything."

"You got it? Kate, you're fabulous!"

Leigh moved around the desk to read the notes over Kate's shoulder, thankful for the change of subject but aware that the issue was far from closed. She still didn't quite buy it, but there was a certain irrefutable logic to Kate's comment. Noah was an adult, and if he wanted to make his own decisions it was not her place to try to stop him.

That might well have been true, but as the days passed Leigh wondered again if it were fair of her to allow things to go on. Noah expected her to change, and she didn't see any change happening within herself. The lack of progress disturbed her. She was able to return Noah's kisses, even to take a vague, nonsexual pleasure in them, but her fear of further intimacy remained, and the brief flashes of passion she had felt in his arms had not recurred. She had been so alone for so long that she saw her own need for human closeness and comfort, but she also recognized what Noah felt when he kissed her.

She could sense the need and the excitement in him, and was equally, painfully, aware of the lack of an answering excitement in herself. She cared for Noah more than she had thought possible, but her feelings were not those of a woman for a man who might become her lover. Bitterly she sometimes wondered if this wasn't Tony's final revenge, the destruction of some vital part of her femininity, leaving her less than a woman. For the first time since his death that mattered to her.

She wanted to change before she was trapped by loneliness forever, but how? She was beginning to doubt her ability to be a woman for Noah or for any man. In the days since Thanksgiving the knowledge of her inadequacy had eaten at her, spawning a growing guilt at her inability to respond to him in the face of his continued caring.

She felt as though she were accepting his affection under false pretenses, and she hated that feeling. She hated to be a taker and not a giver, and somehow she had to give something back to Noah in return for all he had given her. The question of what she would give him in return, of how she would repay his generosity, was one she shied away from, for the answer was at the same time elusive and yet obvious.

"What a way to spend the day before Christmas break!" Leigh muttered sotto voce, then realized that Noah had heard her—he looked up from the affidavit he was studying and met her eyes across the conference table. A partial audit of the budget had been done, and now Leigh, Mike Morris, Dean Anderson, Noah and an assistant bursar were scrutinizing it line by line. This was not how Leigh would have chosen to spend her afternoon. Noah held her eyes for a moment, a conspirator's smile in the deep blue depths of his. Leigh flushed at the message she read there; then he looked down at his papers, and the meeting was all business once more.

"So, you can see," Dean Anderson went on, "that there are no funds available."

"No," Leigh interjected, "that's not precisely true. What we can see is that there is no money in this particular segment of the budget. I want to know if there isn't some little bit of cash somewhere in this huge budget that could be reallocated to salaries and stipends."

"We've already told you, Miss Michaels, that we haven't been able to find any."

"Forgive me, Dean Anderson, but I doubt if you really want to find any. Perhaps if we could look it over?"

"The budget is published each year, Miss Michaels. Feel free to consult it."

"The budget that's published is a synopsis, hardly detailed enough to be useful. We need access to the working budget."

"That budget is confidential," Noah interjected, and she sighed in exasperation.

"I don't think the voters and taxpayers of this state would like to know that the operating budget of the university is confidential, do you, Mr. Burke?"

"Is that a threat?" Dean Anderson asked.

"Of course not. Merely an observation."

The dean cleared his throat and subsided into his chair. "Your 'observation' is noted," he said dryly. "Miss Michaels, will you let Mrs. Weatherly know which sections of the operating budget you need to see?"

"Of course." Leigh was careful to conceal her sense of triumph, but she felt like jumping and shouting. Once they got the operating budget from his secretary and were able to review it, they would have something concrete to present to the legislature.

"Is there any further business?" the dean asked, and when no one replied in the affirmative he sighed in relief. "Meeting is adjourned. I see no reason to reconvene until the first of the year, so I will wish you all a happy holiday. Good-bye."

Amid a chorus of good-byes and happy holidays, Leigh left the room, with Mike at her side. She controlled herself until they were outside the building; then, needing to share her sense of triumph, she grabbed Mike's hand and wrung it, laughing.

"Leigh?" he asked hesitantly.

"Hmm?"

"Will you have dinner with me?"

Leigh searched for the words to tactfully decline. "Mike, I—I appreciate the invitation, but I have plans this evening."

"With me," said Noah from just behind them, startling them both.

Mike dropped Leigh's hand as though it were red hot. "I—ah—I didn't mean to—" He blushed and stammered, and Leigh's heart went out to him.

"That's all right, Mike. It was thoughtful of you to ask me, and I appreciate the invitation."

"Yeah, well . . . I'll see you after the holidays, I guess. Merry Christmas."

"Merry Christmas, Mike." He left them with a last uncertain good-bye, and Leigh scowled at Noah. "Did you have to sneak up and then butt in like the voice from the crypt? You scared him half to death!"

"Good." Noah looked entirely too pleased with himself. "I meant to scare him."

"That was *not* necessary! I was in the process of politely declining when you put in your two cents worth."

"Too politely, if you ask me."

"I didn't ask!"

Noah just laughed and leaned forward to lightly kiss the mutinous pout from her lips. "Go on home, Madame Chairperson; I'll see you there about seven, okay?"

"Okay." Leigh began to smile, undone, as always, by his charm. "I don't know if you deserve dinner after that little stunt though."

"You wouldn't turn down a starving man, would you?" His eyes were pleading, and Leigh broke up.

"No, I guess I wouldn't. Seven o'clock." He left her with another quick, hard kiss, and she walked rapidly home, anxious to have everything ready before he arrived.

Her Christmas tree stood in the center of the living room, half-trimmed, needing only tinsel and candy canes to complete its decor. Working quickly, she finished trimming it, slid it into place by the living-room window and stood back to admire the sight. Glittering with multicolored lights, unbreakable satin balls—in deference to Leon's penchant for removing them from the tree and chasing them around the house—a multitude of tiny wooden toys, candy canes and the tinsel and cranberries, it was beautiful, magical. Leigh reached over to switch off the overhead light, and the tree lit the room with a warming glow.

"Merry Christmas, Leigh," she whispered to herself. She continued to gaze at the tree for a few moments, then checked her watch. "Oh-oh." The mystical mood faded fast; Leigh now had only ninety minutes to fix a meal and get herself ready for the end-of-semester, finals-are-over, leaving-for-Christmas, good-bye dinner they had planned. Noah was taking a plane to New York the next morning; he planned to spend the holidays with his sister and her family in Connecticut, and Leigh would not see him again until after the first of the year. Because it was their final evening together they had also planned to exchange gifts, though they'd agreed not to open them until Christmas Day.

Their final evening together. Leigh paused, holding the pepper shaker poised over the beef tenderloin she was preparing to roast, and thought about that. Of course it wasn't really their last evening together, only their last for about two weeks, but it was still a good-bye. It was to be a special evening for them, a private celebration, yet she wondered just what they had to celebrate.

Probably nothing, she decided as she slid the roast into the hot oven. As a matter of fact, Noah was probably as disappointed in her as she was in herself. And she *was* disappointed, disappointed and guilty, and preparing a luxurious meal for Noah wouldn't assuage that guilt. She owed him more for his caring than roast beef and broccoli with hollandaise sauce; she owed him some progress in her fight to escape her emotional isolation, and she didn't seem to be making any.

Perhaps she was being too cautious. Perhaps she was waiting for some magical transformation when there wasn't going to be a clear-cut moment of change. Perhaps, she thought, she was waiting passively for something to change when what she had to do was *make* a change occur.

But how? How could she *make* herself change? Was there a way to show Noah how grateful she was to him and force a change in herself at the same time? She concentrated on her cooking, a little afraid to consider the conclusion her thoughts had inevitably reached.

It was obvious, though, too obvious to be ignored. She could make love to Noah tonight, before he flew off to New York for two weeks. The idea just sat there in her mind as she completed the meal preparations, gradually becoming less outrageous, more acceptable, more possible. By the time she left the kitchen she realized that she had made her decision.

She would make love with Noah that evening, would force herself past her fear and her lack of response, and would give something to Noah in return for all that he had given her. A strange excitement began to grow in her, fizzing through her veins as she headed for the bathroom to prepare for his arrival.

She sent a steaming torrent gushing into the deep, claw-footed tub, and then, on impulse, poured in a generous dollop of foaming bath oil. It was a seductively scented oil, rich and heady, a gift from Kate. Leigh rarely used it, but tonight it seemed appropriate.

She lay in the bath for a long time, and when at last she pulled the plug and climbed out of the tub she was filled with a dreamy lassitude. She even looked different. She glimpsed her blurred reflection in the foggy mirror, then paused to wipe away the moisture and study herself more closely.

Her hair was wildly disarrayed, a curling, red-gold nimbus about her face; her cheeks were flushed, and her eyes sparkled with a reckless excitement. Even her body looked different, pink and glowing from the heat, warm and alive. She turned abruptly away from her image and began to towel herself roughly, surprised to realize that her hands were trembling.

When she greeted Noah at the door a short time later she had the trembling under control. She was outwardly calm, wearing a softly flattering sweater dress of emerald cashmere, and enamel earrings in the shape of holly leaves, her eyes glowing the same green as her dress, but that core of taut excitement still vibrated within her.

Noah enjoyed the meal, complimenting Leigh lavishly. They didn't really talk, though, until dinner was finished, the dishes cleared away, and they had carried their coffee and dessert into the living room so they could sit by the fire.

"That's a really pretty tree." Noah looked across to where it glowed in its niche by the window, a few gaily wrapped packages piled beneath it.

"Thank you," Leigh said happily, then impulsively leaned close to kiss Noah on the lips.

It was a quick, light kiss, playful, but when Leigh lifted her head she looked into Noah's heavy-lidded, smoky eyes and bent to kiss him again. Startled, he let her take the initiative, and when she didn't call a halt he brought his arms up to hold her. He kissed her eagerly, following the outline of her lips with his tongue tip until slowly, hesitantly, they parted for him.

With growing assurance Noah deepened the kiss, gently searching the sweetness of her mouth as his hands, which had rested unmoving on her back, began to slide slowly up and down her spine. Leigh felt the familiar fearful tension begin to build in her, but she struggled against it, inexpertly returning Noah's kisses, determined this time to overcome her fears.

"Leigh?" Noah surprised her when, after several minutes, he raised his head to look down at her face in the fire glow.

"Hmm?" She peered up at him, then looked quickly away, unnerved by the hunger in his face, the desire in his eyes. She was determined to go through with this; she owed it to him, and she dragged her gaze back to his.

"What is it that you want, Leigh?" he asked, and she looked down again, feeling the heat of a blush wash over her face.

"I want . . ." she whispered, then peered at him through the thick screen of her lashes. "I want to make love with you," she breathed uncertainly, and heard Noah's sharp intake of breath.

He went very still. "Are you sure?" The words were soft, but she heard them perfectly, and after a moment she nodded.

"Yes."

Slowly Noah laid his lips on hers, then, with a suddenness that caught Leigh off guard, he took over the embrace, locking her in his arms, kissing her with a hungry passion she tried to answer, even as she fought her fear of him and what he wished to do. She tried, but she didn't succeed.

She struggled with herself, fighting the instinctive shrinking of her flesh when Noah undid the first few buttons of her dress so he could caress her neck, her shoulders, the pale upper curves of her breasts, and held herself rigidly still when his lips followed his fingers. She struggled with herself, but Leigh was unable to feign a passion she didn't feel, and Noah abruptly broke the embrace.

"What's going on?" he growled. "What's going on, Leigh?"

"I—Noah, I just—just—" Leigh was incapable of a coherent reply.

"Wait a minute!" Noah curtly terminated her stammering. "Just tell me why you suggested making love, when it's painfully obvious you don't want to."

"But I *do* want to!" she babbled. "I *do* want to! You've spent so much time with me, you've been so patient and so kind, you've given me so much, and I want to make love with you—"

"*Stop it!*" His angry shout froze her, and he moved away to sit with his head in his hands. "My God," he said more softly, "do you have any idea how insulting that is?"

She hadn't thought about that, and Leigh felt her face turn scarlet, thankful that Noah didn't look at her.

"You may want to make love to me," he continued, "to fulfill an obligation, but you don't *want* me. And on my part," he said, sitting up and fixing her with an angry glare, "I have no desire at all for you to give your unwilling self to me because you feel sorry for me, or in payment for services rendered. I want to make love to you, Leigh, make no mistake about that, but not this way. I want to make love *with* you, and only when you honestly desire me as a man."

Leigh stared at him with large, stricken eyes. "I—oh, Noah, I'm sorry . . ." she whispered, humiliated by the truth in his words. Utterly miserable, she tried to apologize coherently. "Noah, I was wrong; I'm so sorry. You're right, of course, and I—"

"You don't have to say anything, Leigh." Noah spoke gently now, taking her hand, trying to ease her distress. "I think I understand, but you can't cold-bloodedly plan this. When it happens for us it will be spontaneous, a force stronger than we are. You can't force that, Leigh. You can make yourself receptive to it, you can wait for the feeling to grow, but you can't just decide to make it happen."

Noah was gentle, tactfully attempting to ease Leigh's embarrassment, but she felt incredibly naive and pathetically ignorant of the forces that brought men and women together. She tried to converse naturally, but her words sounded stilted, her laughter forced, and when Noah took his leave well before midnight she felt shy and inhibited as she waited for his good-bye kiss.

"Don't worry so much, Leigh," he said softly, smoothing his fingers over the little lines of anxiety on her forehead, erasing them. He shrugged his camel topcoat on and draped a cashmere scarf around his neck, then looked into her troubled eyes. "Don't worry, sweetheart. These things have a way of working themselves out. Have a merry Christmas, Leigh."

He smiled and took her chin in his fingers, leaning forward to kiss her cheek, then her lips, but so quickly that he had straightened again before she had a chance to respond. "Have a happy holiday, darling. I'll miss you." He caressed her cheek briefly, and then he was gone.

Standing alone in her suddenly empty and echoing house, Leigh hugged herself and shivered, wishing that their good-bye evening hadn't ended on such a note. She wished they hadn't had to part at all, and the strength of that feeling disturbed her. She was surprised to realize that she wasn't looking forward to this holiday with the anticipation she usually felt; the two weeks until Noah's return loomed emptily before her.

Chapter Seven

The night air was cold and biting as Leigh walked home from the Christmas Eve service at the university chapel, her footsteps muffled by the snow that had fallen earlier. Leigh hummed as she walked, Handel and Bach and Christmas carols. She looked up at the inky sky glittering with a million stars and felt a sense of deep peace descend on her.

When she got home she lit only one lamp in the kitchen while she made a pot of Earl Grey tea, and the multicolored lights on the Christmas tree, which complemented the glow of the fire when she stirred it up and added another log from the basket beside it. After changing into a nightgown and a warm, fleecy robe, she carried her tea to the living room and curled into a corner of the sofa to sit gazing at the leaping flames and thinking of nothing.

She didn't know how long she stayed there, yet when the telephone's ring shattered the silence she didn't even start, only reached over to lift the receiver and say huskily, "Hello, Noah."

There was a soft chuckle through the line. "How did you know it was me?" he asked, a smile in his voice.

"A lucky guess?" He laughed, and she shrugged, though he couldn't see. "I just knew it was you, somehow. I didn't expect you to call though. Is something wrong?"

"No, nothing's wrong." Leigh cradled the receiver against her cheek, feeling the deep, distinctive rumble of his voice. "I just wanted to talk to you. I wanted to hear your voice."

Leigh clutched the instrument more tightly. "Oh," she said softly.

"I miss you."

There was a pause, then she said shyly, "I miss you, too."

"Oh, Leigh," Noah half groaned, "you don't know what you do to me!"

"Then shouldn't you tell me?" came the pert rejoinder, and he laughed aloud.

"I'll tell you one day, but this isn't the time." He chuckled and changed the subject. "What did you do today?"

"Nothing much. Why?"

"Because I want to know. I couldn't be with you, so I want to know what you did. Tell me."

"What I did . . ." She didn't consider it particularly interesting, but she briefly outlined her day. ". . . And after supper, I went to the service at the chapel. It was really lovely, Noah. We even had a little bit of snow to make it seem like Christmas."

"I wish I could have been with you." Noah's voice was low and intimate, caressing. "I wish I could be with you now, to sit by the fire and hold you, and keep you warm . . . and to kiss you good-night before I left." He didn't need to be with her to keep her warm; Leigh was warm all over just from his words, from his voice. "Is it midnight there?" he asked after a moment, and she turned to check a clock on the bookshelf.

"It's twelve-fifteen, actually. Why?"

"That means it's Christmas already, and it's time I let you go to sleep. Good night, Leigh, and Merry Christmas."

"Merry Christmas, Noah." Leigh hung up the telephone gently and made her way to bed, at peace and content.

That peace and contentment were still with her the next morning when she carried a cup of coffee and a roll into the living room so she could open Noah's gift. When he'd placed it beneath her tree a few nights before it had been simple enough to guess that the largish, flat, heavy package, wrapped in gleaming gold paper, contained a book. Now Leigh stooped to slide it out from under the tree and saw, behind it, another gold-wrapped box. The second gift was small and oblong, and Leigh looked at it in suspicious surprise for a moment before reaching gingerly beneath the branches to lift it out and lay it beside the other.

Half afraid of it, she left it for the moment and opened the larger package first. It was a book, as she had guessed, a beautifully illustrated work on medieval tapestries, thick, leather-bound and obviously expensive, and she paged through it for a few minutes, deliberately postponing the moment when she would turn to the smaller gift. It was still there, though, the golden gleam of paper and ribbon drawing her eye until she gave in and reached for it.

She weighed it in her hand as she picked it up, aware that it was almost certainly a jewelry box. Slowly, deliberately, she untied the ribbon and unfolded the paper from a gold-foil box, then lifted the lid to reveal a ruby-velvet jeweler's box. Her fingers were suddenly clumsy as she took the velvet box from its nest of tissue paper, and she fumbled with the tiny catch for a moment before she could lift the lid.

Nestled on a bed of ivory satin was a pendant, an oval of gold on a fine gold chain. Of antique design, the pendant had a beaded border surrounding a delicately chased rose-bud set with a brilliant ruby, Leigh's birthstone. It was a gift exactly to her taste, perfect, carefully chosen, and she lifted it almost reverently from the satin. "Oh, Noah," she breathed as the ruby sparkled in the firelight. "Oh, Noah, you shouldn't have."

It was beautiful, and she couldn't help but love it, of

course, but she knew that if Noah were there she would tell him that she couldn't possibly accept such a gift. "And I'll bet you knew that, didn't you, Professor Burke?" she asked the empty room. "And that's why you hid this where I wouldn't find it until today." The ruby winked up at her as she turned the pendant in her fingers. Noah's strategy was well conceived, she had to admit; she had the pendant now, and she couldn't return it until he came back to Bloomington.

It seemed a shame to let it languish in its box. . . . Leigh didn't even pretend to fight the impulse; she reached up to fasten the fine chain around her neck so that the lozenge of gold rested just below the hollow of her throat. She touched it lightly with a fingertip as she crossed to the mirror by the fireplace. It really was beautiful; Leigh lifted her chin for a better view, turning slightly to one side and then the other, watching the play of light on the ruby and the golden rose. It was beautiful, and Noah had chosen it for her.

She knew he was spending Christmas with his sister and her family, and the week between holidays on work for his firm, so she didn't spend the day waiting for a phone call; after all, he had called the night before. It was obvious that he would be too busy to call her again, but all day, as she listened to carols on the stereo, prepared her small Christmas dinner, and watched *Miracle on 34th Street,* she kept reaching up to touch the pendant lightly. Again and again she reassured herself that it was there, feeling as though a bit of Noah were with her.

That evening she was deep in a chapter on weaving techniques in the Middle Ages when the telephone rang. She started, groping for the receiver and wondering who on earth could be calling her at nine o'clock on Christmas night.

"Hello?"

"Merry Christmas, Leigh." Noah's unmistakable deep rumble was unaltered by distance and the telephone lines, and a slow smile crept across Leigh's face.

"Merry Christmas, Noah," she said, soft-voiced, a little shy. "Did you have a nice day?"

"Nice?" He pondered that. "I suppose you could say so, but noisy, clamorous, raucous and overwhelming might be more to the point."

Leigh laughed with him. He was speaking softly, as if trying not to be overheard, and in the background she could hear rock music and youthful laughter. "It sounds a little bit raucous," she agreed. "Where are you, in a disco somewhere?"

"Hardly. Just my sister's little haven of peace and quiet. I think I told you that I have three nephews and a niece?"

"Mm-hm." Leigh was struggling not to laugh.

"And the youngest is twelve, the oldest twenty?"

"Mm-hm."

"And they're all *very* fond of music, the louder, the better?"

"I don't know that you ever mentioned that." She was choking on her giggles.

"Well, if I didn't, I should have!" he growled, half at her giggling and half at his predicament. "If my hearing were tested right now I'd probably need a hearing aid for each ear. Between Terry and his 'golden oldies,' and Marcie and her New Wave, my ears will be ringing for days!"

"Don't play the curmudgeon with me, Noah! You know you love playing uncle, and the pandemonium, and all. Christmas is a family day, after all."

"Yes, I guess it is. How was your day? I thought about you, with no one around on a 'family day.' I hope you weren't lonely."

"Oh, no, don't worry about me. I'm used to being alone, and it doesn't bother me. Anyway, I wasn't so alone this time, because I had extra . . . presents"— she emphasized the plural—"to open, didn't I?"

"You found it, then?" There was a smile in Noah's voice, and Leigh laughed softly at him.

"Not until I took the book out from under the tree, you sneaky devil! Your surprise went just the way you planned."

"Good," he said smugly. "And how do you like them?"

"You tell me, first. How do you like yours?"

"The tapestries are beautiful! I'm overwhelmed at the idea of all the time and effort you put into creating them. Did you make them just . . . for me?"

"Just for you. I chose the colors with you in mind, and the design, after I saw which things of mine you liked best."

"Oh." Noah paused to clear his throat, and when he spoke again, his voice was husky. "I don't quite know how to put this, but I don't think I've ever had a gift that was conceived and created especially for me. Each one is a beautiful piece, in and of itself, and I'll treasure them all for what they mean, for all the work and all of yourself that you put into them. Thank you, Leigh." He was so obviously moved that Leigh felt a thickness in her own throat. "How about you?" he asked after a moment. "Do you like your book?"

"Oh, yes, Noah, of course I do! It's fabulous, but I've just begun reading it. I'll be able to go back to it again and again."

"I'm glad. I spent a lot of furtive moments scanning your bookshelves to make sure I didn't get something you already had."

"Well, you succeeded admirably!" she laughed. The book lay in her lap, and she stroked the tooled leather of the binding. "It really is beautiful, Noah."

"And the other gift? Do you like it?"

Leigh hesitated, searching for the right words. "Noah, it's beautiful, and of course I like it—I love it! But you must know that I can't keep a gift like this—"

"You have to." He interrupted her protest calmly.

"No, Noah, really, I can't. It's lovely, but—"

"You have to," he repeated, "because it can't be returned to the jeweler."

"It can't—?"

"It was made for you, Leigh. If you don't wear it, no one will. That's your birthstone, and the inscription is to you."

"Inscription?" Leigh hadn't noticed any inscription.

"On the back." She turned it over and read the engraved message she had overlooked before. *"Toujours,"* it read, "N."

"Oh, Noah," she sighed helplessly. "Oh . . ."

"It's yours, Leigh. I want you to have it."

"Oh, I . . . Thank you, Noah," she said simply. "You still shouldn't have given me a gift like this. It's too much, really, but it is beautiful, and I'll treasure it." She hesitated, then, "But, Noah?"

"Yes?"

"What do you mean by the inscription? *Toujours?*"

"Do you remember your French?"

"Well enough, I suppose."

"Then you know that *toujours* means 'always' or 'forever.'"

"Yes, of course I know that, but why . . . ?"

"Don't worry about the whys. They aren't important right now; you'll understand why in time. I have something to ask you, though, when I get back to Bloomington, and—damn!" He broke off, and Leigh heard a burst of young laughter from somewhere near him. "Damn!" more softly. "I can't talk now, there are too many *nosy busybodies around, trying to listen to things that are none of their business!*" Leigh could tell he'd turned away from the phone and raised his voice to direct his comment to the unnamed listeners, and another burst of laughter greeted his accusation. "I wish I could be with you now," he said, his frustration obvious at being unable to speak freely, "and instead I won't even be able to talk to you for a week!"

"Why a week? Is someone cutting off your phone?" Leigh tried to mask her disappointment with a light tone and a silly question, and apparently succeeded, because Noah laughed as he answered.

"I don't think so, but I won't be here to answer it. I'm leaving for Stuttgart in the morning to clear up some problems with a client of mine, and I'll probably be in Germany all week."

"That won't be so bad, will it? Christmastime in Germany should be beautiful, and just think of the food!" She forced a smile into her voice, amazed at the depth of her disappointment, which had ballooned at the news that Noah would be out of the country for a week.

"The food I can stand, if I try, but what comes to mind is the weather!"

"Bad?"

"Germany in December is nobody's idea of pleasant weather," he growled. "I don't especially want to spend my holidays picking over clauses in contracts that I don't really care about, and if I'm going to be enjoying cold rain anyway, I'd rather be enjoying it in Bloomington than in Stuttgart, and I'd rather be enjoying it with you!"

"Enjoying rain and sleet and slush? You must be joking!" she laughed. "Anyway, you have work to do, and I do, too. I should be fully occupied until you get back, and it sounds like you'll have enough contracts to keep you out of trouble."

"Oh, I'll be too busy for the beer halls," he grumbled. "But it isn't the way I meant to spend the holidays."

"Just keep busy," she advised, "and the week will pass quickly."

"Will you be busy?"

"I have plenty to do, yes," she replied, a bit puzzled by the question.

"Will you be too busy," he asked softly, "to miss me?"

"Oh," she said in a husky whisper, then cleared her throat. "I—yes, I'll miss you."

"Good, because I'll miss you." He laughed harshly. "I'll miss you every minute of this rotten week!" The angry fervor in his voice surprised her, but when he spoke again he spoke softly. "Merry Christmas, Leigh. Take care of yourself."

"I will, Noah. Merry Christmas."

Long after she had hung up the phone Leigh could still hear the frustration, the throb of emotion, in Noah's voice, and she felt a pang of longing at the memory. She had touted work as a panacea for loneliness; she hoped it was as effective as she'd said.

Midway through the long week between Christmas and New Year's Day she wasn't so sure that work could cure loneliness, but loneliness and a lack of distraction could certainly speed up her work. She was weaving a large wall hanging for an office-building lobby, and her progress had been nothing short of miraculous.

The concentration required to dress the loom for the intricate pattern she was weaving had been enough to block Noah from her mind, and when that was finished she found that weaving until the small hours each night was an excellent way to ensure at least a few hours of exhausted slumber. Her progress on the hanging had indeed been remarkable, but she didn't know just how remarkable until Kate stopped by on December twenty-ninth.

"So, what have you been doing with yourself while Noah's away? Have you been keeping yourself busy?"

"Look at the loom." Leigh jerked her head in the direction of her studio as she took Kate's hat and muffler and went to hang them on the hall tree. "See for yourself."

"Good grief, what have you been doing? Working twenty-four hours a day?"

"Just about. I start as soon as I get up, and I keep at it until I get too tired to work any more, and then I go to bed."

"And just what time do you usually go to bed?" Kate scrutinized Leigh's face. "You look tired," she announced.

"I am—a little. But I'm getting this done really quickly, so it's worth it."

"Maybe it is. You never did say what time you've been going to bed." Kate kept her sharp gaze on Leigh's face as she awaited an answer.

"It's been late." Leigh shrugged. "But not all *that* late."

"*How* late?"

"After midnight."

"How much after midnight?"

"A couple of hours or so."

"You've been weaving all day and all evening and going to bed at two A.M.? It's no wonder you look tired! Are you trying to make yourself sick?"

"Actually," Leigh sighed, "it was three-thirty last night, and no, I'm not trying to make myself sick. I am trying to get this piece done quickly, though."

"Mm-hm." Kate led the way back to the living room and dropped into the wing chair by the fireplace. "I don't suppose there would be any other reason for this insane workaholic attack? Like maybe to take your mind off Noah and the fact that you miss him?"

Leigh rolled her eyes at the ceiling. "You never give up, do you? It's a shame there's no market for matchmakers anymore; you've lost a career by default."

"Do you miss him?" Kate pressed, completely unabashed.

Leigh wrestled with herself only briefly before she gave in. It was easier this way, she rationalized; Kate would win the battle in the end, anyway.

"Yes," she said quietly, "I miss him."

"I'm sorry you miss him, Leigh, but he'll be back in a week or so, won't he?"

"It's not that, Kate." Leigh shook her head. "I can survive until he gets back. It's just that I miss him more than I thought I would—more than I want to."

"But that's a good sign!" Kate cried happily, and Leigh gave her a dirty look.

"A good sign of what? That I'm getting soft in the head? Thanks a lot!"

"You're not getting soft in the head, silly. Soft in the heart, maybe, and it's about time." Leigh sent her a speaking look, and Kate leaned forward, her face earnest. "Don't you see, Leigh? You're finally opening up to a man, finally starting to heal after all this time. You're starting to get over the past."

"I don't know that that's really true." Leigh slumped forward on the sofa and gazed disconsolately at the floor beneath her feet. "Things are different, yes, but you can't assume that everything is all fixed up now, all neat and tidy, and Leigh is just fine, a normal person again. I'm not normal, Kate, not the way you are. I still don't see any future for Noah and me, and it worries me."

"What worries you about it?"

"The fact that I don't see anything happening. I'm worried about the way I'm becoming dependent on him."

"You know what your problem is?"

"Oh, please," Leigh drawled, "I can hardly wait to find out."

"Your problem is that you worry too much. Just let the future take care of itself. Don't anticipate trouble, Leigh. I know you're trying to be clear-sighted and fair to Noah and all of that, but just wait and see, and stop trying to predict the worst. Just relax," she advised, "and let things happen."

Kate's advice undoubtedly had merit, but Leigh couldn't rid herself of the feeling that she shouldn't be missing Noah, or at least missing him so much. And she did miss him; she missed him a lot. No matter how busy she kept herself, no matter how she tried to turn her thoughts in other directions, they returned, time and again, to Noah.

She was lonely for him in so many ways, lonely for the sight of him, for his presence. She was lonely for the sound of his voice, that deep, velvety rumble.

Oh, but she was lonely for him. One afternoon Leigh sat back on her bench, the shuttle in her hand, and stared blankly into the distance. She was lonely for the sight of him, the sound of him—and lonely for his touch. The realization was almost frightening, certainly it was surprising, but she missed his touch, the solid warmth of him, giving comfort, consolation, congratulation—and more. She wanted to touch him, to be held in his arms, to kiss him.

She would never have imagined it possible, and yet she remembered with longing the comfort and security she felt in his presence, the pleasure she had begun to take in his undemanding kisses. He was indeed bringing her out of the half life she had lived for so long, but that emergence carried with it risks that frightened her.

She was becoming dependent on Noah. No, she corrected herself, she had already become dependent on him, and that brought the potential for disaster. Noah's time in Bloomington was limited, and when the semester ended in May, he would return to New York, his law firm and the fast-paced life he had led before.

He would return to his "real" life, but things might not be so easy for Leigh. Whether she could ever return to her previous existence, she didn't know, because Noah had breached her defenses and made her need him in spite of herself. That need was both a blessing and a curse, bringing her out of her cocoon of isolation, while condemning her to a bleak and empty future once he had gone.

New Year's Eve arrived at last, but the ordinarily festive evening meant little to Leigh beyond the fact that Noah was expected to return in a few days, days that loomed like an eternity. In a token gesture of observing the day, she carried her portable television into the studio and positioned it where she could watch the ball drop in Times Square as she sat at her loom. All ready to celebrate the New Year, she thought with a touch of mockery, then went to find herself something to eat.

Her appetite had dwindled to almost nothing, so she merely selected an apple from the bowl on the kitchen table. She had just finished eating it when the doorbell rang. She wasn't expecting company, and if it was a salesman, Leigh promised herself belligerently, he'd definitely get a piece of her mind about pestering people on holidays.

A large silhouette was all Leigh could distinguish through the wavy beveled glass of the door, and she prudently left the security chain on as she opened it.

"Can I—" The phrase died unfinished on her lips as she stared at the man standing there. "Noah?"

"Happy New Year, Leigh." He smiled, and she jerked on the door, intending to throw it wide for him. The brass chain twanged fiercely in its fittings, but held fast.

"This rotten chain!" she babbled, laughing and suddenly

breathless. "Just a minute . . ." She slammed the door and fumbled with shaking fingers to slip the chain from its anchor, muttering under her breath at her own clumsiness. ". . . such a klutz! There!" The chain slid free and clattered against the doorframe as she finally swung the door open. "Noah? Is it really you?"

"It's really me." He grinned, opening his arms wide, and Leigh hurled herself into his embrace, shyness forgotten in the surprise of his unexpected arrival. His arms closed around her, and he leaned back to lift her and twirl her in an exuberant circle before setting her down again in the warmth of the entry hall and closing the door behind them.

"That would be easier to do, you know," he observed with a grin, "if you were just a little bit shorter."

"Or if you were taller," Leigh pointed out as she helped him off with his coat. "But that doesn't matter. What are you doing here? I thought you were still in Germany. How did you get away? And when did—?"

"Whoa! Hold it!" Noah laid his fingers across her lips to silence the spate of questions. "I'll tell you all about it as soon as I have a cup of coffee and warm up."

"Oh! I'm sorry!" Flustered, Leigh took his scarf and fur-lined gloves and put them away. She belatedly remembered her role as hostess. "Have you had supper? I can fix you something more than just a cup of coffee."

"I'd appreciate that." Noah shrugged off his suit coat as he followed her to the kitchen, flexing his shoulders tiredly. "They gave us what they fondly refer to as a 'snack' on the flight from New York to Indianapolis, but it was too early for them to serve dinner, and a prefab sandwich didn't have much appeal. I don't need anything special; the leftovers from your dinner will be fine."

"Sit down, and I'll get the coffee going." Leigh pushed him toward the table. "I don't have any leftovers, though, since my dinner was an apple."

"An apple? That's all you had?" She nodded. "Then you can eat with me," he said firmly. "That's no meal at all."

"It's enough, really," Leigh protested.

"No, it's not; you need real food. Would you like to go out somewhere?"

Leigh laughed. "Don't be silly. After a week of just feeding myself it'll be fun to cook."

"You haven't been cooking?" he asked sharply, and Leigh shrugged.

"Not really. Just soup and sandwiches and stuff. It seemed silly to cook just for me."

"Well, it's not silly at all." Noah came around the table to take her chin in his hand and turn her face to the light. "You look tired, Leigh. What have you been doing?"

"Just working." She avoided his eyes and tried to pull away, but he held her firmly.

"Working too hard, it looks like." She knew he had seen the shadows beneath her eyes, the pallor from too little sleep and a minimum of food. "You're going to eat a decent meal tonight, but I'm not going to sit on my backside while you cook. We'll fix this together. I've done too much sitting in the last twenty-four hours."

A little seed of suspicion began to sprout in Leigh's mind, and it was her turn to take Noah by one massive shoulder and turn him toward the light. He looked as tired as she did. He had shaved recently, perhaps on the plane, but his face was paler than usual, and there were lines of fatigue around his eyes. He looked weary, older, and it hurt Leigh to see him that way.

"Just how long," she asked accusingly, "have you been sitting?"

He shrugged. "Since Stuttgart."

Leigh stared. "You flew straight through from Stuttgart? And then you drove down here from Indianapolis?"

"I changed planes in Paris, and then in New York."

Leigh sighed in exasperation. "Big deal, you walked from one gate to another. Was that all the time you spent in New York?"

"Yeah, about three hours."

"You came back from Stuttgart and didn't even see your sister?"

"I thought I'd call her tomorrow."

"Do you mean that she doesn't even know you're back?" He shrugged again, and Leigh studied him, narrow-eyed. "When, exactly, were you supposed to come back from Germany, Noah?"

"On the second."

"So how did you manage to get back two days early?"

"I pushed and got my business finished sooner than I planned to, so I came straight back."

"To Bloomington?" Leigh asked.

"To you," Noah corrected her.

Chapter Eight

$\mathcal{L}$ eigh looked into Noah's eyes for a long moment; then color washed into her face and she looked quickly away. "Oh," she said after a moment, her voice faint. "Why—why did you do that?"

"Because I missed you." Noah took her shoulders and made her face him again. "And I realized that I didn't want to spend New Year's Eve with a bunch of strangers in Germany, and I didn't want to spend it at a big, noisy, crowded party in New York. I wanted to spend it with you." His hands slipped from her shoulders to her back, and he pulled her closer.

Mesmerized by his eyes, reading his intent in them, Leigh waited as he leaned forward to kiss her, a light, teasing kiss, brushing his lips back and forth across hers. Her eyes fell closed at the first touch of his mouth, and as their lips met and clung at last, she swayed against him, unconscious of her hands moving up to clasp behind his neck, holding him close. It was a long kiss, a kiss of tenderness and yearning and the easing at last of their loneliness and frustration, and Leigh found that she could return it freely.

When at last the kiss ended she was flushed and trembling. Noah clasped his hands behind her waist, keeping her there with him when she would have moved away, smiling into her eyes.

"I think," he said with the air of a man who has made an important discovery, "that I like kissing tall girls."

"Oh?" Leigh's eyebrows rose. "And why is that?"

"Well," he said thoughtfully, "I don't have to hunch over, and you don't have to stand on tiptoe. I'll bet you could prove that it's much more efficient to kiss someone your own height than someone shorter."

"You think so?"

"Mm-hm."

"And just how many tall girls have you tested this theory with?"

Noah's gaze darted guiltily away. "Well, actually it hasn't been a real, scientific study, you know. . . ."

"How many, Noah?"

"Actually . . ." He struggled, not very successfully, to keep a straight face. "Actually, there's been only one test subject."

"Oh."

"You know, I don't think the theory's really been tested all that thoroughly yet."

Leigh considered that for a moment. "You could have a point. Aren't scientific theories supposed to be *very* thoroughly tested?"

"Mm-hm, they are," Noah murmured, and proceeded to do so.

Had Leigh been capable of conscious thought she would have rejoiced at the realization that she was no longer just tolerating Noah's kisses, she was enjoying them. If he had become aggressive, tried to force her lips apart, she might have been frightened again, but under the tender persuasion of his mouth her lips first softened, then shyly parted. He didn't push her too far, too fast, but contented himself with caressing her soft inner lip with his tongue tip, letting her relax and enjoy this new step they had taken.

Suddenly Leigh jumped guiltily away from him. "I'm sorry! I just remembered! I'm supposed to be feeding you and I . . . and we . . ."

"We had other things on our minds," Noah said gently. "More important things." Leigh felt her color rise as he held her gaze for a moment. Then he grinned, and the spell was broken. "Now, however, what I have on my mind is food. What shall we fix?"

"I'm sure I can come up with something. Just let me see . . ." She rummaged in the refrigerator, eventually producing the ingredients for spaghetti carbonara. Noah made a passable salad from the contents of the crisper, and she even stole five minutes, while the spaghetti was boiling, to slip into her bedroom and change.

The faded jeans and ancient sweater she was wearing were warm and comfortable, but they were hardly festive, and even though Noah had shed his coat and tie, opened the collar of his shirt and turned back his sleeves, she felt severely underdressed. She put on burgundy trousers, a soft, matching sweater and strappy sandals with heels that would make her slightly taller than Noah. Somehow she didn't think he would mind. As a final touch she added the pendant he had given her and emerged feeling considerably better about her appearance.

She found Noah draining the spaghetti over the sink. It was a matter of only a few minutes to add the bacon, eggs, cheese and cream, to toss the salad and open the wine, and dim the kitchen light while they took their meal to the table lit by three long tapers.

Noah poured wine, handed a glass to Leigh and raised his own. She waited expectantly, but when he spoke his words were simple. She would have been disappointed if not for the expression in his eyes.

"Happy New Year, Leigh," he said.

She read the message in his gaze, smiled and replied, "Happy New Year, Noah."

He held her gaze for a heartbeat longer, then nodded, as if satisfied about something, and attacked his meal hungrily. Leigh stole glances at him between bites, marveling at him, at his presence.

He reached for his wineglass, and Leigh noticed his hand, strong and square and brown, with long, straight fingers. She watched in fascination as he raised the glass to his lips. He drank, and her enraptured gaze moved to his throat, then up to his face, to find that he was watching her, amused.

She flushed and quickly lowered her eyes to her plate as Noah chuckled, then looked up at him again. "Laugh if you like, smarty," she said tartly. "I know I was staring, but it's still hard to believe you're actually here."

"Sometimes it's hard for me to believe it," he agreed, and rubbed the back of his neck in a weary gesture. "When I remember that trip, though, it all becomes very clear. . . ." His statement trailed off into a huge yawn, and Leigh frowned at him in concern.

"When did you last sleep?"

"I'm not sure. . . ." He thought about it, concentrating. "Sometime yesterday, I think, or maybe the day before. I left last night, and I didn't really sleep on the plane."

"Then shouldn't you get some sleep now? You look awfully tired."

"Go to sleep on New Year's Eve? No way!" He sat back and pushed his plate away. "No, I'm going to stay up and ring in the new year just like everyone else. Although"—he thought for a moment—"it's probably already January first in Stuttgart."

"And you've been without sleep since yesterday? Or whenever yesterday was in Germany? Noah, you really need to sleep!"

"I will, I promise—after midnight." Noah rose to carry his dishes to the sink. "Shall I make coffee?"

"I will. You sit down and relax."

"I'll sit in a minute. I have something in the car that I want to bring in." In seconds he was gone, but he returned in about two minutes with an impressive, gold-foil-embellished bottle of brut French champagne. "Here," he said, plunking it on the table with a flourish, "all the way from Orly Airport in my flight bag, just for us at midnight."

"You managed to get this between planes?"

"I had a couple of hours to wait." He shrugged, then added more vehemently, "And if I don't see the inside of an airport, *or* a plane, for a while that's fine with me!"

"Noah," Leigh said dryly, "you were crazy to make such a long trip on no sleep just to be here for New Year's Eve. You realize that, don't you?"

Noah smiled into her eyes. "I had my reasons," he said softly and enigmatically.

Leigh blushed and glanced away, picking up the dessert tray to have something to do. "Let's take this into the living room." She heard Noah chuckle knowingly as he followed her.

"Five . . . four . . . three . . ." Some ninety minutes later they stood side by side, counting along with the televised mob in Times Square as the ball dropped, and on the stroke of midnight they touched glasses lightly and toasted each other.

Leigh met Noah's eyes over the rim of her glass, and her own eyes widened. He held her gaze, reaching out to take the champagne from her fingers and set it aside, then slowly, carefully, he took her into his arms. Entranced by his eyes, drunk on his presence more than the wine, Leigh waited for his kiss. At the first touch of his lips she melted against him.

He kissed her slowly, seductively, brushing his lips over hers, kissing the corners of her mouth until Leigh wound her arms around his neck and clung to him, returning the caress. Very gradually the kiss deepened, Noah's tongue seeking her mouth, outlining the velvety contours of her lips, then probing the sweet warmth inside. Hesitant, embarrassed by her own inexperience, Leigh answered him, half-afraid, yet half-eager, following the outline of his lips as he had done hers.

Something was happening to her, something momentous,

something so startling that it wasn't until much later that she realized that she had felt the faint stirrings of desire, that for the first time since her marriage to Tony had begun, she wanted to feel more. She only knew that she wanted to kiss Noah, wanted to go on kissing him, that she never wanted to stop. She had slipped her sandals off some time before, and now she was nearly Noah's height; she had only to tip her head to the side to meet his kiss. His arms around her waist held her close, and she could feel the muscles in his legs move against hers as he shifted to take more of her weight against him. She delighted in him, in the differences that so perfectly complemented each other, the differences that had for so long frightened her and now fascinated her.

He was broad where she was slim, heavy muscled where she was delicately made, strong in ways she could never be, hard where she was soft. Leigh tangled her fingers in the crisp curls that just touched his collar, probing the muscles there as Noah's arm tightened around her waist and one hand came up to cradle the back of her head for a last, hard kiss.

He must have felt her response, must have known what she was feeling, and though he could have taken advantage of it, and of her, he did not. When he broke the kiss he took his lips reluctantly from hers, sighing with regret when she gave a little murmur of protest against his mouth. Keeping her close beside him, he steered her to the sofa, tucking her securely within the circle of his arm.

"Noah?" Leigh whispered, snuggling into his side and reaching up to turn his face toward her with a light touch of her fingers.

"Hmm?"

"May I kiss you?"

"Leigh!" He gave a strangled laugh; then as her lips brushed the corner of his mouth he groaned and turned that extra millimeter to meet her kiss, though he tore himself away with difficulty after a few moments. "Leigh, I want to talk to you!" he protested when she reached for him again.

She sighed with exaggerated disappointment and pouted,

inwardly amazed at her own flirtatiousness. "Do you really want to talk?"

"I do," he said firmly, then took her hands from his face and folded them demurely in her lap. "And since when did you start flirting, anyway?"

"Was I flirting?" she asked innocently.

"Give me strength!" he pleaded, then frowned at her in reproof. "You know exactly what you were doing. Now behave yourself!"

"Oh, all right." She folded her arms and looked at him expectantly. "What do you want to talk about?"

Noah looked down at the floor for a moment, and when he lifted his gaze to Leigh again his face was sober, grave. She felt her heart lurch, then begin a rapid hammering.

"Noah, what is it?" she whispered. "What's wrong?"

"Nothing's wrong," he reassured her quickly, and the arm about her shoulders tightened in comfort. "Don't worry about that. You were surprised that I came back early, though, weren't you?"

"I—yes, I was."

"There was a reason, you know, beyond just wanting to see you again. I didn't come back just on a whim."

"What was . . . ?" She hesitated, then took the plunge. "What was the reason?"

"I came back early because I have something to ask you, and something to give you. I'm glad you like this"—he reached out to lightly touch the pendant that sparkled at the base of her throat—"because I hope you'll like the other gift I have for you. They kind of—kind of go together."

"Oh, no, Noah. You really can't give me anything more!" she protested, and touched the pendant lightly, as he had done. "This is beautiful, and you know I love it, but you really can't give me anything more."

"Oh, yes, I can." He reached out to pluck his jacket from where he'd dropped it and fished in an inside pocket. "I can give you this." He extracted a small, velvet-covered box from the pocket, and even as Leigh's mind was frantically trying to deny that it was what it appeared to be, he opened

it to reveal a ring, a beautiful, emerald-cut diamond soli-
taire.

Speechless, transfixed, Leigh stared at it as she might
stare at a serpent about to strike, and when she moved again
it was to shake her head, recoiling from Noah and the ring.

"I want you to marry me, Leigh," Noah said, ignoring her
reaction. "I want you to be my wife."

"But I can't!" she cried, and stumbled to her feet. "I can't
marry you; you know that!" Her voice rose. "You know
why I can't marry you!"

"No, I *don't* know." Noah stood and faced her from a few
feet away. "I know what you *think* you can't do, but I don't
believe that. I believe that your problem can be overcome.
With time I think we can work through the trauma and the
fears, work through the aftereffects of all you suffered."

"You think so, do you?" Leigh stared at him as if she'd
never seen him before. "That's nice and optimistic, isn't it?
We'll work together and have faith, and pretty soon everything will be all right, and poor little Leigh will be cured of
her affliction! Just like in a bad novel, huh?" There was a
bitter twist to her mouth, a hard edge to her voice. "Some
very big-time psychiatrists have tried some very sophisticated therapies on me, and finally they all came to the
conclusion that there was nothing more that could be done
for me, Noah. Nothing at all!"

"Maybe that's what they decided—then," he argued.
"Maybe. But time has passed, and things have changed, and
you have, too. You've changed with me, haven't you?"
Leigh started to argue, but he cut her off. "If this sounds
egotistical, I'm sorry, but you've told me yourself that
you've changed since you've known me, and I happen to
think that we can build on that!"

"I don't know whether we can or not," Leigh said,
shrugging off his assertion. "That vague and very likely
pointless hope is hardly a basis for a marriage, though, is it?
Sort of like trying to build a skyscraper on quicksand. No,
don't say anything!" She flung up a hand when he started to
speak, took an agitated step away, then turned to him again.

"You can't marry me just on the hope that I can magically be cured someday. You can't do that because there's the possibility—the very strong possibility—that I can't be cured! And what if that happens?" she demanded. "What if I can never be a wife to you, never be a woman for you? Think about it, Noah! You don't want a wife who's damaged, who's less than a real woman!"

"Stop it!" Noah exploded in anger, seizing her arms in a grip that hurt her and pulling her roughly against him. "Just stop it! You are not less than a woman! You aren't *less than* anything! You're the woman I want to marry, the woman I love!"

Leigh knew she hadn't heard him correctly, she couldn't have heard him correctly, even though she heard him repeat his unbelievable words. "I love you, Leigh, and I want to marry you."

She struggled to assimilate the impossible fact, gulped and stammered. "L-love?"

"Yes, love," Noah said, still half-angry, though his expression softened when he saw the stunned astonishment in her face. "Of course I love you, Leigh. I hope you love me."

She hesitated for a long, painful moment, unable to freely give the answer he wanted. "I don't know," she finally muttered in distress. "I really don't know. I care for you, yes, but love?" She shook her head again, her unhappiness evident. "I don't know about love, Noah. I honestly don't know if I'm capable of loving you or anyone. I don't know if I ever will be capable of it." She pulled free and walked a few steps away to stand with her back to him, head bent and hands twisted together. "I can't honestly say I'm in love with you, Noah."

She turned again, forcing herself to meet his eyes. "I can't honestly say that. I wish I could, but I can't. And I can't be a real wife to you now, we both know that. It wouldn't be fair of me to marry you under these circumstances."

"Can't you let me make that decision?"

"Noah, I'm not in love with you!" she cried, and ached inside when she saw him flinch from the words. She couldn't withdraw them though, couldn't deny their honesty. "I won't marry you—I *can't* marry you—until I know I can love you the way you deserve to be loved, until I know I can be a wife to you in every way."

"I might be able to accept that if there were another man—"

"Don't be stupid!" she snapped, glaring at him, and he shook his head ruefully.

"I'm sorry. That was unnecessary. I wish you would let me worry about what I do or don't deserve though. If I want to marry you, no matter what—"

"Noah, *listen* to me! I'm not even going to consider this insane proposal of yours until I've proven to myself that I can be the woman you want me to be."

"You were a woman when we toasted the new year," Noah reminded her, and she scowled.

"In a way," she grudgingly admitted, "if you mean the fact that I was able to kiss you, and yes, I've even begun to be able to enjoy it, but—"

"All this flattery is killing me!"

"That's not funny!" She was torn between anger and tears. "I can kiss you now, but that's a long way from being your wife, from being—being your lover."

"It may be a long way, but haven't you ever heard"—he came close and took her by the shoulders—"that the longest journey begins with a single step?"

Noah gathered her into his arms to kiss her with a tender sweetness that wrung her heart, but though Leigh wanted to, she couldn't respond to him. Upset and agitated, too highly strained to feel again the warmth and closeness of their midnight embrace, she tried to force a response and Noah knew it. She wasn't able to deceive him, and with a gentle kiss on her forehead he ended the embrace.

"Don't try to pretend, Leigh," he said quietly, and a little sadly. "Don't ever try to pretend something you don't feel. That feeling, love or desire, will come on its own, or it won't come at all. It can't be simulated." Leigh could feel her face flush with shame and a stifling sense of failure, and she turned away, not wanting Noah's eyes on her. "Don't blame yourself, Leigh, please. You didn't do anything wrong, anything to feel bad about."

She shrugged, the bones of her shoulders fragile under his hands. "I'm sorry, Noah. I know it was a stupid thing to do. I know it was, but—" Her voice wobbled, and Noah wrapped her in the security of his arms again.

"Don't apologize and don't worry, okay? It's late, and you're upset, and I've had a long day." He looked at the mantel clock and corrected himself. "Or *days*. We won't accomplish anything by arguing tonight. Let's just let it wait a while." He rubbed a hand over his face. "I'm too tired to think right now. I'd better get going and let both of us get some sleep."

He turned toward the door, but Leigh saw his face, white and strained, the weary slump of his broad shoulders. He had gone beyond tired to the far reaches of exhaustion, and she reached out impulsively to touch his arm. He stopped and turned.

"Noah, you don't really have to go." His tired eyes widened in surprise. "I mean, it's so late," she explained, "and you look exhausted. Your apartment will be cold, and I'll bet you don't have any food there, do you?"

"Guilty." He shrugged with a weary smile.

"You can stay in the guest room. The bed's made up, and I can get you an extra blanket, and you even have your suitcase out in the car, don't you?" He nodded. "Stay here and get some rest, Noah. I don't like to think of your going home in the cold and all. Just stay here."

He looked at her for a long moment, then sighed, his shoulders slumping with fatigue as tension drained out of him. "All right, I will, if it's no trouble." He ran a hand around the back of his neck in a weary gesture. "I don't like the sound of that cold apartment with no food either. I'll go get my things."

"I'll get the room ready." In the few minutes it took Noah to pull on his topcoat and dash through the beginnings of a snowstorm to retrieve his suitcase from the car, Leigh prepared the room. Thankful that she kept the bed in her guest room made up, she lit the lamp beside it, dug an extra blanket from the cedar chest and was taking fresh towels to the bathroom when Noah appeared in the hallway, suitcase in hand. "I brought you an extra blanket," she said unnecessarily, indicating the fluffy blue cover folded at the foot of the bed. "And I was putting these in the bathroom for you."

He looked at the armload of towels she clutched and smiled gravely. "Thank you. That's very considerate."

"I—it—it's nothing. I mean, you have to have towels, you know." Leigh knew she was blushing and stammering like a silly teenager, but she couldn't seem to stop. She turned and preceded Noah across the hall to the bathroom, where she rapidly arranged the towels on the rod. "Is there—do you have everything you need?"

"Yes, this is fine." Noah was still smiling, and Leigh struggled to relax. "You're taking better care of me than I would of myself. Thank you."

"Well . . ." She hesitated. "Well, good night, Noah. I'll see you in the morning."

"Good night, Leigh." He brushed his fingertips over her cheek. "Sleep well."

Alone in her bedroom, Leigh stood in the dim glow of her bedside lamp and listened to the small sounds of Noah moving about on the other side of the wall. They were oddly comfortable, comforting sounds to someone who for so long had jealously guarded her independence.

The first thing Leigh noticed when she awoke was Leon's absence from his usual spot atop her feet. She stretched groggily, but there was no dead-weight heap of cat anywhere on her bed. She thought about it for a moment, then decided that he'd probably left to have an early-morning snack. Or a late-morning snack. She rolled over to check the time, and her eyes opened wide in chagrin when she saw the glowing 9:48 on her clock's digital display.

She stared at it for a bleary moment, trying to work out

why she was just waking up at 9:48, then the number blinked to 9:49, and it all came back in a rush of recollection. It was New Year's Day, and Noah was sleeping in the next room, and it was chilly in her room and very cold outside, judging by the frost she could see on the windowpanes. Oddly she found that having Noah in the house didn't make her uneasy, even in the cold light of day. It still felt comfortable, just as it had the night before, and Leigh was surprised at that.

How strange. How strange to have Noah in the house and how strange to find it comfortable, secure—nice. She slid out of bed, shivering in the chilly air as she stepped into fuzzy slippers and wrapped herself in her warm, fleecy robe. Moving quietly, she washed her face and brushed her hair, then padded down to the hall to the kitchen to make coffee.

While it dripped she stood by the window, gazing out at a dusting of new snow and an even, light-gray cloud layer that promised more to come. It looked like a good day to stay indoors, and she wondered if Noah liked to spend his New Year's Day in the traditional manner, with football games and beer. She grinned and went to pour the coffee. If that was what he wanted, she had no objections.

Softly, in case he was still sleeping, she carried a cup of coffee to Noah's door, listened for sounds of activity within, and when she heard none, eased the door carefully open. Peering into the room, dimly illuminated by a shaft of watery light slanting through a gap in the curtains, she saw Noah sprawled across the bed, with Leon curled up at his feet.

Smiling, Leigh stepped farther into the room as her eyes adjusted to the murky light and stood looking down at Noah. He was still deeply asleep, recovering from jet lag and too much travel. When even the seductive aroma of fresh coffee failed to rouse him, she could have turned and left, but Leigh was unable to resist the opportunity to study him at her leisure.

The blankets had slipped to his waist as he slept, and for a moment the artist in Leigh simply savored the pure male beauty of him, the long, taut curve of his back, the broad, heavily muscled shoulders tapering to a narrow waist, the strong, brown arms. He really was beautiful, she thought, strong and utterly male, and yet in sleep, face buried in the pillow, hair wildly mused, she could see the boy he had been. Leon raised his head to yawn hugely at her, and she grinned at him, backed out of the room and softly closed the door.

She drank her own coffee at the kitchen table, staring unseeingly out at the snow and the pale-gray sky, and watching a procession of images in her mind, images of Noah as she had known him in the past months. He was infinitely more complex and interesting than the smooth-talking flirt she had first taken him for, and she felt a little ashamed of her first superficial judgment of so complicated a man. He had forced her to get to know more of him, and as she'd learned about him, she had let him into her life.

He had become such an integral, even vital, part of her, that it was now difficult for her to imagine life without him. Of course, she reminded herself, if she accepted his proposal she wouldn't have to live without him, but the question then became: Could she live with him? And that was the sixty-four-thousand dollar question. How could she know? How could she be certain she loved him?

If only there were some way to find out if she would ever be capable of loving again. Certainly she cared for Noah, but the element that separated caring from "being in love" was missing, and for all Leigh knew she might never be capable of feeling it. She had felt a prickling of desire the night before, while Noah was kissing her, but she refused to pin false hopes on such an isolated moment.

Her feelings could have been a reaction to the champagne and the firelight, to being with Noah again after a long, lonely week, or even, she thought with ironic humor, a momentary rebellion of female hormones too long ignored. She knew better than to make too much of that. The fear hadn't closed over her while they were kissing, but if he had caressed her breast, her stomach, her hips, her reaction could as easily have been the familiar blind hysteria.

She rose to refill her cup, then walked back to the table, where she sat deep in thought. She *could* accept his proposal; certainly he wanted her to, in spite of all the problems and her reservations. Would it be fair though to either of them? Would it be right to make that sort of commitment when she couldn't say that she could ever be a wife to him in the fullest sense?

She shook her head. No, she would never feel right about that. She had no idea how long she sat there, wrestling with the problem, seeing no solution, her coffee cooling.

"Why so glum?"

"Oh!" She jumped, startled, and spun around to see the object of her thoughts lounging in the doorway, sleepy-eyed and smiling. "I didn't hear you!" She pushed the brooding thoughts away and returned his smile. "I'm not glum, just thinking."

"Thinking about what?" Noah picked up the coffeepot and shook it, but it was nearly empty.

"Nothing important." Leigh walked over and took the pot from his hand. "I'll make some more; it'll take only a minute. You sit down." She got the coffee going, then leaned a hip against the counter and looked across the room at Noah. "You look as though you slept well."

Noah smiled ruefully. "How you can tell anything at all from the way I look now, I can't imagine. I did sleep well, though, thank you."

He had dressed in yesterday's slacks, with his shirt pulled on but hanging open; his hair was ruffled from sleep, and it only became more unruly when he combed his fingers through it in an attempt to subdue the wayward curls. His jaw was dark with stubble, and he rubbed a hand over it, scowling, as Leigh set a cup of fresh coffee in front of him.

"Thank you. I'm afraid I'm one of those people who isn't normal until he's had some coffee to open his eyes." He sipped and rubbed his chin again, then looked apologetically at Leigh. "Would you excuse me long enough to get presentable?"

"Of course." She smiled. "You should find everything you need in the bathroom."

"Okay. Thank you." He disappeared down the hall, and after a moment Leigh followed. She'd fix a brunch while he got cleaned up, but first she'd get dressed herself. In love with him or not, she didn't intend to subject Noah to any more of the sight of her in a flannel nightgown and robe.

Moving quickly, she wriggled into snug jeans and pulled on a green crew-neck sweater, applied some light makeup and stepped back into her slippers before returning to the kitchen to fix sausages and blueberry waffles, and mull over some new and disturbing realizations.

A few minutes of bustling got the meal started, to the accompaniment of the rushing shower down the hall, but she paused in the middle of beating eggs, the dripping whisk poised above the bowl, and looked over at the chair where Noah had sat. He'd had none of the urbane veneer of the big-city lawyer as he sat there, unshaven, with rumpled hair and sleepy eyes, the open shirt revealing his broad, deep chest and the dark hair across it. Even half awake, without the gloss of tailored suits and handmade shoes, seen at what he would probably consider his worst, he was a potently attractive man, the kind of man Leigh had scrupulously avoided since her disastrous marriage.

She had always been afraid of men who looked so naturally, completely male, yet she was startled to realize that she hadn't been at all afraid of Noah. She'd been a little embarrassed to be seen in her robe, a little shy, after all that had been said the night before, but she had felt safe with him, secure. She'd felt safe sitting in the kitchen with a man who had spent the night in her house, though neither of them had been fully dressed. She'd felt safe in a situation that was almost painfully reminiscent of marriage, her own private hell. She'd felt safe.

She heard the guest-room door open and footsteps in the hall, and hastily returned to beating the eggs, her cheeks warming with embarrassment.

Noah didn't seem to notice anything amiss though, as he breezed into the room, rolling up his sleeves and asking, "What can I do?"

"You could sit down, have some coffee and wait for this to be cooked. Are you sure you want to work for your breakfast?"

"I offered," he said simply, and Leigh nodded.

"You got it." She handed him a spatula and directed him to the stove and the sausages. With his help they soon sat down to their breakfast.

Something had changed though. Noah had become quiet as they cooked, and he munched his waffles in thoughtful silence. Leigh tried to keep eating, trying not to let tension creep up on her, but the food stuck in her throat, and she jumped when Noah spoke again.

"Leigh?"

Leigh took a slow, careful breath. "Yes?"

"Have you considered my proposal?"

She smiled sadly at him. "You know I haven't thought about anything else."

"And have you come to any conclusions?"

"Don't you mean any *new* conclusions?" she asked. "And no, I haven't. It wouldn't be fair for me to marry you when I don't know if I'm capable of loving you, or of making love to you. I haven't changed my mind about that."

"If I'm not worried about whether it's fair or not, why should you be? I can worry about my own emotional health, you know."

"Of course you can, but what about mine? I'm not being entirely altruistic, Noah." She stared at her cup as if there were something fascinating about the familiar salt-glazed stoneware, and struggled to remain calm. "My emotional health is at issue, too, and we're both aware that it's not what it should be. Right now you're confident that I can change, that I *will* change, and that you can make everything all right. And I have to admit that there's a possibility that you could be right."

"Then why not let me—"

"*Listen* to me, Noah," she interrupted urgently. "Let me finish, please. It's impossible to completely rule out that possibility, but it's totally unrealistic to assume that it will come to pass just because you want it to. There is also a strong possibility that I won't change, that you won't be able to make it all better, and what then?" She scowled at him, frustration and hurt in her eyes. "Think about it, Noah!" she cried. "What happens one, or two or ten years from now, when the problems haven't magically vanished? What happens when you meet a woman who can love you and make love to you? What happens when you meet a woman like that and you don't want me for a wife any longer? What happens to me then, Noah?"

Leigh shoved her chair back and ran sobbing from the kitchen.

Chapter Nine

Noah followed and found her leaning against her bedroom window, her forehead pressed to the cold glass. She was no longer sobbing, but she scrubbed her hands over her cheeks when she heard him enter the room, erasing the evidence of her tears.

"Leigh, come away from the window; you'll get cold." He took her by the shoulders and gently turned her around, steering her back across the room. "Come back to the kitchen, where it's warm, and we'll talk about this, all right?"

"All right," she said weakly and sniffled. "I'm sorry to be so stupid."

"You're not stupid, Leigh, but I am, for making you cry."

She managed a watery smile. "You didn't make me cry, Noah; the thought of what it would be like if you left me did."

"Leigh, you know I wouldn't do that to you," he protested.

Leigh met his gaze calmly. "I don't know the future, Noah, and neither do you, but I won't put myself in a position where that could happen. I won't put myself through that, and I won't put you through it either, whether you're worried about it or not. You may not want to admit it, but you have to realize that getting married under these circumstances would be insanity."

There was a long, taut silence; then Noah sighed heavily. "Very well," he said at length, "Do you have any solutions to suggest?"

She looked at him, her answer in her eyes. "It has nowhere to go, Noah. It has to end."

His mouth tightened into a hard line. "Leigh, I love you! I have no intention of letting things end between us!"

"I don't want to end things either," she cried, very near tears again. "But what else can we do?"

"Find a compromise," he suggested. "A good lawyer ought to be able to find a compromise solution to any problem." He wasn't smiling, but there was a gleam deep in his eyes that took the edge off Leigh's frustrated unhappiness, and she began to relax.

"Okay, big-time lawyer, let's hear your ideas." She folded her arms, waiting.

"Well-l-l, so far all we've discussed are the all-or-nothing ends of the spectrum. There must be lots of gradations in between."

"Okay." Leigh sat up straight, getting into the game with him, though she sniffled and had to grab a tissue to blow her nose. "Okay, what are some of the gradations?"

Noah thought for a moment. "We could go steady?" he offered.

Leigh gaped at him, afraid for a fleeting instant that he wasn't kidding. "You mean like in high school? I'd wear your class ring, and you'd take me to the sock hop?"

"Yeah, or if you don't like that idea, we could be pinned. I must have my Sigma Chi pin around somewhere. How'd you like to be the sweetheart of Sigma Chi?" Leigh began to giggle helplessly as he leaned across the table with a crack salesman's air of "have I got a deal for you!" "Maybe," he leered, "I'll even let you wear my ID bracelet!"

Leigh collapsed onto the tabletop, her head on her arms, and gave way to laughter. It broke the tension they had both tried to ignore, and when Leigh finally had herself under control again she propped her chin on one hand and smiled across the table at him.

"Okay," she said, "you've made your point. In lieu of my wearing your ID bracelet or your Sigma Chi pin, what are our alternatives, really?"

"They're unlimited. All we have to do is consider all the possibilities along the continuum, from no relationship at all to marriage. Dating, for instance, which is what we've been doing—sort of." He shrugged. "Or something on the order of 'going steady,' whatever the equivalent is for those of us beyond high school."

"Since I don't think I really understand how one goes steady without a class ring, do you have any other ideas?"

"An indefinite engagement, maybe? We could just be engaged until such time as the situation changes."

"Do you mean 'engaged,' as in a ring and an announcement and everything?"

"We could skip the announcement."

"No." Leigh shook her head. "An engagement is a declaration of intent to marry, and people ask you when the date is and buy you presents and everything. That's too public, Noah, and it's too official, and if it didn't work out there would be no end of embarrassing explanations."

"There is another possibility," Noah said carefully, so carefully that Leigh felt a twinge of trepidation. "We could try . . . perhaps . . . living together."

This time Leigh stared at him for a long, long moment. "Living together . . . in what way?" she asked at length.

"At first as roommates, not as lovers," he reassured her. "The proximity, the closeness on a day-to-day basis, might help you become more at ease around me, and then, later, the problem might just work itself out. Does that sound like a possibility to you?"

"I—I don't know. Do you really think it could work?"

Noah looked into her eyes, then nodded. "Yes, at least as well as anything else. And you?"

Leigh thought about it for several minutes. "It could help," she said slowly. "I'm sure the psychiatrists have a word for it, some kind of conditioning or desensitization or something."

"I do have one reservation," Noah said, and Leigh looked across to see him frowning uneasily at his hands on the table.

"What's that?"

"I wonder if you'll be comfortable in a situation like that? It isn't something you can hide, you know. Will it be an embarrassment to you to have your friends and your colleagues aware that you're living with a man? Or even worse, will it hurt your career?"

Leigh was touched by his concern, but it was misplaced, and she told him so. "In this day and age?" She laughed shortly. "I can't imagine that anyone involved with my career would even be interested, and my friends would just think I'm finally acting normal and not like a trainee nun!" She shook her head. "No, no one will care who I live with, or why, but what about you?"

"Me?"

"You, the law professor. As you say, it's not something you can hide, and it might be more of an embarrassment to you than me. After all, lawyers and law professors are a notoriously conservative bunch, aren't they?"

"No problem," he replied lightly. "Things have loosened up a lot lately. I won't suffer any embarrassment; my only worry was that you might."

"An artist? Be serious, Noah." She grinned. "Artists are supposed to live the bohemian life. I can see a problem though."

"And that is?"

"The committee and the administration. If people got upset over our having lunch together, what are they going to say about our living together?"

"They have no right to say anything," Noah told her grimly, "but if they do I'll force them to prove that any allegations they make have merit in a court of law. Neither of us is going to compromise his or her principles, and we know it. Anyone who questions that will have to deal with me!"

"I hope *I* never have to deal with you in a court of law! You're scary when you're legally outraged." Leigh grinned, and Noah relaxed, smiling.

"That's one problem settled, then." He sat back with an air of satisfaction.

"Uh . . . Noah?" Leigh asked, hesitant.

"Hmm?"

"Are we really going to do this?"

He looked startled. "I thought so, but I guess we haven't made it official yet, have we?" He reached across the table to take her hand in both of his. "Leigh, will you do me the honor of living with me?"

She looked at their clasped hands for a moment, then into the bottomless blue of Noah's eyes, her face grave. "Yes, I will, Noah."

He bent his head to kiss her fingers, then turned her hand over and pressed a kiss into her palm, folding her fingers over to hold it there when he lifted his lips.

"Thank you, Leigh." He seemed to sense that she was at a loss for words and let the almost unbearably poignant moment pass. After releasing her hand, he poured the last of the coffee into his cup, looked at it and made a face. "Yuck. Do you suppose we could take a few minutes to clear these dishes away and make some more coffee? I think we need to replenish our supplies."

"Sure." She wrinkled her nose at the remains of breakfast. "This all looked a lot better when it was fresh." She rose and carried the dishes to the sink. "You know," she said after a moment, "we do have another problem."

"Oh?" Noah bent over the refrigerator, replacing the butter and milk. "What is it?"

"Well, if we're going to live together, where are we going to live?"

"Good question." Noah closed the refrigerator and came to stand beside her, taking the dishes as she rinsed them and stacking them in the dishwasher. "I hadn't thought of that. I guess we have three options."

"What three are those?"

"We could live at my apartment, or get someplace new, or live here, in your house."

"What's your opinion of each of them?"

"Okay, the first option is my apartment." He looked across the dishwasher at her, eyebrows raised.

"It's a nice apartment," Leigh said, trying to be fair, "but where would I put my loom?"

"Hmm, that is a problem." He pondered the issue with mock gravity. "I don't suppose the loom could go in the bathroom?"

"Then what would we do with the quilting frame?" Leigh closed the dishwasher and began getting the coffee started.

"If I draw a conclusion from all this, it's that the apartment is too small."

"I'm afraid so."

"Please don't feel bad about that. The Law School arranged for me to rent it because it's close to campus, but I've never been that crazy about it."

"Okay, you won't mind moving out anyway, so what about the other choices? We could rent someplace together."

"We could," he agreed, "but would you really want to move?"

"Not a lot," Leigh admitted. "It would mean renting this house to someone else, and I have it fixed up the way I like it. . . ." She looked searchingly at him. "I'm comfortable here, Noah, but would you be comfortable in this house?"

"Of course. I've always liked this house and the way

you've decorated it. It's big enough, too. What about chores?"

"What about them?" Leigh didn't understand.

"Well, I've never done this before, lived with anyone, I mean. Aren't you supposed to make a list or something and divide up the housework fairly?"

"I doubt if we really need to get that specific." Leigh grinned at his earnest question and poured more coffee for them. "If you don't have any serious objections to vacuuming or dishes or anything, we can just do what needs to be done as it comes up."

"Are you sure?" he asked uncertainly. "I don't want to be chauvinistic about this or anything."

"Oh, Noah," she giggled, "that's sweet of you, but I don't think you need to worry. Anyway, I promise I'll complain if you start imposing on me, okay?"

"I'm being dumb, aren't I?"

"No, you're being considerate, and I thank you for it. It's not dumb, it's sweet."

Noah looked a little disgruntled, as if he weren't entirely pleased to be called sweet. Leigh watched, amused, as he sipped his coffee in silence for a moment. "Do you know what else we're forgetting?" he said suddenly.

"What? I thought we'd covered everything."

"Everything except when we start this new arrangement."

"Oh." She thought about it for a moment. "Do you have any suggestions?"

"How about starting it now?"

"Now?" Leigh's voice came out in a strangled squeak. This idea, which she'd been able to regard in the abstract, was coming to life with a vengeance. She had been treating their decision making as a game, but Noah was suggesting that they begin playing immediately, and she wasn't certain she was prepared for that. "Do you mean 'now,' as in today?"

"Not necessarily today, but this week, before classes

start," Noah replied. "Since my lease runs one semester at a time, I can call my landlady tomorrow to tell her I won't be renewing it."

"That makes sense," Leigh acknowledged with counterfeit calm while the realization dawned that a decision had been made. She and Noah were going to live together.

Within a week she and Noah would be living together. It was a fact now; she had unleashed something she couldn't stop. Strangely, as they discussed the mechanics of the move she felt no regrets or reservations, only a fizzing, percolating excitement that was part anticipation, part fear, part just plain nerves. She let it carry her along during the next few days, strangely content to be out of control, going passively with the flow of events.

Noah slept at his apartment for the next several nights, while they packed and prepared, and the move itself was accomplished with an almost miraculous smoothness. Leigh had anticipated a great deal of tension between them as the moment neared, yet she found that any constraint there might have been was lost in the bustle of sorting and packing, carrying and unpacking.

Finally, on Sunday evening, exactly one week after they had made the decision to live together, they did a final cleaning of Noah's apartment, received his security deposit from the landlady and returned to Leigh's house, tired, grubby, burdened with the vacuum and buckets piled with cleaning supplies, and laughing over the landlady's gimlet-eyed scrutiny of the apartment.

"What on earth could she have been looking for? She acted like she suspected a law professor of running guns or something."

"She was suspicious, all right, but it wasn't guns she was worried about. More likely burns on the carpet or stains on the wallpaper. She wasn't about to give that security deposit back until she knew everything was perfect."

"I guess we did a good cleaning job, then, didn't we? Maybe we can go into the cleaning business, huh?"

"Never! I'm not used to all that hard work!"

"You will be by the time we finish in here," Leigh said ominously as she looked around her living room, which was crowded with boxes of Noah's books. The only furniture he'd brought was a desk, which fit nicely into the living room, but the logistics of finding space for all his books on Leigh's well-filled shelves had them stymied.

"Don't remind me!" Noah groaned. "I had no idea how many books I had until we started putting them in boxes."

"They *will* fit," she told him determinedly. "We just have to figure out a way."

"Can we eat while we figure? I'm starving, and I think I'm in the mood for a nice pizza, delivered to the door."

"That sounds perfect, and no dishes to do!"

By the time the pizza arrived they had cleaned up and changed out of their rather dirty working clothes, and Noah had opened a bottle of inexpensive red wine. Leigh slouched on the sofa, sipping her wine and surveying the room.

"Maybe," she said thoughtfully, "if I drink enough of this I won't mind the chaos all around us."

"If you drink enough of that there won't be any left to go with the pizza."

She checked her watch. "No, we're safe. He should be here any time."

"I hope so! I'm wasting away from starvation while we wait."

Leigh eyed his powerful frame, sprawled beside her, and grinned. "I don't think you're in danger of shriveling up and blowing away any time soon."

"And what's that supposed to imply?" He scowled at her in stagy outrage. "Are you accusing me of being—ah—" The doorbell pealed before he could come up with an appropriate epithet.

"Saved by the bell!" Leigh escaped to the front door to pay for the pizza. To her dismay she found that the bell had not been rung by the pizza man but by Kate Holland.

"Guess what!" She bounced into the entry hall as Leigh opened the door, grinning happily. "I just got a commission to do the illustrations for a series of children's books!"

"Oh, Kate, that's terrific!"

Kate was too excited by her good news to notice Leigh's confused surprise or the ten-dollar bill in her hand. "It's a series of nature books, and they want . . ." Bubbling over, Kate walked into the house, and Leigh followed, at a loss to know how to handle the situation.

"I know I should have called first," Kate was saying, "but I was out anyway, and I wanted to borrow your book on still-life drawing for—" She fell suddenly silent as she stepped into the living room.

"Good evening, Kate." Noah rose to greet her, smiling from amid the clutter of boxes, and for a second or two Kate was at a loss for words.

"Hello, Noah," she said finally. She smiled at him and then surveyed the room with raised eyebrows. "I didn't mean to intrude, but obviously I've been a little out of touch." She looked from Leigh's stricken face to Noah's bland one. "I take it you've moved in, Noah?"

"I have." He inclined his head with a tiny smile.

"Then congratulations are in order. I hope you'll both be happy, and I won't intrude. I can get the book anytime, Leigh."

"No, it's handy enough, Kate." Leigh quickly searched along a crowded shelf and produced the book in question. "Here you are."

"Thanks a lot, Leigh. This will be a big help." Kate tucked the book under her arm and smiled at Noah. "Good night, Noah, and congratulations again."

"Good night, Kate." Noah's face was still calm and untroubled, but Leigh could feel herself blushing as she accompanied Kate to the door.

"Why didn't you *tell* me?" Kate whispered, and Leigh shrugged.

"There wasn't anything to tell."

Kate rolled her eyes, exasperated. "Come on, Leigh!

You—" The doorbell rang again, and Leigh moved gratefully to answer it. This time it *was* the pizza man.

Leigh dug in her pocket for the money. "Good night, Kate. It's been lovely seeing you, and congratulations on the commission. Have a nice evening."

"Not as nice as yours, I bet."

With that Kate left. Leigh paid the delivery man and headed back inside, but she didn't meet Noah's eyes as she set the pizza on the coffee table.

"It's still hot," she said as she tested the temperature of the box bottom.

"At this point I don't think I'd care if it wasn't. I'm too hungry." Noah lifted out a piece and set it on a paper plate which he passed to Leigh, then served himself. "Mmm, this is wonderful!" he said around a mouthful, and for several minutes they ate in silence.

Noah ate, at any rate. He ate his way steadily through three pieces while Leigh toyed with her first. Noah seemed not to notice, but at last he broke the lengthening silence to ask, "Are you having second thoughts?"

"Am I . . . ? Oh, no, of course not."

"'Of course not,'" he repeated dryly. "Kate's visit made you uneasy, that's obvious. Are you having second thoughts about our living together?"

"No," she replied after a moment, "not second thoughts, exactly. It's just . . . more embarrassing than I'd thought it would be, knowing what Kate must think."

"That's what everyone will think," he reminded her gently, "and they won't all be as pleased about it as Kate is."

"Oh, I know." Leigh shrugged helplessly. "And what people think doesn't bother me, really. It's just that this is all so strange."

"My living here is strange?"

"The two of us living together, but not as lovers," she clarified. "It's just not the most relaxing situation, knowing that you want to marry me, and that you've said you love me, while I don't know if I'm capable of loving you, emotionally or physically. I care about you, but there's a big difference between that and being in love with you," she finished unhappily.

"I've told you that I'm willing to live with that uncertainty, Leigh. It doesn't bother me."

"Maybe it *should* bother you. Have you thought about that? Maybe you shouldn't settle for a situation like this. Maybe you should find a woman who can give you what you deserve, instead of trying to rehabilitate me."

"Don't say that!" he commanded. He slid close on the sofa, took the plate from her hand and set it aside, then pulled her into the curve of his arm. "We've been through all this already," he said patiently. "It's not a question of what I deserve, it's a question of what I want, and I want you. I love you." He bent his head to look into her unhappy face. "Don't worry about it, okay? We'll handle it together; you'll see."

We'll handle it together, Leigh thought as she attacked her pizza with renewed appetite. *Together*. She liked the sound of that; she liked it a lot.

When her alarm clock awakened her the next morning at 6:30 she fumbled blearily for the button, then heard an echoing buzz from Noah's room. It went on a lot longer than hers, and she heard a couple of thumps and a smothered curse before it fell silent. She grinned to herself and slid shivering out of bed, pulling on her robe.

"Do you want the bathroom first or second?" Noah called through the wall.

"First, if you don't mind," she called back.

"That's fine. Will there be enough hot water for a shower?"

"Plenty!"

"Thanks. I'll start coffee while you get ready."

"Terrific!" Leigh replied, and hurried down the hall. Not wishing to abuse her bathroom privileges, she took even less time than usual to shower, letting the steam fluff the natural curl in her hair, then brushed her teeth and made up with record speed. Wrapped in her robe again, she returned to her room, knocking on Noah's door as she passed. "It's all yours."

"Thanks!"

The coffee was ready when she entered the kitchen after dressing. She poured herself a cup, added milk, and put bread in the toaster, belatedly wondering if Noah expected a bacon-and-eggs breakfast every morning. She hoped not; she couldn't work up a lot of enthusiasm for that much food so early in the morning. "I just hope that's not what he eats," she muttered to herself as her toast popped up.

"Talking to yourself?" he said, and she jumped.

"Oh! You startled me!" Turning, she found him directly behind her, dressed for business in conservative navy-blue trousers and a vest, his suit jacket over his arm. She grinned ruefully. "I know, talking to myself is a bad sign. I was wondering what you have for breakfast, since I didn't ask you last night. I can fix you eggs and bacon, or something, if you'd like."

"At this hour?" He shuddered. "Thanks for the offer, but no, thank you, Leigh. I usually have just toast and coffee."

"Me too," she said thankfully. "Do you want me to fix you some toast?"

"Sit down and eat yours while it's hot. I'll make mine."

"Are you sure?"

"I don't want you to wait on me, Leigh." He dropped bread in the toaster. "Go on, eat your breakfast." Leigh carried her plate to the table. "How long does it take to walk from here to the Law School?"

"Twenty minutes, if you move fast."

"In this weather I'll be moving fast, all right." He carried his toast to the table and sat beside her. "Do you have any idea just how cold it is outside?"

"The weatherman on the radio said six."

"Degrees?" She nodded. "Yeesh. Above zero, or below?"

"Six above."

"Well, thank heaven for small favors, I guess." He took a bite of his toast and chewed reflectively, fingering his tie. "Leigh?"

"Hmm?"

"Is this straight? It doesn't feel right."

"Look at me." Noah turned to face her, and Leigh studied the knot in the cranberry silk. "It is a little bit crooked." She reached over to straighten it. "There. Perfect."

"Thanks." He touched the knot again and nodded. "Some days I just can't get it right. Is there more coffee?"

Leigh nodded and watched him pour it, the cozy domesticity of the scene suddenly hurting her. They could be man and wife, making toast, drinking coffee, listening to the morning news on the radio. They could—almost—be married, but when the sun set and the winter night turned bitter, married couples clung together in the darkness, while Leigh and Noah lay alone in their cold beds, separated by so much more than the wall between their rooms. With an abrupt, jerky urgency she rose and carried her dishes to the sink.

"I have to get going," she announced, and Noah joined her, stacking his plate and cup in the dishwasher.

"I do, too," he said placidly. "I'll walk with you as far as Dunn Meadow." Leigh replied with a silent nod and filled her tote bag while Noah checked the contents of his briefcase; then they spent five minutes at the coat closet, muffling themselves to the eyebrows in coats, scarves, hats and gloves, preparing to brave the elements. Leigh was about to pull a thick fold of her emerald muffler over her mouth when Noah reached out to take her hand and still it for a moment.

"Don't worry, Leigh," he said softly, looking into her eyes, into her heart. "Please don't worry. It will all work out, you'll see."

"I hope so," she whispered. "I really hope so."

"I'm right about this. You'll see." He leaned forward to kiss her lips, then pulled the muffler into place. "Come on, Admiral Peary, out into the blizzard."

"You're Admiral Peary." Leigh followed him out the door, catching her breath as a frigid blast rocked her. "I'm Dr. Cook, racing you to the North Pole."

Heads down against the wind, arms linked, they trudged off into the icy morning, giggling idiotically. It was just as well, Leigh thought, that no one could hear them above the wind.

Chapter Ten

"And how they expect me to figure *this* out, I'll never know!" Halfway through that morning, Leigh glared at the schedule in her hand, struggling to figure out a way she could teach a class when no room was available. It couldn't be done. Where she was going to find a studio for her afternoon class she didn't know; all the studios were already booked, and she was going to have to make do with an ordinary classroom, or persuade another instructor to change rooms. That would be no easy task. She scowled at the schedule again. "Rats!"

"Not rats, Danish!" Kate shouldered the door open and eased into the office, carefully balancing two large Styrofoam cups of coffee on a white, string-tied bakery box. "Cherry Danish, to be specific." She set a cup in front of Leigh, laid a napkin beside it and placed a luscious-looking pastry on that. "Just take a coffee break for a few minutes, and we'll talk."

"That's considerate of you, Kate," Leigh said quickly, "and I'd love to, but I just have too much to do."

"Ah-ah-ah!" Kate wagged a reproving finger at her. "You're not getting out of it that easily, my sweet. We *are* going to talk." She dropped into her chair and sipped cautiously at her coffee. "First, I want to apologize for dropping in without calling last night. It was awkward for you, and I'm sorry about that. And I also want to congratulate you on your new domestic arrangements. I think it's absolutely wonderful that Noah has moved in with you. I really am glad for both of you."

Leigh's eyes widened. "You're glad? Really?"

"Well, of course I'm glad! What else?"

"You know it isn't the most socially acceptable kind of arrangement, after all," Leigh said, hesitant, and Kate laughed.

"These days I don't think there's any such thing as a socially *un*acceptable relationship, Leigh. I'm glad it's Noah, too." She smiled, but Leigh was more concerned with correcting her mistaken impression of the relationship.

"Kate, wait, you're wrong. We're not—we're not sleeping together."

Kate frowned, puzzled. "Then why did he move in?" The question popped out as though Kate were helpless to keep it in, but she immediately shook her head vigorously. "No. No, that was an unforgivable question, Leigh. Just forget I said it; it's none of my business."

"That's okay, Kate. I don't mind. It is kind of a strange situation, after all. It all came up in kind of a strange way, too. You see, he asked me to marry him, and—"

"He asked you to *what?*"

Kate was so rarely taken by surprise that Leigh began to smile at her astonishment. It was nice to be the one to render Kate speechless for a change. "He asked me to marry him," she repeated demurely. "And I told him no, I couldn't."

"You told him *no?*" Kate's mouth hung open.

"Well, I had to." Leigh shrugged and sobered, wondering how to explain. "Kate, you know I couldn't agree to marry him when I don't know if I can be a real wife to him. I only

agreed to live with him because he thinks it will help."
Leigh's eyes were dark with a plea for understanding.

"I see," Kate said after a moment, and smiled at Leigh.
"Don't worry about the way it looks, Leigh; that's of no
concern to anybody but the two of you. It could very well
work, too, you know. It's platonic for now, but you two are
living together, and things may change—sooner than you
think!"

"Kate, come on!" Leigh begged, blushing furiously.
"We're just roommates, that's all!"

"Mm-hm," Kate teased. "I never had a roommate who
wanted to marry me though!"

"Kate!"

Kate was finally persuaded to submerge herself in her
own mountain of papers while Leigh resumed wrestling with
the question of where she was to hold her class. She was
embarrassed by the teasing, but at the same time she was
reassured by her friend's acceptance and approval, her
vague fears and tension subsiding.

That sangfroid persisted until Leigh walked into the
house that evening to find Noah sitting in the living room,
drinking coffee with Marge. Her hard-won confidence vanished in an instant. "I-I'll just get out of my coat and—and
things. . . ." Her voice trailed off as she retreated to the
entry hall and fumbled with shaking fingers to unbutton her
coat.

"Hi." Noah joined her in the hall and reached around her
to help her out of her coat, brushing a kiss over her cheek as
he did. "Don't worry, Leigh. It won't be so terrible."

"Oh, Noah." Leigh turned within his arms and looked at
him with stricken eyes. "What am I going to say?"

"Tell the truth. You'll be fine, Leigh; you'll see."

"I wish I thought so," she whispered. Noah hugged her
close for a moment before walking with her into the living
room, where he excused himself to Marge, saying that he
had some reading to do.

"Would you like more coffee, Marge? I'm going to get
myself a cup and thaw out."

"I'll come with you." Marge followed Leigh to the kitchen, where Leigh poured coffee for both of them, then sipped at hers, at a loss for words.

"I—I was going to tell you about this, Marge," she said after an awkward pause, avoiding Marge's eyes. "But it all happened kind of suddenly."

"I know it did, and don't worry about me. You don't owe me an explanation. If this will make you happy, Leigh, then just let me congratulate you on taking such a big step." Marge smiled.

Leigh looked up uncertainly. "Well, thanks, Marge. . . . This situation is just so strange." Leigh sighed helplessly. "It's not what it appears to be on the surface, but explanations are much too involved, and what it appears to be is what Noah would like it to be eventually. It's all so complicated!"

"Don't worry about it, Leigh, and remember that you don't owe anyone an explanation. And if you're saying what I think you are, I think you have a good chance of succeeding. But you have to work at it; remember that. You have to face your fears, understand them and defuse them. It will require effort on your part, but it can be done." Marge looked steadily into Leigh's eyes. "It can be done, but remember, Leigh, it all depends on you."

By the end of that week Leigh wondered why she had ever worried. It was late Sunday afternoon, and things had gone so smoothly that she found herself wondering what all the fuss had been about. She threw the shuttle one last time, then slid off the bench at her loom.

"All finished?" Noah looked up from the syllabus he was revising at his desk.

"For the time being. The committee meeting's in half an hour, so I'd better get ready and go."

"Would you like me to drive you over there?"

"No, thanks. It's not that far, and I can use the walk to organize my thoughts."

"And clear your head?" Noah suggested with a grin.

"That may be a good idea. Do you expect this to be a rough meeting?"

"Not at all. Probably we'll just review what everyone learned over the holidays." She left him with a confident smile and a jaunty wave.

Everyone, she thought an hour into that meeting, is entitled to be wrong once in a while. She sat listening quietly while the fourth speaker in a row harangued the membership to approve a resolution to picket the financial offices if the university did not agree to petition the state legislature for more money. The resolution was couched in what Leigh considered inflammatory language, but her suggestion that they modify the phrasing had been quickly voted down. Her plea that they refrain from threatening to picket would no doubt receive the same quick rejection.

And so it did. She left the meeting in the unenviable position of having to present a resolution with which she disagreed to the administration the following night, and to follow that with a threat, with which she also disagreed.

About the only thing she still agreed with, she thought disgustedly as she made her way home, was the need for more teaching assistants and the money to pay them. Everything else seemed to have grown out of control, fed by frustration and a few rabble-rousers. She couldn't just opt out of the committee and its problems at this point though; she felt a responsibility to see this through, and to act as the voice of reason as long as she had the power to do so. She just wondered how Noah was going to react to this new development.

"How did it go?"

His first words as she walked in the door did nothing to help, and she struggled to find an acceptably noncommittal reply. "Not the best," she told him, turning to hang up her coat. "But everyone gave their reports and got caught up on what was done over the holidays." She pinned on a smile and walked into the living room. "I'm glad that's done, at any rate. What's for dinner?"

Noah let her change the subject, for which she was

grateful, but all evening she was abstracted, wondering what was going to happen when she presented her ultimatum to the administration. It was too much to hope that her preoccupation would go unnoticed.

"Care to tell me about it?"

"What?" Leigh looked up from putting her loom "to bed" for the night.

"Care to tell me what's bothering you? You've been on another planet since that meeting this evening, and it doesn't take a genius to guess that something went on that you aren't happy about."

"Oh." She shrugged. "Well, I'm not too happy with it, you're right, but do you mind if I don't tell you about it right now? I have to bring it up at the meeting tomorrow, and I'm not too comfortable with the idea of discussing this stuff at home."

"You still don't trust me." His voice was flat, his eyes cold, and Leigh dropped her shuttle and hurried across the room to him.

"Noah, that's not it at all!"

He looked down at her hand on his arm, but his face didn't soften. "Then what is it, Leigh? You tell me."

She took her hand from his sleeve. "It's the propriety of it all. You know I'm not comfortable with the two of us being on opposite sides in this mess, and when we agreed to live together I promised myself that I would keep committee business separate from us. I intend to do that, Noah," she said firmly. "You'll hear what I have to say tomorrow, along with everyone else. I hope you can understand that."

After a moment he nodded. "Yes, I can understand. I think you may be taking things to something of an extreme, but I can understand."

"I'm glad." She reached up to press a light kiss on his cheek. "Good night, Noah."

" 'Night, Leigh." She could feel him watching her walk down the hall and was well aware that though he said he understood, he wasn't happy.

Well, she wasn't very happy either, and frankly she was

wondering if this living-together situation wasn't going to cause more problems than it solved. Maybe she'd been overly optimistic about how well everything was going that afternoon, and maybe Noah had been wrong about its being such a good idea. It might solve some problems, but the problem that had introduced them in the first place was still between them, and until someone compromised it was destined to remain there.

Damn! Sometimes she felt she'd have been far better off if the committee had never been formed and she'd never heard of Noah Burke.

"Since we have examined the budget, we have satisfied ourselves that sufficient funds to adequately augment the teaching staff cannot be found." Leigh stopped speaking for a moment and looked around the conference table, her eyes sliding quickly past Noah's lest any message be seen to pass between them. "Since there are not adequate funds presently in the budget, and since we share with the administration a commitment to quality education, we feel it necessary to petition the state legislature for an addition to the budget. We have arranged to speak to the appropriate legislative committees next week, and we expect that the administration will do likewise."

She paused, scanning people's faces, mentally assessing their reaction to her words. Only Noah seemed relaxed, leaning back in his chair, arms folded across his chest, a smile lifting one corner of his mouth as he watched her. She wondered if he'd still be smiling when she finished.

"The committee has instructed me to inform you that if the administration does not see fit to join us in presenting a unified front to the legislature, we will perceive it as an indication that the administration is not seriously interested in resolving this issue with all possible speed. The committee will take this as a sign that our efforts at compromise have been fruitless, that our concerns are not being addressed seriously, and we feel that a public demonstration of our concern and commitment will then be necessary. This will take the form of informational picketing outside this building, and if that is not effective, a job action remains a distinct possibility." Leigh sat down in the middle of what could only be described as a thunderstruck silence.

Dean Anderson was the first to recover. "Young lady, are you threatening us?"

"No, sir." Leigh shook her head. "I assure you this is not a threat. We have exhausted all other avenues, so an approach to the legislature is necessary."

"I'm not talking about the legislature!" He waved that off in irritation. "I'm talking about this business of picketing! And striking!"

"Neither of those will occur if we can present a petition to the legislature together," she pointed out. "They'll be forgotten, *if* we can work together on this."

"Well, we *can't!*" Dean Anderson half rose, leaning over the table to glare at Leigh, his face nearly purple. "I take that as a threat, young lady, and I assure you that we will not knuckle under to this kind of pressure!"

"We're not trying to put pressure on you!" Leigh retorted. "We're trying to solve a problem that has dragged on unresolved for more than a semester and that could be solved with alacrity—*if* you would cooperate!"

"Cooperate? How can you imply that we have been anything but cooperative?"

Leigh snorted, too angry for tact. "I don't have to imply anything; all I have to do is look at the record of the past six months. It speaks for itself! And," she added, "my name is not 'young lady,' it is Michaels."

"Very well, *Miss Michaels,*" he drawled. "Let me assure you that we will not accede to your demands. As far as I'm concerned the budget will remain as it is for the rest of this fiscal year, and the appropriation for next year will not be altered either. As for what will happen if you stoop to hooliganism such as picketing, I will let Mr. Burke address the issue of the probable consequences."

Everyone turned toward Noah, but Leigh hesitated. Help me, Noah, she found herself thinking, as if she could communicate telepathically with him. Say something that will make him see how unreasonable he's being, something that will end this arguing. She couldn't hide what was in her eyes, the frustration and the plea for assistance, but when she finally looked across the table at Noah, she saw that she would get no help.

He leaned back even farther in his chair, watching them all with detached amusement. No, she'd get no assistance from that quarter, and Leigh felt a surge of fury at his attitude. This might not seem like a big deal to him, but it was important to her, to all the rest of them, and the least he could do was act interested! Her anger only grew when he spoke.

"The course of action open to the administration is clear-cut," he said calmly. "An injunction can be obtained to prevent picketing on university property. If that injunction is violated, those in violation may be arrested and charged."

Leigh couldn't quite suppress a gasp of shock. Then she shoved her chair back and rose, stuffing papers haphazardly into her briefcase.

"I think we've gone as far as we can," she said curtly. "I assure you, Dean Anderson, that your bullying tactics will not work, and I'd advise you to consider how it will look to the press when your teaching staff is jailed for their commitment to quality education." With that, she turned and stalked out of the room, hurrying away before she could say something she would later regret.

It took Noah two blocks to catch up with her. "Slow down! You're going to trip over something and fall down, the way you're going!"

"A lot you'd care!" she snapped. "You're the one who's going to put me in jail for picketing, aren't you? Why should you worry if I fall and break both my legs?"

"Leigh, don't be ridiculous," he began. "You kn—"

"Ridiculous?" He'd struck a nerve and she stopped short, glaring at him. "I'm ridiculous because I'm working for a cause I believe in? How convenient! The next thing you'll tell me is that I'm hysterical, and isn't *that* a convenient male cop-out? Well, I'm not hysterical, and I'm not ridiculous, and I won't even tell you what I think of you for your performance in there!" She spun on her heel and set off again.

"Be reasonable, Leigh. I had to—"

"Damnit, Noah, I *am* being reasonable! But unless you stop accusing me of being out of control just because I'm angry, I won't be for long! Don't do that to me, Noah."

"Do what?" Noah kept pace with her easily, his unruffled calm infuriating.

"Shift the argument so you're blaming me for being a woman," she snapped. "You say I'm ridiculous, but in the same position you would be 'firm in your convictions.' I'm unreasonable; you would be 'justifiably angry.' You know, Tony used to do that, too. If he was angry it was always because I was unreasonable, or—"

Leigh was cut off sharply as Noah seized her arm and jerked her roughly to a halt. His face was thunderous, his eyes dark with fury, and Leigh felt a pang of fear as he held her there.

"Don't you ever compare me to him," he snarled, then took a deep breath. "Don't you *ever* even suggest that I might be in any way like him, do you hear me?" Leigh hesitated, and he shook her slightly. "Do you hear me?"

Her anger burst through again, overcoming that moment of fear. "Of course I hear you! The whole block can hear you, but it doesn't alter the fact that you're accusing me of being irrational when I'm simply standing up for what I believe in!"

"Don't compare me to him."

It was a flat order, and Leigh didn't like it. "I won't unless you give me reason to." She looked pointedly at his hands on her arms. "Don't bully me, Noah." He followed her gaze, and he flushed as he took her point. Carefully, spreading his fingers wide, he released her.

She walked on. "I *am* angry, and I don't see that I have any reason to apologize for that. I am sick and tired of Dean Anderson and his stonewalling, and the more time I spend around him the less I like him. Calling me 'young lady,' trying to diminish my credibility by treating me like a child! And you're not much better!" she shot at Noah. "Sitting there smirking at us, as if it were all a game. What was so funny, anyway?"

"It's all funny, when you think about it. Dean Anderson having apoplexy, you and your committee ready to carry signs and stage a sit-in, just like the sixties—"

"What about you?" Leigh demanded. "You're involved in this, too, aren't you?"

"Not really. I'm just there as legal adviser, that's all."

"Are you kidding?" she gasped, and he shook his head. "Then why the hell are you there at all? Why do you even bother with it, if you're not involved, if you think it's nothing but a joke? My God, Noah, I thought better of you than that!"

"What do you mean, 'thought better of me'? I'm doing a job, and that's all I ever pretended to be doing!" Her words had stung, and his retort was sharp. "I'm doing a damned good job, too!"

"Regardless of right or wrong, is that it?" Leigh sneered.

"I'm doing a good job. Right and wrong don't enter into it."

"Of course they do! I always thought you believed in what you were doing, Noah. I didn't know you were just doing it for the money!"

"I'm not getting paid."

"Then for what? The ego gratification? Does it give you some kind of high to know that you can send a lot of people to jail just because they want to guarantee the quality of education? Does that give you a feeling of power, Noah?"

"No, it doesn't give me a feeling of power," he snapped as they strode up the walk to the house, "but I don't regret what I said." Leigh sucked in her breath in a furious hiss, but he ignored her, just followed her into the house and closed the door very carefully behind them. "I don't regret it because I think you're wrong, Leigh. I've always thought you and the committee made a good case for mandating a limit on the size of basic classes, and that hasn't changed, but I think your methods are wrong. I see nothing wrong in trying to prevent those methods from being used."

"Even if you get me thrown in jail?" Leigh shoved her coat into the closet and slammed the door. "Thanks a million, Noah! And, by the way, if you think the threat of arrest or jail will deter my fellow committee members, you are sadly out of touch with human nature. Most of the ones who voted to picket will look on the opportunity to get themselves arrested as too good to be missed!"

"Including you?"

"No, *not* including me! I'm sure you've figured out that I voted against it, but my one vote didn't carry much weight. I will do my best to support the course of action the committee chooses, Noah, because I believe in what we're working for, even if some of the methods are not what I would have chosen. I'll do that because I believe in our cause. I wonder why you're doing what you are though. Can you honestly say that Dean Anderson's methods are all that admirable?"

"I'm not there to question the man's methods; I'm there to provide legal assistance when I'm asked for it. I'm a lawyer; that's what I do."

"I don't see how you can do it! You could help both sides to reach a workable compromise, but you choose not to get involved; you just stay on the sidelines, watching us, speaking your little piece when you're asked to and never really caring about any of it. I wonder how much farther along we'd be if you *had* chosen to get involved in this, Noah. I wonder how much you could have done."

She turned and strode down the hall, and moments later Noah heard the very definite closing of her bedroom door.

He smiled a little at that, in spite of his own anger. She hadn't slammed it, not quite, but he knew just how badly she had wanted to. She was wrong though. He wasn't prostituting himself and his skills by remaining detached from the emotional issues; he was preserving his objectivity. She didn't understand that, but he had to remain objective. As a lawyer it was his primary skill, one he was proud of and had carefully cultivated.

He wasn't so sure about the other accusation. He'd been furious when she accused him of acting like her dead husband; he was not—and could never be—like that man. And yet he had to admit that he had been falling back on a cliché when he had called her unreasonable. She had a point, and he would apologize, but he would also make it clear that he didn't feel he deserved to be compared to that sick . . . After a few seconds he followed Leigh and tapped on her door.

"Leigh? We need to talk."

There was a long moment of silence; then the door swung open and Leigh looked stonily at him. "Do we? I thought we had said all there was to say."

"I don't think so."

She considered that for a moment. "I don't like what you're doing, Noah, and I don't like our being on opposite sides of this. It makes me uncomfortable."

And that, he thought with a trace of amusement, was the understatement of the century. It didn't make her uncomfortable, it made her livid. "I don't like being compared with a sick, sadistic monster, either, Leigh. I may have deserved what you said about diverting the argument, but I didn't deserve that."

They faced each other in silence for a long moment; then Leigh nodded, slowly. "I apologize for that. It was unfair."

"I apologize for my male-chauvinist remarks," Noah said, "but not for my professional performance. What I said before still stands. I intend to remain objective and do my job, no more. I know you don't like it, and I'm sorry, but that's the way it is."

" 'That's the way it is,' " she repeated, and shrugged. "I guess that's as far as either of us is willing to go, isn't it?"

"'Fraid so." Then Noah asked with a half smile, "Do you realize what this is?"

Leigh frowned, puzzled. "What what is?"

"This. It's our first fight."

"Our first—" Leigh stared for an instant, then choked back a giggle. "Yes, I guess it is . . . unless you want to count that first meeting. I wasn't too happy with you then, either."

"Good point." Noah grinned. "But I think we can call this our first official fight, don't you?"

"I suppose so, if there is such a thing as an 'official' fight." She smiled ruefully. "I never heard of one."

"Well, this was one, and I think it's time we made up, don't you?"

Leigh shrugged. "Can we make up? I mean, we haven't resolved anything yet, have we? We still disagree."

"There's no law against disagreement." He put an arm around her shoulders and led her back to the living room, where he sat her beside him on the sofa. "We can disagree and still be friends, Leigh. Even if we were lovers we could still disagree. You accused me of being overly objective, but that objectivity is something that's absolutely vital to my work. It's what enables me to interpret the law fairly and accurately. I *need* it."

Leigh thought for a moment, then nodded slowly. "I can see that." She looked sharply over at him. "But I'm still not crazy about the idea of being arrested!"

"It won't come to that."

"How can you be sure? I saw the way Dean Anderson's face lit up when you started all that stuff about injunctions and arrests and everything. He looked like he just saw Santa Claus coming his way!"

"Believe me, if Marty Anderson saw Santa Claus he wouldn't be smiling. He'd probably have a heart attack."

"I still don't see how you can be so sure he won't have us arrested. He was absolutely thrilled with the idea, and you've already said you won't do anything to talk him out of it."

"Well, I can't promise anything, but I don't see the situation going that far. Be optimistic, Leigh. Things aren't all that bad, you know."

"Maybe not from where you're sitting," she replied dryly, and he pulled her closer to his side.

"I'm sitting right where you are, and things aren't all that bad, trust me."

"Can I?"

"Can you what?"

"Trust you. After all, you've threatened to have me arrested."

"I promise you, if you're arrested, I'll be right there to bail you out," he murmured.

"I'll hold you to that."

"Mm-hm, you do that." He was silent for a moment, his face against her hair. "Leigh?"

"Hmm?"

"Have we made up?"

She thought about it. "I guess so, if we can make up without agreeing."

"We can."

"Then I guess we've made up."

"Good." Noah's arms tightened about her. "I don't like fighting with you."

I don't like it either, Leigh thought fervently. I don't like it at all.

Chapter Eleven

*T*heir first fight caused definite ripples in the smooth progress of their relationship, and though the surface disturbance was quickly smoothed over, a certain agitation persisted underneath. Despite what Noah had told her about objectivity being a necessary part of his working personality, Leigh didn't like it, and she didn't agree with it. She just didn't see how he could lend his talents and his effort to something he didn't believe in.

They had made up, after a fashion, but she knew that nothing had really been resolved, and she was left with the feeling that a lot of very unpleasant things had been conveniently swept under the rug. They were out of sight, sure, but they were still there, and one of these days a draft would blow that rug up and scatter them all over the room, and there was no telling what they would have grown into by then.

Despite those undercurrents, her days with Noah quickly settled into a pattern, the adjustment period made easier by the fact that they were both very busy with the opening of the new semester. The bustle of registration and preparing class materials kept them too busy at first to worry about subtle nuances of emotion, and when Leigh finally had time to catch her breath and think, she realized that they had fallen into an easy routine almost by accident. The first hurdle had been almost ridiculously easy to leap: She was completely and utterly comfortable living with Noah.

She was sifting through a stack of proposed student projects late on a gray afternoon when the telephone interrupted her. She reached over a bag of yarn samples and knocked the bag flying. "Whoops!" She lifted the receiver, grabbing too late for the errant bag, and managed to knock a couple of books after it as the yarn spilled in a colorful cascade across the floor. "Oh, rats!" She set the receiver on her shoulder. "Hello?"

"Leigh? Is something wrong?"

"Oh! Hi, Noah." Leigh propped the receiver on her shoulder, to reach across the floor for the yarn, and predictably the receiver slipped, falling with a deafening clatter to the floor. She dragged it back up by the cord and apologized breathlessly. "I'm sorry about that! I knocked a bunch of stuff off my desk, and then when I tried to get it I dropped the phone. I hope you're not deaf after all that!"

"My ear may ring for a while," Noah told her dryly, "but I think I'll live. Do you know what day it is?"

Leigh didn't see why he needed to know, but she glanced at her desk calendar. "It's February first."

"Yeah, but do you know what day that is?"

"Aside from the day after January thirty-first, I don't think so."

"*Think*, Leigh!"

She thought, but to no effect. "I give up, Noah. What day is it?"

"One month to the day since New Year's Day—when we decided to live together!"

"Oh!" She hadn't realized that. "It is, isn't it?"

"Mm-hm, and I think we ought to do something special, so how about dinner out?"

"I'd love it. Would you like to dress up and go somewhere really fancy?"

"It's kind of cold to dress up, so why don't we stay as we are and go somewhere sort of medium fancy?"

They arranged to meet at a Greek restaurant near the campus, and Leigh hung up, smiling.

"Are you ready to give your testimony next week?" Noah propped his chin in his hand and studied Leigh across the table. The waitress had brought their drinks and departed with their order, and as Leigh sipped her tea, her face was thoughtful.

"I hope so. I have my presentation ready, and I think the questions they'll ask should be pretty predictable, but you never know, do you?"

"You never know," he agreed. "Your presentation should give them some direction to follow when they question you though, so keep that in mind while you're speaking."

"I will. Thanks for the hint."

"My pleasure. Are you sure you don't want me to go to Indianapolis with you? For moral support or anything?"

"Thank you, but there's no need. There are four of us going."

Noah stirred his thick Greek coffee, then grinned at her. "I still wish I knew how you got them to postpone the picketing until after you talked to the legislature. Maybe I could learn something from you."

"I doubt it," she said dryly. "That was not one of my finer hours as a chairperson. I ended up yelling at them that we wouldn't impress the legislators with the reasonableness of our cause if we were all arrested for carrying signs. The signs are still in Jonas's garage though, just waiting for someone to pick them up and turn this into a big, messy 'situation.'"

"Well, let's hope it doesn't come to that."

"I'll drink to that!" Leigh raised her teacup as the waitress appeared with their dinner, and serious discussion was shelved for the moment.

She wondered though just how serious Noah was in his "professional, detached" hope that the situation would remain calm, and how much he was simply enjoying watching the rest of them play out their charade. She sometimes had the feeling that this problem, important as it was to the university community, was nothing more than a diversion to Noah, accustomed as he was to directing the course of international commerce.

Logically, she knew that she shouldn't be disappointed that he might be more entertained than involved, and yet she was disappointed, a little angry and a little sad. She was grateful for the arrival of their meal. This was supposed to be a celebration, and she didn't want to dwell on Noah's disconcerting detachment tonight; tonight she wanted to enjoy him.

Sated with stuffed grape leaves and shish kebab, they walked from the restaurant into spitting snow and a cold, raw wind. Leigh pulled her knit cloche lower on her brow and clung to Noah's arm, shamelessly using his bulk as a shield from the wind.

"Here." He pulled off her glove and tucked her hand deep in his coat pocket, holding it in his, holding her beside him. "Is that warmer?"

"It's wonderful! I feel kind of bad using you as a windbreak though. You must be cold, too."

"I'm all right." They were quiet for a few minutes as they walked toward home. "I'm glad you suggested this place, you know. I had no idea you could find good Greek food in the wilds of Indiana."

"Spoken like a true New York culinary snob!" she laughed. "I've always thought it was good, even if it isn't in New York. I don't think I should have had the feta-and-olive salad, though. I'll probably have bad breath for a week!"

"Let's see." Using the hand imprisoned in his pocket,

Noah pulled her to a halt and swung her around to face him, took her chin in his free hand and kissed her cold lips. "Hmm," he mused, "maybe another . . ." He pulled her close with his free arm for another kiss, longer this time, unconcerned by the occasional passersby.

Leigh might have been a bit embarrassed had she been able to think coherently about it, but the sweet, seductive movements of Noah's lips against hers, the cold freshness of their faces and the rasp of his day's growth of beard on her skin were an intoxicating combination. She leaned into him, her right hand still in his coat pocket, her left coming up to clutch the soft cashmere of his lapel as her knees weakened beneath her. She began to tremble.

Noah mistook her reaction for shivering. "You're cold; let's get you home." Keeping her close at his side, he set a brisk pace, walking in a silence broken only by the sound of their feet on the pavement. Leigh understood why he didn't speak; words would be superfluous, but a bubbling, effervescent excitement was growing in her. Still silently, they climbed the wooden steps to the porch, and Leigh clung to Noah's hand as he unlocked the door and let them into the dark entry hall.

"Oh!" Her soft gasp was smothered against his mouth as he caught her to him before she could even unbutton her coat. She swayed into the curve of his body, clutching his coatsleeves as he tugged her knit hat off and tangled his fingers in her curls, holding her imprisoned. It was a sweet prison though, and Leigh made the most of it, returning his kisses eagerly, linking her hands behind his neck as their mouths teased and tasted, met and clung again and again.

The winter chill vanished as their bodies heated with passion, and clumsily they struggled out of their coats. Leigh found herself on the sofa with no real idea of how she had come to be there, but that didn't matter, because Noah was there with her. She took him into her welcoming arms, shifting her body to make room for him, kissing him eagerly.

She could sense the passion in him, but felt no fear of it;

never, since he'd learned the reasons for her fear, had he failed to keep that passion under strict control. Leigh had been free to savor his lovemaking without worrying about where it might lead, to give herself over to him, as she did now. Dizzy with her own reckless bravado, she clung to him as his hands moved over her sweater, shaping the soft curves under the wool, then moving to the hem to slide beneath it. She made no move to resist when he caressed her ribs, none even when he hesitated, then moved his hand up. With a sensation of abandoning herself to forces she could not deny Leigh let her body arch up against the curve of his as he gently caressed her breasts, taking their weight in his palms, her nipples tightening to hard peaks at his touch.

With the one tiny corner of her mind that was still capable of thought Leigh realized that Noah's caresses didn't frighten her in the least, and more than that, that she was actually taking pleasure in them, desiring them. She could still feel desire for a man; the womanly part of her had not been completely killed off after all, and yet . . .

And yet there was still something missing, just as there always was. Her surrender, startling though it was, was incomplete. It was as if she were waiting for the fear to strike again, as if she expected it, and therefore couldn't abandon herself to Noah's lips and hands. When the fear did strike, it overwhelmed her easily.

Noah's lips, dropping little nibbling kisses along her jawline and onto her throat, distracted her at first, but as his fingertips slipped open the button at the waistband of her slacks and the zipper rasped down, she froze, the familiar panic knifing through her. Noah's hand moved over the soft skin of her stomach, and she was galvanized into action, twisting out of his arms and off the sofa, frantically pulling her clothes into place again.

"Leigh—"

"Noah, I can't. I'm sorry, but I just can't." She turned her back on him, muttering her apology.

"What is it this time?" His voice, angrily sarcastic, brought her around to stare at him, eyes wide and shocked. "Have I stepped over some new line you've drawn? Have I acted too much like a man for you?" He shoved himself off the sofa and walked with abrupt, angry strides across the room, then turned on her. "Well, if I have acted too much like a man, Leigh, maybe you should remember that I *am* a man! I'm a man, and you're the woman I love, and I'm damned tired of being treated like your brother!"

"Noah, that's not what I—"

"No!" He interrupted her rudely. "*You* listen to *me* this time! I moved in with you so our relationship, such as it is, could grow and mature, not so that it could stagnate. I've been pretty accommodating, as far as I can tell. I've put my own desires in the background in deference to you, and I've tried, far harder than you can ever know, to make things as easy as possible for you. As far as I can see though, you haven't done anything at all! You don't have any idea what you do to me, do you?" he snarled. "You haven't looked at any of this from my point of view. Well, let me tell you, lady, I've done my damnedest to look at everything from your point of view, and right now I don't especially like what I see!"

"But, Noah, you knew what the situation was when we decided to do this!" Leigh protested, and he chopped savagely at the air in denial.

"We both knew! But didn't we agree that we were going to work together to change things? I know you're emotionally fragile and traumatized by the terrible things that happened to you, Leigh. Well, I happen to think you're a lot stronger than you give yourself credit for, and I *don't* think you're trying! So far I've done all I know how to do to aid the process of change, but I can't see that you've done anything!" He stared at her from across the room, then added quietly, "Right now I don't feel like making any more futile efforts."

He turned on his heel and strode out of the room,

grabbed his heavy jacket from the hall tree and stormed out
of the house, slamming the door behind him with enough
force to rattle the windows.

For an endless moment Leigh could only stare, frozen in
shocked surprise, at the door through which he'd disappeared. She would never know how long she stood there,
unable to absorb what had happened, but when the realization at last began to penetrate she moved slowly to the wing
chair and sank into its depths.

She gazed with blank eyes into the fireplace, but instead
of the dead ashes of yesterday's fire she saw the secrets
within herself. What she saw, sitting there while the minutes
and then the hours passed, while the house grew cool and
then cold around her, was not pleasing.

She didn't want to admit it, but the accusations Noah had
hurled at her were true. She had been so comfortable with
the status quo, with the essentially platonic, nonthreatening
relationship they'd developed, that she had made no effort
to move on to the uncharted territory that frightened her so
much. If she were brutally honest with herself, she also had
to admit that she had almost welcomed that stab of panic,
the familiar fear that protected her from that which was so
terrifying.

Noah had been right when he said she'd never considered
his feelings. With her narrow, self-absorbed view of things
she had concerned herself only with what *she* felt, what *she*
thought. She had never once considered what sort of strain
this situation might have placed on Noah, what efforts he
was making to help her. Thoughtlessly, selfishly, she had
allowed herself to float passively along, had assumed that
that was enough to ask of herself, even though Noah had
told her that he loved her, that he wanted to marry her, that
he wanted to make love to her.

He had bared his soul to her, had given and given of his
strength, his comfort, his understanding, and Leigh had
taken everything while giving nothing in return. No wonder
he was angry, she thought despairingly. No wonder he had
walked out.

How many times in the past month, she wondered, had she hurt him with her casual indifference to his love and caring? How many times had he longed to hear her say she loved him, even a little, while the words went unspoken, unthought? How many times had he wanted her? How many times, as she was dashing to the shower in the morning, when she was sitting close beside him watching TV, or sleeping in the next room, had he wanted her, and concealed his need and his wanting out of consideration for her?

How could she have been so blind? Leigh had always considered herself a fairly sensitive human being. She had just discovered how fallacious *that* assumption was, hadn't she? She shifted in the chair, squirming away from the unpleasantness she saw in herself. She wasn't made any more comfortable by her awareness of just what Noah must think of her. He had told her that she was stronger than she thought, so it was undoubtedly nothing but laziness and cowardice that kept her locked in her narrow little world.

Of course there were huge, gaping holes in her perception of Noah, too. She had spent this last month thinking about, relating to and dealing with a figment of her imagination. Noah wasn't a brother or a platonic friend or a roommate; he was a man. More than that, he was a man who had admitted his love and his desire for her.

He was a man. Images of him began to unreel in her mind, and this time she saw those images with a new insight and a clearer vision. She saw pictures of Noah sleepy-eyed in the morning, his jaw dark with stubble, wearing only royal-blue pajama trousers and doing sit-ups in his bedroom, a light sweat sheening his chest. Or lounging by the fireplace in the evening, reading a student paper, his shirt half-open in the warmth, his eyes following her as she moved about the house. She watched those and so many more images pass like a film montage, seeing them clearly for the first time. As she watched them she could feel her perception of Noah changing, feel herself changing.

It was subtle, but with her new awareness, with her

reexamination of her feelings, came the tentative beginnings of sexual awareness. He was a man, she saw that now, with a piercing, crystalline clarity: He was a man, and she was a woman.

He had been living with her all this time, but she had regarded him more as an asexual, nonthreatening room-mate than as a man. Just how insulting that dismissive attitude was had never occurred to her before, but now the realization struck her with the force of a blow. Noah was a great deal more than a "roomie," and he had begun this arrangement confident that she understood that.

She had let him down badly, so badly that, as she sat alone and waited for him to come home, she was terribly afraid that he might decide not to return at all.

He did return, but very late, long after she had gone to bed, where she lay staring at the ceiling. She knew that she wouldn't sleep until Noah returned, but even when he did, moving quietly through the house to his room, she remained wakeful. An idea had come to her during those long hours of waiting. It had captured her imagination, and though it was very late before she slept, she woke early the next morning, filled with a giddy, tremulous, nervous excitement.

It was Saturday, and neither of them had any appointments or obligations that would interfere with her plan, but she lay for a few moments wondering if she dared carry it out, and then wondering if she dared abandon it. No, she resolved, she would not back out now. If progress were ever to be made, it had to start somewhere.

Moving quietly, she slipped out of bed and pulled on her robe, then tiptoed to the bathroom to wash her face, brush her teeth, and put on a light touch of blusher and lipstick. She brushed through her unruly curls, then hesitated before leaving the room. She turned back, took a small perfume flacon from the shelf above the sink and touched the silver stopper to her wrists and throat.

The house was chilly, and as she passed the thermostat on

the wall she pushed it up a few degrees and listened to the distant "whoosh" as the furnace lit. In the few minutes it would take to make coffee the early-morning chill would be gone. When the coffee was ready she poured herself a cup and sipped it, but her heart was pounding, her stomach jumpy, and she poured the bulk of it away.

Her hands trembled very slightly as she poured another cup, but she ignored the sign of weakness and slipped her robe off her shoulders, dropping it over a kitchen chair. The edge had been taken off the air, but she shivered a little as a draft plucked at the sheer white batiste of her nightgown. She picked up the coffee, holding it carefully in both hands, and carried it to Noah's room.

She pushed the door open slowly, blinking to accustom her eyes to the dimness within. Noah was still sleeping, as he had been on that first morning when she'd brought coffee to him, but this time she didn't leave, as she had done then. Standing in the doorway, her slim form faintly visible through the thin gown, the cup cradled in her hands like an offering, she looked at the man who shared her home.

As before, he was sprawled facedown across the bed, his face turned away from her and buried in a pillow, his shoulders broad and brown against the white sheets. Leon was curled comfortably against his legs and looked up as Leigh opened the door, regarding her with lazy emerald eyes for a moment before his face disappeared behind an enormous yawn, all pink tongue and gleaming teeth.

"Go away, Leon," she whispered, and flapped her hand at him in a shooing motion. "Go *on!*" Grudgingly the cat heaved his bulk off the quilt and hopped to the floor, where he stretched luxuriously before ambling out of the room, his progress hastened by a prod from Leigh's toe as he passed.

The small commotion didn't wake Noah, but he moved against the pillow and muttered something unintelligible before he subsided again. Leigh put the coffee on the nightstand and moved to the bedside, then sat carefully on the edge of the mattress. Noah slept on, and she reached to touch his shoulder lightly.

"Noah?" She stroked his shoulder, marveling at the warmth and smoothness of the skin under her fingertips, the firm muscle of his shoulder. "Noah? I've brought you coffee."

"Mmm?" He moved restlessly, not quite awake, and she stroked his shoulder again. "Hm?" he said more clearly, then rolled onto his side and blinked at her. "Leigh?"

"I brought you coffee," she said shyly, and glanced at the cup.

"Oh. Thank you." Holding the blankets to his waist with one hand, a gesture that gave Leigh a moment's pause, because she understood its significance, he heaved himself up against the pillows.

"Here you are." She handed him the brimming cup. "Good morning."

"Good morning." He drank, then studied her for a minute. "This is nice." He sipped again. "Thank you."

"You're welcome." Leigh blushed a little and looked down, pleating a fold of the sheer cotton. She blushed again when she realized just how sheer her nightgown really was, but it was too late to do anything about that now.

"Why did you bring me this?"

Leigh's head jerked up at the question, and she stared at him, eyes wide with emotion. "I want to apologize," she said softly, and looked down at her hands again, "for being insensitive and selfish. You were right—you were absolutely right in the things you said last night. I thought about it for a long time, and I'm ashamed of myself and the way I've acted." She looked up again, her eyes dark and pleading and a little bit frightened. "I'm sorry," she whispered and leaned forward to kiss his lips.

When she lifted her head Noah sat absolutely still for a moment, watching her face, then his gaze dropped to her bare shoulders, crossed by ribbon straps, to her breasts, faintly visible through the light gown, and to the thinly veiled lines of her hips and thighs. She bore his scrutiny bravely, but her cheeks were very pink when he met her eyes again. Carefully, slowly, as if a sudden movement might frighten her away, he set his cup aside and took her into his arms.

Leigh melted against him as his arms closed about her, her hands sliding up to cling to his shoulders. He was big and strong and warm and male, and as his mouth closed over hers, she was aware of a myriad of delicious sensations. The thick mat of hair on his chest prickled softly against her breasts as he pulled her to him; the night's growth of beard rasped her cheeks. Beneath the blankets his legs moved, sliding close to form a cradle behind her. She ran her hands over his shoulders, arms and back, wondering at the warm smoothness of his skin, the hard ripple and bulge of muscle underneath, the implication of a strength so much greater than her own, marveling at all the complementary differences between them.

Noah kissed her deeply, tenderly, savoring the sweetness of her mouth, teasing and tasting while his hands moved over her back, her naked shoulders, then slowly, delicately, over the fragile line of her collarbone and lower, to the soft upper curves of her breasts. She shivered when his fingertips, hard and slightly rough, slid across her breasts, then dipped beneath the lace-edged neckline of her gown. Her nipples tightened into hard buds under his fingers, and desire washed through her as a man's touch gave her the pleasure she had thought she would never know.

She responded helplessly to him, drowning in these new sensations, clinging to him almost desperately as her only security. When he withdrew at last she moaned softly in protest, burying her hot face against his neck. She felt him groan deep in his chest; then he gently took her arms from around his neck and with a brief kiss on her forehead lifted himself away to put a slight distance between them.

"Leigh?"

"Hmm?"

"I meant what I said last night—"

"I know you did, but—"

"Wait, Leigh." He stopped her protest with a gentle smile and a finger laid across her lips. "Let me finish. I meant what I said, but as I told you before, I'm not asking for a human sacrifice from you."

"But I want to . . . with you," she said shyly. "I want . . . I want you."

Noah took her hand to pull her up beside him. "You're beginning to," he said gently. "You're beginning to, you're learning to, but it's too soon. A time will come, *the* time will come, when it will be right for us to make love. We'll both know when that is, when your desire is strong enough to overwhelm everything else."

Leigh thought about that for a moment, then snuggled closer, smiling into Noah's eyes. "Now isn't the time?" She ran her hand over his chest in a light caress, and he covered her fingers with his own, stilling their provocative movements.

"Not now," he told her, a spark of amusement in his eyes. "But you seem to be learning awfully fast."

Leigh dropped her eyes shyly. "I want to learn," she whispered.

"You will," he promised, his voice husky. "For now, though, I really think you ought to go get dressed—for both our sakes."

"You think so?" She flirted with her eyes, and Noah's darkened as he met her gaze.

"The time will come, Leigh; I promise you." His arm tightened to pull her close, and he kissed her, a quick, hard, hungry kiss that echoed that promise. When he lifted his lips he held her tightly for a moment, then gave her a little push. "Go get dressed, Leigh."

She went.

Over the next days Noah watched with frank enjoyment and not a little amusement the changes that took place in Leigh. She was growing, changing so rapidly that he found it hard to adjust. She was testing her wings as a woman, learning to accept and enjoy the vulnerable, feminine side of herself, even learning, with a shy playfulness that wrung his heart, to flirt with him. She was learning and growing before his eyes, but Noah realized that he was learning as well.

He was thirty-seven years old. Thirty-seven. He had reached that disgustingly "advanced" age free of personal attachments, unencumbered by emotional entanglements, a carefree, high-living, jet-setting bachelor, the man no woman could catch. If asked, he freely would have admitted that he had contrived to avoid the ties of love and commitment; he would have been unembarrassed by, almost proud of, that admission.

He'd been selfish and self-satisfied, he realized, and now, looking back at the man he'd been, he found he didn't like that shallow, narcissistic playboy at all. He'd spent all those years skimming over the surface of life, working hard, playing hard, but hardly *feeling* at all. Leigh was learning, but he was learning too, learning to care for someone more than he cared for himself, learning to put her needs before his own, learning for the first time to deny his own desires in deference to her feelings. If he had helped Leigh, then Leigh had helped him as well, and he had grown in as many ways as she had.

She was an odd mixture, the shy girl contrasting with the self-possessed and committed woman who had testified before the state legislature's finance committee for four consecutive days. Though she hadn't felt he needed to go with her for moral support, on the third day of her testimony Noah had driven her to Indianapolis, since he had business of his own with the state supreme court. He had been able to conclude matters quickly, and had slipped into the rear of the small hearing room in time to listen as she calmly fielded questions.

He had been impressed, even though he'd already seen her in action as she crossed swords with Dean Anderson, and privately he thought that her request had a good chance of being approved, though he had had to caution her that the wheels of government ground slowly, and that she and the committee would have to be patient.

"Patient?" she'd cried on the drive home, exasperated.

"*Patient?* We've been nothing *but* patient for months now! How much patience do you expect us to have?"

"Enough, Leigh. That's all the patience you have to have: enough to see it through."

"Hmph! Easier said than done."

As he sat in his office one afternoon the telephone on the desk beside him buzzed its peremptory summons. He punched the blinking button and lifted the receiver. "Yes?"

"Miss Michaels is here to see you, Mr. Burke."

Chapter Twelve

"Hi!" She breezed into his office moments later like a breath of spring air. Her coat was open, her hair was a windblown red-gold tousle, her cheeks flushed from the cold and her eyes sparkling with laughter. Noah felt his heart lurch. She didn't even know how beautiful she was, what the sight of her did to him. And that knowledge would scare her to death, he thought wryly, so perhaps it was just as well that her new understanding of him didn't go quite that far.

"She didn't tell you"—Leigh's laughing voice pulled him back to reality—"that I'm stealing you away from all this drudgery. Are you ready to go shopping?"

"Just as soon as I get my coat. I hope this thing is worth the trip though."

"It is." Leigh grinned. "You'll see. I told you about it last night, remember, just so you'd know what a terrific buy you'll be getting."

"I know what you told me, but I'm still not sure if it's what I think it is," he said over his shoulder as she helped him with his coat.

"So I'll tell you again. Obviously you didn't pay attention." They set out for the shop, laughing together at

Leigh's flamboyant reprise of her description of the book cabinet they were going to see. "You're going to love it," she concluded. "It's the most gorgeous piece of furniture I've ever seen. I know it's the one thing you want!"

"Oh, I don't know," Noah drawled, tucking her hand more tightly in the crook of his arm. "I think I already have what I want."

Leigh looked sidelong at him and flushed a little at what she saw in his eyes. She looked down at the sidewalk for a moment, then grinned, teasing again. "You silver-tongued devil!" She poked him in the ribs. "Here's the store." She steered him toward a seedy storefront with a sign reading FURNITURE—ANTIQUES.

"Not a very prepossessing place, is it?" Noah surveyed the dusty treasures piled in the window. "Are you sure this is the greatest bookcase of all time?"

"Come on." She pulled him toward the door. "These little places are where you find the best things. Anyway, it really is perfect. It matches your desk, and it'll fit into the alcove between the windows. Come on, you're going to love it!"

"If you say so." With a last dubious glance at a battered banjo reposing amid several pieces of chipped cranberry glass in the window, Noah let himself be led inside. "A veritable Aladdin's cave," he muttered, looking around the shop at the dusty jumble of old furniture, lamps and bric-a-brac stacked in haphazard, and probably dangerous, piles.

Leigh strode purposefully toward a murky corner, and Noah followed, picking his way through the maze, wondering how on earth she'd ever managed to find anything of value in this chaos. It was typical of her, though, and he smiled as he sidestepped a hideous mahogany curio cabinet. She had an uncanny knack for finding the perfect item at the perfect price, and he had grown used to following in her bargain-hunting wake.

"Here it is!" she called, waving him toward the darkest corner, pulling a rickety lamp table out of his way and sneezing when she raised a cloud of dust. "Isn't it gorgeous?"

Noah wasn't really surprised to find that it was indeed gorgeous, in spite of its unpromising surroundings. It was a tall, glass-fronted library cabinet, golden oak like his desk, a graceful piece of furniture, its beauty marred only by a liberal coating of dust. As Leigh pointed out, it would go a long way toward relieving their ongoing shortage of book space. He looked it over carefully for nicks and scratches, opened and closed the doors, gave it a push to see if it was steady on its legs, and finally turned to Leigh, carefully keeping his face deadpan. He was interrupted before he could give his opinion, though.

"Brought him in, did ya?" The proprietor, a tiny, wizened gnome aged somewhere between seventy and infinity smiled ingratiatingly at them around a fat, malodorous cigar. "Great piece, ain't it?"

"What do you think, Noah?" Leigh was still smiling, but she was watching his face intently.

Noah hid his amusement as he answered the shopkeeper. "It's not bad," he said noncommittally. "The price is a little steep, though, isn't it?"

"Steep?" The gnome's bushy white eyebrows climbed the steep slope of his forehead. "I'm takin' a beating on it!"

"Oh, come on," Noah drawled, and Leigh watched narrow-eyed as he pointed out flaws. Surely he could see what a bargain the cabinet was, or was it . . . ? He called the gnome's attention to a nick here, a scratch there, and as he bent to point out a chip on one of the legs he looked over the old man's shoulder and one eyelid dropped in a conspirator's wink.

She almost laughed aloud. So that was his strategy! Folding her hands demurely before her, she stood back and let the negotiations run their course. Noah pointed out flaws, the gnome countered with the cabinet's fine points, and when it was all over the price had been reduced by forty dollars, and Leigh was as impressed as the gnome was disgruntled.

"You're one sharp customer, I'll tell ya, mister." He took the check from Noah and scrutinized it carefully, but when Noah offered identification he waved it away. "Nah, that's okay. I kinda wish the little lady woulda come by herself though."

"I might be just as tough a customer as Noah, you know." Leigh grinned, and the gnome shook his head.

"I don't think so, ma'am," he drawled ruefully. "I'll see this gets delivered tomorrow, and thank you for the business, Mrs. Burke."

"Oh, but—" Leigh's protest was cut off by the impact of Noah's elbow in her ribs.

"Just thank the man, Leigh," he muttered.

"Thank you very much," she repeated dutifully. Noah added his farewell, and steered her outside again to the chilly evening. "Noah, he thought we were married. Shouldn't we have told him?"

"We didn't have to tell him anything. Whatever conclusions he draws are his business, and our situation is our business. Anyway"—he grinned—"I kind of liked the sound of it." He took her hand and tucked it in his arm again, walking quickly through the dusk toward home.

Home. Their home. Mrs. Burke. Yes, Leigh realized, she liked the sound of that, too.

Other things were also changing for her. She noticed things now, things to which she had previously been oblivious. She noticed Noah, the way his hair curled wildly when he came in from the rain, giving him the look of a Greek statue; the way he developed a vertical line between his brows when he concentrated on something; the way he absently caressed her shoulder when she sat beside him on the sofa. She was always aware of him now, stealing glances when he wasn't looking, fascinated by the texture of his skin, the play of muscles as he moved, and the play of expression over his face. She was aware, too, of his potent, powerful maleness, so sharp a contrast to her own femininity.

She had also begun to notice other women. They had always watched him, she supposed, but she had been too involved with herself to see them. Now she noticed them, watched them watching Noah with their hungry eyes, smiling inviting smiles at him, and she found herself wanting to assert her claim, to shout, "You can't have him, he's mine!" She wondered, though, if she had any right to feel that way after the things she had said and done. She wondered, too, if Noah might not change his mind, and how she would bear it if he did.

The new cabinet had just been delivered the next evening, and Noah and Leigh stood admiring it when the telephone shrilled behind them. Leigh picked it up.

"Hello? Oh, hi, Marge. How are y—" She broke off abruptly, and Noah turned to see a stunned expression spread over her face. She listened intently for a moment, then cried, "You *what?*" Her voice rose. "You *did?* Oh, Marge, that's wonderful; that's *fabulous!* Yes, of course. We'll be right over." She banged the phone back onto its rest and grabbed Noah's hand, hopping up and down with excitement. "Marge and Joe are getting married!" she cried, pulling him toward the door. "Come on! We're going over to celebrate!"

Marge opened the kitchen door to them, her flushed cheeks and ruffled hair evidence that she and Joe had been celebrating privately. "Hi, Leigh, Noah," she greeted them with a smile, but could say no more before Leigh threw her arms around her in a bear hug. When Leigh turned to hug Joe, Marge smiled shyly up at Noah. "I guess Leigh gave you the news."

"Yes, she did, and we both think it's wonderful." He bent to kiss her cheek. "When did you decide?"

"Tonight, actually."

"Tonight?" Leigh shrieked. "You mean, just now?"

"Mm-hm." Marge smiled, her eyes sparkling as she looked at her husband-to-be. Joe had been pouring champagne for them all, but when Marge looked in his direction he turned toward her as if pulled by an invisible thread. The look they shared, full of tenderness and promise, intimate and sweet, brought a lump to Leigh's throat.

"Well, you certainly surprised us," she said, her voice oddly husky.

"You did indeed, Marge. I have a feeling you're a pretty surprising lady." Noah saw that they each held a glass of champagne and lifted his own in a toast. "To Marge and Joe," he said. "May you have a long and happy life together!"

"Hear, hear!" They raised their glasses together.

More toasts were proposed and drunk, and they talked and hugged and laughed a lot, and even cried a little, and Leigh laughed and talked and cried right along with everyone else. She felt pulled in two though, as if one part of her were enjoying the party while another part stood on the outside, looking in.

Marge and her Joe were beautiful together, possessing a beauty that seemed to glow from within when they looked at each other. When Marge looked at Joe, Leigh knew she didn't see the lines around his eyes or his thinning hair. She saw the man who loved her, who would care for her and protect her, strong and brave and tender and loving. When Joe looked at Marge, slim and pretty, glowing as she smiled at him, he saw glamour, allure . . . and love. Most of all, love.

Leigh wasn't sure what she saw when she looked at Noah, but the rose-colored glasses were slipping over her eyes, as well. She didn't even remember, most of the time, that Noah was barely an inch taller than she, that at one time she had found that strange. So what if she were taller than he when she wore heels? When she looked at Noah, she saw a strong man, an utterly male man, a man who would protect her and care for her.

And so, she wondered, watching the happy faces around her, what was the fatal difference between herself and Noah, and Marge and Joe? Why had they found their happiness together, while she and Noah still struggled? Was there a fatal flaw hidden within her? Leigh wondered sadly.

Was it something that could be changed, or was it destined, eventually, to drive them apart? Would they ever be as happy together as Marge and Joe were tonight?

Noah moved over to stand beside her, draping an arm around her shoulders to hold her close, but the caring gesture couldn't bring her into the magic circle with the rest of them. She felt isolated, imprisoned in a glass bubble, watching the others but apart from them, hearing their happy laughter from a great distance.

"It's wonderful!" Kate exclaimed. "How did Joe ever convince her?"

"I'm not sure he did." Leigh shrugged. "I think she more or less convinced herself." The setting sun poured in the west-facing window, flooding their office with golden light, and Leigh had to blink against the glare when she looked across the room at Kate. "She didn't tell us her reasons for saying yes last night. I think Joe had kissed her into incoherence."

"I'll bet he had. Joe's quiet, but you always have the feeling that there's a lot going on under that mild-mannered surface." Kate stuffed sketches and papers into her portfolio, zipped it closed and took her coat off a hook. "Are you about ready to go?"

"Just about." Leigh was gathering the papers she would need for the committee meeting scheduled to begin in fifteen minutes. "I wish we had time to eat; I'm starving."

"Me, too." Kate pulled on her coat. "He's kind of like you, you know."

"Who's kind of like me?" Leigh asked absently, accustomed to Kate's conversational non sequiturs.

"Joe is; you both have a lot going on under the surface. So when are *you* going to get married?"

"Why do I have to get married?"

"Because marriage is a wonderful institution!"

"You're just prejudiced, Kate! You really should start taking a broader view of things."

"But I like *my* view!" Kate protested plaintively as Leigh reached for the telephone on her desk.

"I want to let Noah know I may be late."

Noah picked up the telephone on the second ring. "Hello?"

"Hi, Noah, it's me."

"Oh, hello there! What's up?"

"The committee, what else? We have an emergency meeting tonight, so I'll be a little bit late getting home. I just wanted to let you know."

"How late will you be?"

"Another hour or so, probably. No later than that."

"It'll be pretty dark by then. Do you want me to drive over there and pick you up?"

"No, don't bother. It's not far to walk. I'll see you later, okay?"

"You're sure you want to walk?"

"Sure. What's for dinner?"

"Ham and sweet potatoes. Will that get you home any sooner?"

"I'll be there as soon as I can!" Leigh promised, and heard Noah's laughter rumble through the phone.

"Everything under control?" Kate asked as they left the office, and Leigh nodded firmly.

"He's got dinner going, so I hope this meeting is a short one, or I'll fade away from starvation just thinking about food!"

They laughed at that, but Leigh knew that the dinner wasn't the primary reason she would hurry home as soon as she could. She was anxious to get home to Noah, to share the comfort and warmth and privacy they had there, to be with him. Was that love? she wondered; was it a part of love? She had been turning her feelings over in her mind ever since the impromptu party the night before, trying to decide how she felt about Noah, trying to decide just what constituted love.

Certainly her feelings for him had been changing at a dizzying rate, but when that evolution would be finished she couldn't guess any more than she could guess the end result. The only thing she knew was that she very much wanted to get home to Noah.

The large classroom where they were meeting was already buzzing when they arrived, and Leigh's request for the first item of business brought Jonas Petersen to his feet.

"I have some new business!" he shouted. "I move we quit putting up with Anderson's stalling and lying! It's time for action, and I move we start picketing tomorrow, and the hell with all their threats to arrest us! They can arrest us if they want, but we *will* be heard!"

The room erupted with applause and shouts, and Leigh had to hammer her gavel for several minutes before order was restored and she could call for discussion. Others spoke, some in favor and some opposed to Jonas's motion, and finally Leigh herself rose to speak.

"I agree with you, Jonas. We have put up with enough stalling and evasiveness. We must be heard. I couldn't agree with you more, *but—*" The noise level rose again, and she waited patiently for quiet before she continued. "I agree, but we *are* being heard. We're being heard in the one place where our collective voice can have the greatest impact.

"As I'm sure you know, your officers and I have spent four days testifying in the state legislature, and we will testify again if asked to. The legislature is considering our case, they seem to be sympathetic, and if we can keep them on our side we have an excellent chance of getting what we're asking for. *If* we can keep them on our side."

In the end it was close, but she failed to persuade them that their cause would be ill served by the notoriety they would receive if they picketed and were arrested. Though she argued and even pleaded, the final vote was narrowly in favor of picketing, to begin on the following Monday if the administration did not agree to support their request to the legislature. Leigh knew she should have felt anger, defeat and frustration when she left the building at last, but she was conscious only of exhaustion and an overwhelming desire to go home to Noah.

"Do you want a lift?" Kate asked as they were donning their coats in the lobby.

"No, thanks, Kate. I don't have far to go, and it's in the wrong direction for you. I'll see you in the morning."

"Leigh, I'm sorry the vote went the way it did, but don't worry, okay? It will work out."

"Thanks, Kate. And I don't intend to worry. Right now I'm not even going to think about it. I'm just going home."

Of course, Leigh reflected a few minutes later, she wouldn't tell Noah that she was hurrying to him. She'd tell him that she'd hurried home for the ham and the sweet potatoes, and maybe the warmth of the fire, she thought with a tired smile. She'd tell him she missed Leon. She wouldn't tell him that she was hurrying toward the sight of his face, the sound of his voice, the warm, hard strength of his arms around her; she was still too shy for that, but she knew it was the truth, and she had an idea that Noah knew it, too.

Walking quickly, shivering a little, she turned from a wide, well-lit thoroughfare onto a narrower residential street, dimly illuminated by widely spaced streetlights. It was really awfully cold; she wouldn't be at all surprised if they got more snow. She was glad she was only a few blocks from home.

Leigh never saw the blow coming. Her mind on other things, she walked into a pool of inky shadow cast by some thick pine trees near the sidewalk and was struck, hard, from behind. The blow had been meant for the back of her head, but went wide, glancing off her skull and striking her shoulder with enough force to make her stumble to her knees. Before she could regain her feet a rough hand seized her arm and jerked it behind her back while another hand brandished a knife in front of her.

"Don't scream!" her attacker snarled, and Leigh choked on a sob of fright. "Gimme your purse!" She shook it off her shoulder, and as it fell to the ground she tried to pull free of the punishing grip on her arm. It tightened, sending pain writhing through her shoulder. "You got any jewelry?"

"N-no," she choked out. "That's all I have. Just take it and let me go!"

"Oh, no. You ain't goin' yet, baby," her assailant whispered. "You an' me 're gonna have a little fun first!"

Oh, no, Leigh thought, gagging in panic. No, not that! Her knees scraped across the rough sidewalk, and her shoulder felt like it was breaking as she was dragged toward those thick, black pines, toward the violation he intended for her, and something inside her broke. He had a weapon, he could hurt her, even kill her, but she was more afraid of the other weapon he possessed.

"No," she whimpered, then dragged an agonizing breath into her burning lungs and screamed, knife or no knife. "*No*! Let me *go*! *Let me go!*"

He tried to cover her mouth, to silence her, and she struck out blindly, frantically, her earlier passivity gone, clawing at the mugger's face, struggling to her feet, kicking and scratching. Her sudden attack took him off guard, and he grunted an obscene epithet as she raked her nails across his face. She screamed again, and he slapped a hand over her mouth. Her stomach heaved and she bit him, hard.

He spat another obscenity, and she kicked out at him, bucking and writhing in his grasp. She felt a quick, burning pain slice across her upper arm, then she lashed out at his face and tore free. Free. She couldn't let him catch her, couldn't let him—

Sobbing in fear, her breath whistling from her lungs in painful gasps, she staggered a few unsteady steps, then found her balance and raced for home, driven by terror, by the fear of running steps behind her. She didn't know if he followed her; she couldn't spare a glance over her shoulder to see. Her one need was to get home, to Noah. Noah would protect her. Noah would take care of her.

Noah. Noah will help. I have to get to Noah. I have to get to Noah.

Over and over, in time with her pounding feet, the desperate words pounded through her brain like an incantation, like a spell to see her safely home to him.

Chapter Thirteen

*A*fterward she never had any memory of running those blocks, never remembered anything until she stumbled up the steps of her front porch and hammered on the door, crying for Noah.

"I'm coming!" he called from inside, and she heard his rapid footsteps. "Just a minute!" The lock rattled, the door swung open, and Leigh half fell into the house. "Oh, my God!"

He caught her in his arms as she stumbled inside, and she clung to him desperately, sobbing out her pain and terror incoherently against his chest. Leigh was half-aware, beneath the sound of her sobs, of Noah swearing steadily, words she had no idea he ever used. She knew that in different circumstances she would have been amused by that, but now she couldn't seem to stop crying.

Noah's arms closed around her, strong and warm, and he lifted her to carry her to the sofa where he cradled her across his lap, rocking her gently, murmuring soothing nonsense to her until she had finally cried herself back to a shaky semblance of calm. He smoothed his hand over her back in rhythmic circles, seeking, she knew, to comfort and calm her, but she was helped more than anything simply by having him there with her.

She felt him lift his face from her hair when her sobs tapered off into little tremors that shook her spasmodically. He shifted his grasp to lean back and look at her, but as he moved he closed a hand on her upper arm.

"Ahh!" She gasped and flinched away from the pain lancing along her arm, and Noah snatched his hand back, then stared in horror at his fingers.

"Dear God, Leigh!" She looked at his hand, at the scarlet smears on his palm and fingers. "That's blood! What in hell *happened* to you?"

"Blood?" she whispered, beginning to shake again as she stared down at her arm. Noah slid her from his lap to the sofa cushions, turning her toward the light.

"Yes, blood," he said grimly. "Look at this."

Her coat sleeve, reddened and sticky, had a slash across it, and as she looked at it, Leigh began to realize she was in pain. Suddenly lightheaded, she looked quickly away.

"Leigh, are you okay?" Noah asked urgently. "Are you?" He seized her chin and turned her face toward the light to scrutinize her features.

Leigh blinked at the bright light and nodded. "Y-yes. I—I'm okay."

"I don't think so. Let me get this coat off so you can lie down." He lifted her toward him, and she winced when he touched her bruised shoulder. "You're hurt there, too? I'm sorry, darling; I don't want to hurt you, but we have to get this coat off. . . ." He eased her uninjured right arm out of the sleeve. "I have to see how badly you're hurt. You know that, don't you?"

"Yes . . . I know." Leigh's voice was faint and shaky in spite of her efforts to steady it, but at least she was able to speak. "Ohh!" She couldn't suppress a gasp of pain as her arm slipped out of the sleeve. She glanced down, saw blood welling from a slash on her upper arm and looked away again. She wasn't usually squeamish, but she found she didn't want to look at this. "Is it—is it very bad?"

"I can't tell," Noah grunted. "I can't see. . . . I'm going to have to cut off your sweater, I'm afraid."

"Go ahead and cut it. I don't want this sweater anymore," she said unevenly, and Noah nodded.

"Okay. Are there scissors by your loom?"

"In the bench. There's a drawer in one end."

"Right." He returned in seconds with her long, sharp fabric shears and carefully began to cut the sweater away. "Can you tell me what happened, Leigh?"

Something in his voice, a sort of barely suppressed violence, got through to Leigh at last, and she realized just what it had cost him to put off questioning her this long. "Yes, I can," she said softly. His hands paused in their cutting. "I was mugged. That's all. It happens all the time, I guess. I was just so . . . so scared, and . . ."

Her voice wobbled, and she took a deep breath to steady herself. She had to tell Noah—and would have to tell the police—everything she could recall, and she had to be coherent. "We . . . we had the meeting, and they decided to picket, and Kate asked if I wanted a ride home, but I said no, and I . . . I was walking home, and . . . and—"

"Wait, Leigh, I'm sorry." Noah interrupted her compulsive attempt to tell him everything. "Don't try to tell me now. Let me stop the bleeding and then call next door for Joe. You'll have to tell the police anyway, so I won't make you go through it twice." He peeled the blood-soaked sweater off her arm and tossed it to the floor, then eased her down on the sofa, slipping a pillow under her head before he examined her arm. "This isn't too good. Where's your first-aid kit?"

"The kitchen. Above the sink."

"Right. Lie still." He left the room in a hurry and returned a minute later with his hands full. "Here." He dropped the kit in her lap and used a wet towel to sponge the blood away so he could better assess the damage. "Okay, it's a pretty long cut, but I don't think it's too deep or anything." He laid a clean, folded towel over the cut and put her right hand on it. "Hold this on it and press hard, okay? I'm gonna call Joe." He went over to the phone and looked back at her as he dialed. "You lie still, got it?"

"Yes, General." Leigh managed a wan smile and subsided into the cushions, carefully holding the towel on her arm. Behind her she could hear him talking on the phone.

". . . yeah. Mugged! Damnit, *yes*! Can you come over, Joe? She hasn't told me the story yet; I don't want her to talk any more than necessary. . . . Yes, she's hurt. Was she . . . ? Oh, God, I hadn't thought of that! I don't know. She'll have to go to the emergency room, though. . . . Yeah. . . . The front door's unlocked." He hung up and came quickly back to kneel beside her. "Are you hurt anywhere else, Leigh? Besides your arm?"

"Not—not much." She shook her head gingerly. "My knees hurt." She raised one foot and surveyed her scraped knee and the wreckage of her pantyhose. "He knocked me down. I guess he hit my face, too; it's kind of sore." She touched her cheekbone, where a bruise was already beginning to darken. "Oh, and he hit my head, too."

"Your head? Where?"

"Back here." She felt for the bump and explored it carefully with her fingertips. "He hit me with a pipe or something. It hit my shoulder, too, I think."

"It did. I see a bruise there." Noah ran his fingertips lightly over the ugly blotch beneath the ribbon strap of her teddy, his face grim. "You're going to get cold," he said shortly.

His movements were tightly controlled as he unfolded an afghan and covered her with it, but Leigh could see a muscle twitching in his cheek when he bent over her to tuck the soft wool around her injured arm. He stood looking down at her for a long moment, then spun around, startling Leigh as he erupted into furious action, seeking an outlet for his rage. "By God, I'd like to kill that bastard!" He smashed his fist against the white-painted brick of the fireplace, leaving a streak of blood there.

"Why don't you leave the retribution to us, Noah?" Joe walked into the room with Marge just behind him. "I don't want to have to arrest you, too."

"Can't blame me for how I feel, Joe," Noah replied, unsmiling. "Thank you for coming."

"Do you feel well enough to tell me about it, Leigh?" Joe asked.

She nodded. "Yes."

"Make it short, Joe." Noah lifted the towel from her arm. "This may need stitches."

Joe grunted assent. "We'll be brief, then. What actually happened, Leigh?"

Carefully, trying to remember everything she could, Leigh recounted the assault, her struggle and her final escape, doing her best to ignore periodic exclamations of outrage from Noah and concentrate on Joe, who was writing quickly in a notebook.

"Okay, Leigh, did he have a gun?"

"I didn't see one, but he had a knife, and whatever he hit me over the head with."

"He demanded your purse and your jewelry, and then he threatened to rape you?"

"Y-yes." Noah took her good hand and held it tightly when her voice shook.

"Did you see his face?"

"No. It was dark, and he was behind me."

"Anything you can tell me about his appearance?"

"Well, he was about my height, and he had on a leather jacket. It was some dark color. He didn't have gloves on."

"Did you?"

"I did but . . . I guess they came off. I scratched his face."

"You did? Good! Have you washed your hands?" She shook her head, and he nodded in satisfaction. "Okay. The hospital can take scrapings. I'll drive you there now. One more thing, though—"

"Yes?"

"Where are the clothes you were wearing?"

"Over there." Noah showed him.

"Okay, we'll take fiber samples from them, too. Let's go."

Leigh was wrapped in a blanket, carried to Joe's unmarked car and driven to the hospital while Joe radioed for a car to be sent to the site of the attack. Exhaustion blurred her awareness of her emergency-room experience, but she was cleaned up. The gash on her arm required stitches; it and her knees were painted with antiseptic. Her fingernails were scraped and the material carefully sealed in plastic envelopes for the police lab; her head and shoulders were x-rayed.

She slumped limply against Noah on the way home, woozy from the pain medication she'd been given, but she was not to be allowed to rest just yet. There was a police car parked in front of the house when they returned, and the two officers came inside with them, conferring with Joe while Marge took Leigh to her bedroom to help her into a nightgown and her warm velour robe.

She reassured Marge that she was indeed up to dealing with more questions, and realized, as they returned to the living room, that she was actually hungry. Not so surprising, she thought, when she considered that she'd never had that ham and sweet potatoes she'd been looking forward to so much.

"Noah?" she asked as she sat beside Marge on the sofa.

"Yes?"

"Is the ham okay?"

"The ham?"

"Yes. I never had dinner, and I'm really hungry."

"Oh, no!" He struck his forehead with his open hand. "It's been in the oven since seven!"

"I don't smell smoke." Marge grinned as he sprinted for the kitchen, and Leigh giggled with her, grateful for some light relief.

"It was set on warm," he shouted, and they waited for the

verdict, the patrolmen looking a little bemused by this slapstick in the middle of an investigation. The oven door slammed. "It's not dead!" came the shouted verdict. "A little dry, maybe, but we can eat it!" He returned to the living room, smiling in triumph. "You won't have to starve tonight, Leigh."

"You won't have to wait long for dinner, either," Joe promised her. "This will be short." He was as good as his word, returning her purse and wallet—which had been found near the site of the attack minus most of their contents, asking a few more questions, making a few more notes, and then rising, along with the patrolmen. "That's it, I think. We'll prepare a statement for you to sign, Leigh."

"Okay."

He stepped over and patted her hand. "If you need to talk to me, just call. Anytime."

"Thank you, Joe. I will."

Leigh said good-night to them all, then remained on the sofa while Noah walked them to the door.

"Are you ready to eat?" he asked as he returned to the room.

"I'm starved!" She rose awkwardly, not yet accustomed to moving with her left arm in a sling, and favoring it, because it was beginning to throb.

"Do you want me to bring a tray in here for you?"

"Oh, no. I'll eat in the kitchen." She managed a grin as they walked into the other room. "You'll have to cut my meat for me like my daddy used to do, though."

"I'm not *that* old!" he protested, holding a chair for her. "But I suppose I can fill in, since you're indisposed."

Leigh subsided into the chair. "Is the ham really okay?"

"It seems to be, just a little dry." He carved several thick slices. "The sweet potatoes are fine—they had a lid on—but the green beans are awfully well done. They're only so-so." He brought the plates to the table, and Leigh surveyed hers.

"It looks fine. As a matter of fact, it looks great to me. I'm too famished to care if it's dry."

She ate hungrily, and Noah tactfully avoided the subject of the attack.

"You said they voted to picket," he said after a few minutes. "How did that happen?"

Leigh groaned. "Suffice it to say that it was not a good meeting. Jonas has had it with waiting for some action, and even though I talked myself half to death, practically got down on my knees and begged, the final vote was to picket on Monday unless the administration agrees to go to the legislature with us. I can hardly wait to see how that looks on the six o'clock news!" She chewed moodily on a mouthful of rather tough ham. "Knowing Jonas, he'll be dragged into a police car on the evening news, kicking and screaming about human rights and police brutality. Will you get that injunction, Noah?"

He looked down at his plate for a moment, and when he raised his eyes to hers they were unreadable. "I'll do my job. There's no point in worrying about that now though. Monday is a long way away, and a lot can happen between now and then."

"That's pretty much what Kate said," Leigh replied, subdued. "I just hope the two of you are right."

"We are; you'll see. There's no point in worrying about it tonight, anyway." He pushed his plate away. "Are you finished?"

"Mm-hm. It was all really good, too. I didn't know you could cook so well, Noah."

"I can't." He grinned, but the grin didn't reach his eyes; they were shuttered, and Leigh felt a prickling of unease. He was withdrawing from her, and she could feel it, and she didn't understand why. "You have some pretty good cookbooks."

"That explains it." Leigh let him clear away her dishes and bring her a cup of coffee, her mind returning inevitably to the attack as she stirred the fragrant brew.

"Leigh?" She looked up to find Noah watching her closely. "How are you really?"

"I'm all right. The bruises and my knees and all aren't too bad. It's just my arm that hurts."

"You'll take another pain pill before you go to bed."

It was a command rather than a question, but Leigh nodded obediently. He had a point, after all. She looked down at her arm. "I'm going to have a scar."

Noah frowned. "A scar doesn't matter!" he said harshly. "It's your life that matters, and your mind and your emotions!" He hesitated, then said more quietly, hesitating as he tried to put the right words together, "I don't quite know how to put this, Leigh, but did the attack bring it all back?"

Leigh looked down, tracing the pattern on the tablecloth with her fingertip, uncertain how to answer him. She waited so long that Noah reached out to capture her hand in his.

"Leigh, please tell me! What is it? What's wrong?"

There was a harsh demand in his voice, and when she looked up she saw it reflected in his eyes and in the tense, rigid lines of his face.

"Don't worry, Noah; I'm not going to crack up or anything." She spoke quickly to reassure him but her voice was more bitter than she meant it to be. "I haven't been traumatized beyond my limits."

"The attack didn't bring it all back?" Noah chose to ignore the edge in her voice, and Leigh wondered, not too kindly, if he were afraid of pushing her too far. She was glad to know that he was concerned about her, but his lack of faith in her mental health was hardly flattering.

"No," she replied rather sharply. "You don't have to worry that I'll crack up because of it. It wasn't the same, really, if you think about it. It wasn't the same because this was a stranger. This wasn't somebody I thought I loved. This was someone who wanted my purse, my money. He wasn't doing those things because he hated me, but just because he wanted whatever I had." She laughed, a tight, angry laugh. "There's something refreshingly impersonal about that. Only . . ." Her voice dropped, the anger now directed at herself. "I just gave it to him. I just simply *handed* it over when he told me to!"

"For God's sake, Leigh, that's what you're *supposed* to do! If a mugger wants your money, you give him your money! That's basic survival for New Yorkers!"

"Well, I'm not a sophisticated, big-time New Yorker, am I?" she cried angrily. "I don't know basic New York survival. I just know that I was so scared at first that I didn't even fight!"

"Of course you were scared!" Noah barked back at her. "Anybody in their right mind would have been scared!"

Leigh's lips twisted in a humorless smile. "I suppose they would, but then the question of whether or not I'm in my right mind has never really been resolved, has it? Anyway" —her voice went flat—"I did fight him in the end."

"And that's how you got hurt, how your arm got cut?" He glanced at the sleeve of her robe, lying lumpily over the thick bandage.

"Mm-hm." Leigh looked down at the tablecloth again, but what she saw was not the pattern of flowers and leaves there.

"Tell me about it, Leigh."

She nodded, knowing she needed to talk about it, even though she dreaded the reliving of it. Taking a deep breath, she began, her eyes focused blindly on the tablecloth.

". . . I asked him to let me go," she concluded, "but he wouldn't. He said he—we—were going to have a little fun first." Her voice had dropped to a whisper, and Noah reached for her hand, holding it tightly, helping her face what had happened, helping her work through the trauma and the shock. "That was when—when I started to fight . . . when he dragged me toward those trees, and I knew what . . . I knew what he was going to . . ." Her voice wobbled and died away.

"It's all right now, Leigh," Noah said firmly. "It's all over now, and that didn't happen. How did you get away from him?"

"I don't really know. I fought him, and I finally got free, and I ran. I didn't even know he had cut my arm until you saw the blood."

"Did he chase you, try to catch you?"

"I don't know. I was afraid he would, but I don't think he did. I didn't look to see. I just ran as fast as I could." She looked at their tightly clasped hands for a moment, hers slim and pale, his big and square and strong, with a sprinkling of dark hairs on the back. She looked at their joined hands, then up at Noah's face. "I ran as fast as I could. I ran home, back to you. I knew I'd be safe with you, that you'd take care of me."

"God, I wish I could have!" Noah stood abruptly, shoving his chair back with a protesting screech, and took several agitated steps across the room. "I should have!" His fist crashed onto the countertop with a violence that was sudden and shocking in the quiet warmth of the kitchen. He spun around and glared at her from across the kitchen. "I should have kept you safe; you realize that, don't you?" he said harshly. "I should have come and driven you home. I should have kept you safe, and I didn't!"

"Noah, don't say that!" Leigh rose and crossed quickly to his side. She laid a hand on his arm. "You can't blame yourself, Noah. You offered to come for me, and I told you not to. You're not to blame for it; the mugger is!"

He might not have heard her at all. "You'll never know what it did to me," he whispered. "Seeing you stumble in, beaten, terrified. Your face . . ." He reached up to touch his fingers to the rapidly darkening bruise on her cheekbone. "He hit your face, he hit you over the head, cut you with a knife, and I wasn't there to protect you! He tried to rape you, and you had to fight him off alone! Do you know how I feel about that?" He finished on an angry shout and took Leigh's free hand to pull her close.

He didn't mean to be rough, Leigh knew that, but the sudden movement jarred her wrenched shoulder and cut arm, and she couldn't suppress a cry of pain. He snatched his hand away, his face a mixture of alarm, remorse and self-disgust that tore at Leigh's heart.

"I'm okay, Noah. It just kind of jolted me, that's all, and my arm is . . . is kind of sore, and . . ." She tried to keep her voice level, but it shook in spite of her efforts, and tears of pain glittered in her eyes.

"I'm sorry, Leigh," Noah groaned. "God, I'm sorry."

Carefully this time, with infinite tenderness, he gathered her battered body into his arms, cradled her close against him and kissed her brow, brushed his lips over her bruised cheekbone, her chin and eyelids and the tip of her nose, and finally, like a drowning man seeking air, her mouth. His lips slanted across hers, caressing, probing, then parting hers to seek the sweetness within.

Leigh needed Noah's kiss, needed *him*, but she needed more than his tenderness and care. She needed his passion, that declaration of life and hope and love, and she kissed him eagerly, with all the need and yearning she had denied for so long. His response was as immediate and as hungry as her insistent demand, and his arms tightened convulsively around her. He tried to be gentle, careful of her injuries, but the aches and pains paled into insignificance beside the pleasure he gave her. Her injured left arm lay motionless in the sling, but her right was wound around his neck, holding him tightly to her as the kiss went on and on.

She was weak-kneed and dizzy when he dragged his mouth away and buried his face in her hair. "I don't know what I'd do if that sick little—" He bit back an epithet. "I don't know what I'd do if he had hurt you more than he did. I don't know what I'd do without you." He gave a soft, choked laugh which stirred the strands of hair around her ear. "To be frank, I don't know what I'm going to do as it is. I don't know how I'll live with myself, knowing that I could have prevented this and I didn't."

"Noah, it wasn't your fault!" Leigh protested, and he raised his head.

"Not in the sense of my actually causing the incident to

happen, no, it wasn't. In the sense of my having been able to prevent it, and failing to do so, though, it was my fault."

Leigh felt a weak giggle bubble up. "You talk like a lawyer at the strangest times, Noah."

He didn't share her amusement. His face was a grim, almost angry, mask, and she reached up to cup her hand around the back of his neck, brushing her fingertips through the short curls there.

"Kiss me, please, Noah." She leaned forward the inch necessary to find his mouth, and with a smothered curse he did as he was bid, kissing her with a desperate, furious intensity. He braced himself against the countertop, set his feet apart and moved Leigh between them, where she lay slack against his body, her bones turned to water. One of his hands slid up her spine to cradle her head, his fingers molding her skull, while the other moved down past her waist and over the curve of her hip to cup her bottom, lifting her up into the curve of his body.

Nothing could penetrate her consciousness except . . . except the pain in her arm. Noah held her close, his arms warm and strong and secure around her, but she wanted to be even closer, she needed to be as close as she could possibly be, needed to taste what she had so nearly lost, and instinctively she tried to reach up, to clasp him tightly to her.

"Oh!" Pain knifed through her arm, and she let it fall, cradling the injured limb with her good hand. "I'm sorry, Noah," she whispered, biting her lip, fighting back tears. "It—it hurts when I move it. I didn't think . . ."

"Don't apologize," he muttered, and Leigh looked up to see that the grimness was back, his face set and hard, his eyes no longer warm. "I'm the one who should apologize. Come here." Keeping one arm around her for support, he steered her over to the sink, where the little bottle of painkillers stood. "You need one of your pain pills, and a cup of tea and a good night's sleep."

"You make me sound like an eight-year-old."

"Here." Noah ignored her protest and shook one of the

white tablets into her palm. "Take it." He ran cold water into a glass, passed it to her and watched while she swallowed the medication.

"You're wrong about what I need, you know," she said softly. "I'm not an eight-year-old, Noah, and you're not going to give me my little cup of tea and send me to bed." Some of the anger left his eyes, and Leigh pressed her advantage. She was a woman, and she wanted to make sure he understood that very clearly. Her lids lowered, shielding her eyes provocatively beneath the thick brush of her lashes. "You know what I'd really like, instead of that tea?" she asked him.

"What's that?" He was softening; she could see it.

Leigh took a step closer, smiling into his eyes, and pressed her lightly clad body sinuously against him. "I'd really like a brandy. Some of that wonderful stuff you brought back from France."

"The Cordon Bleu?"

"That's it." She kissed the corner of his mouth.

"Sorry." He moved his mouth just far enough to kiss her briefly, then set her slightly away from him, his hands on her shoulders holding her when she swayed toward him again. "That pill you just took has codeine in it. No booze for you tonight."

"How do you know so much about my medicine?"

"I asked the doctor while the nurse was painting your knees with that orange goop."

"Oh."

"Yes, oh." He turned her around and steered her toward the hallway. "Come on. I've kept you up too long as it is. You get into bed and stay warm, and I'll bring your tea in a few minutes."

Leigh wasn't thrilled with the idea. Actually, she felt a lot better now than she had earlier, no longer shocked and fearful, and she was sick of both this avuncular treatment and that stony courtesy he reverted to when he began blaming himself for the attack. She acquiesced though, letting Noah lead her to her room and help her out of her

robe and the sling, easing it carefully over the bulky
bandage on her upper arm. The gauze was already stained
with blood, and Noah surveyed it grimly, then swept back
her bedcovers. He held them while she climbed in, then
covered her tenderly, tucking the quilt in around her with all
the solicitous care of a doting grandmother, and went to
make her tea.

She didn't mean to be ungrateful, and certainly it was nice
to be taken care of, but, Leigh thought peevishly, there
were limits. Carefully, leaning on her good arm, she sat up
against the pillows; then, still carefully, she folded her arms
and waited for Noah. She was glad he wanted to take care of
her, really she was, but he wasn't her grandfather, and she
wouldn't have him acting as if he were. That attitude was
beginning to grate. She knew exactly what she needed, and
she would make certain Noah understood that when he
returned.

"Here you are." He carried two mugs into the room and
perched on the foot of the bed as he handed one to Leigh.
"Drink it all."

She heaved a gusty sigh. "Thank you for the tea, Noah.
I'll drink as much of it as I want."

"You'll drink it all," Noah said like the parent of a
recalcitrant child. "Go on."

"Noah, quit acting like a pushy auntie!" she said sharply.
"I'm not six, I'm twenty-six, and I'll drink as much of this as
I want, okay?"

"Okay, okay." He leaned back against the bedpost and
lifted his legs to stretch them out on the mattress beside her.
"Are you sleepy?"

"A little bit." She sipped her tea and set it on the
nightstand. "I'm kind of cold, though. Would you sit up
here, by me?" She patted the mattress next to her and sent
him a wistful smile.

He gave her a hard look, almost suspicious, then
shrugged. "All right." He reversed his position to sit
leaning against the headboard beside her, his arm around
her shoulders. "Is that better?"

Leigh snuggled close, her head on his shoulder. "Mmm, thank you. That's nice and warm."

"Relax," he murmured, brushing a wayward curl off her forehead. "Just relax."

This was what she needed, her man beside her, big and strong, taking care of her. Turning her head, she watched the slow rise and fall of his chest beneath his half-open shirt, studied the slanting, golden light of the bedside lamp sifting through the mat of dark hair there. She breathed deeply, filling her senses with the scent of him, of warm, male skin and traces of the spicy after-shave he wore, and rubbed her cheek against him in a catlike caress. This was what she needed, the reassurance of him there with her, the contrast of his powerful, heavily muscled body and her slimmer, softer one. She could feel his muscles bunch and flex as he shifted his position to make her more comfortable.

His fingers made little circles on her shoulder, his breath moved the soft strands of hair by her ear, and the rest of the world faded away, leaving only the two of them, alone in the warm, dimly lit privacy of her bedroom. Leigh shifted position slightly, careful of her arm, and reached out to brush her palm over Noah's chest, sensing all the textures— smooth skin, crisply curling hair and hard muscle that tensed at her touch. He caught his breath as she traced the line of his half-open shirt, stroking down and then up, resting her hand over his heart, absorbing the quickening rhythm of its heavy beat.

Slowly, very slowly, she trailed her fingers down to the buttons that still held the fabric together, slipped a finger under the first button and opened it. Noah's hand came up as she moved her fingers toward the next button, trapping her palm against the taut, corrugated muscles of his stomach.

"What are you doing, Leigh?" he asked, his voice husky. She could feel his pulse beneath her fingers. His heartbeat was more rapid than it had been.

"Don't you know?" she whispered, her own heartbeat a wild flutter in her breast. She turned her head a fraction further to kiss the upper slope of his chest. Her body was lax, heavy with a voluptuous languor, warm and soft and waiting for his touch, for his loving.

"Leigh," he growled, "stop it. I know what you're doing, but I'm not sure you do."

"I know, Noah." She kissed his shoulder, nudging his shirt aside with her lips. "Make love to me."

He went very still, then took her hand and lifted it away as he levered himself away from her. "I can't do that, Leigh."

"Yes, you can." She lifted her lips to kiss the angle of his jaw. "You can, Noah. I want you to."

"Not tonight, Leigh." He sat up, disentangling himself. "You've been attacked tonight, and hurt, and scared to death, and no doubt you're a little out of it from that pain pill. You're probably suffering from shock or stress or something, and you're exhausted, and now is not the time."

Leigh looked sidelong at him, a little angry, a little hurt by his reluctance. She would have sworn that he was as affected by her presence as she was by his, would have sworn that he wanted her, so why was he suddenly so cool? "What do you mean, 'I'm suffering from stress'?" she asked sharply. "Why don't you say what you mean, Noah? You're afraid I'm going to crack up on you because I've been that way in the past, aren't you? Well, I'm not crazy, and I'm not a child, and I'm not so dopey that I don't know what I'm doing or what I want!"

"You know I didn't mean you're—"

"I know *just* what you mean, and I resent it! I'm tired of everyone treating me like I'm a borderline mental case!"

"Now, Leigh," he began soothingly, placatingly, "you know that isn't what I meant." He reached out to put an arm around her, but she shrugged it off angrily.

"Don't patronize me, Noah. You know that's exactly what has been going on all night! Everyone's been treating me like I might fall to pieces any minute, and I'm tired of it! Marge did it, putting me in my nightie like a little girl; Joe did it at the hospital and with the other policemen, trying to soften the questions, just in case I couldn't handle it. And now you!"

"What have I done? What has any of us done, except try to make things easier on you?"

"You've all treated me like I'm crazy, and the fact that your intentions were good doesn't make it any easier to take. I'm not disturbed, or unstable, or anything else, but you all seem to think I am, and I'm starting to resent it!"

"Leigh, you know we don't think you're crazy, but we care about you, and you know we have reason to worry about you when something like this has happened. I'm sorry, Leigh, but what you need now, more than anything else, is sleep." He gathered her into his arms again, and this time she allowed it. "I'm sorry that you think I'm being patronizing, because I'm not. I just don't want you to be hurt. You need to rest; everything else can wait." He set her back on the pillows and took her clinging hands from his neck. "Go to sleep, Leigh."

"I wish . . ."

"Go to sleep."

Chapter Fourteen

They lay in silence for several minutes, and Leigh drifted into the first light stages of sleep, only to start violently awake when she felt Noah begin to move away. She clutched his arm in panic, holding him there with her. "Don't go, Noah! Please, don't!"

"I'm only going to my room, Leigh. You'll be all right. And you need to sleep."

"I'll sleep, I promise, but not alone, not tonight. Stay with me, please, Noah? Sleep here, with me?"

"Leigh, you know you'd sleep better alone."

"I don't want to be alone." The green depths of her eyes were cloudy with fear, and after a second's intense scrutiny of her frightened face, he relented.

"Okay," he said slowly, "I won't leave you alone. I'll sleep in here."

"In this bed, with me. I want to know you're here," she said urgently, not caring if his acquiescence were unwilling, only knowing that she needed him there. Long seconds passed; then he nodded again.

"I'll sleep with you." She relaxed back into the pillows. "I just need to get undressed first, all right? Will you be okay while I go to my room?"

"Mm-hm," she replied drowsily, then added more sharply, "You won't be long?"

"I won't be long."

"Okay." She let her eyes fall closed as he left her, secure in the knowledge that he would return. She must have dozed in the few minutes he was gone, because the next thing she was aware of was someone moving quietly into the darkened room. His silhouette passed across the pale rectangle of the window; then she pulled the covers back for him as he slid carefully into the bed beside her. His arms came around her to cradle her in the curve of his body, and he settled her snugly in the nest of quilts, curled comfortably against him. Her last conscious thought was a hazy realization that he had broken his custom of the last weeks and worn pajama trousers to bed.

Somehow, in spite of all the trauma and upheaval of the day, she slept deeply and dreamlessly that night. The nightmares which by rights should have been hers never intruded on her deep and exhausted sleep, kept at bay, perhaps, by a sense of safety she had never known before.

She slept so deeply that she had to struggle to wake the next morning. She was groggy and slow-witted, and aware that it was very late. She had a hazy memory of hearing the telephone ring and some half-intelligible conversation, but that could have been a snatch of dream as she rose slowly toward consciousness. Surely, she thought, the telephone would have brought her fully awake.

The light slanting through the curtains was brilliant and clear, and Leigh squinted at it, then turned over to wake Noah, only to find the bed empty beside her. Of course, she realized after a moment, she could smell fresh coffee. In fact, that rich, seductive scent was probably what had finally awakened her. Noah must be making coffee before he rejoined her.

Leigh stretched luxuriously and smiled to herself, her

mood undimmed by a twinge of protest from her arm and a general, all-over stiffness. Whatever had been wrong last night, whatever misdirected guilt had been driving Noah, making him cool and distant, it must have dissipated by this morning, or it would when he saw how much better she was feeling. He had no reason to feel guilty about anything. The arm felt much better this morning; in fact, *she* felt much better this morning, and she fluffed her hair before settling back to wait for Noah.

"Awake at last, sleepyhead?"

She hadn't heard Noah's approach, but as he spoke she turned her head to see him standing in the doorway, coffee mugs in hand. Her anticipated scenario was wrong, though, because he obviously hadn't overcome whatever had been disturbing him. He was wearing jeans and a flannel shirt with a sweater over it, and he had evidently been up for some time, because he had showered and shaved. He looked alert and refreshed and ready to face the day, but though his lips curved, the smile didn't reach his eyes. Her fantasy of a happy morning together burst like a pricked balloon.

"Yes," she said, pushing herself into a sitting position against the headboard, "I'm awake at last." She managed a smile, but her disappointment was acute. "What time is it, anyway?"

"Nearly noon. Eleven forty-eight, to be precise." He leaned over to kiss her quickly, then sat at the foot of the bed and handed her a mug. "You look pretty good, except for this." He reached out to touch the bruise high on her cheekbone. "I was beginning to wonder if you were going to wake up before suppertime, though."

"Is it very bad?" She fingered the tender area.

"It's not as bad as I thought it would be. It'll fade quickly, anyway. Don't worry about it."

Leigh looked into his eyes for a moment and saw no evasion there. She nodded. "Okay, I won't." She sipped the coffee, black and strong and bracing. "Mmm, I need this! I feel like I've slept for a week, sort of groggy and dopey."

"I'm not surprised, after a pain pill and nearly twelve hours' sleep."

"Good point." She took another long swallow, then remembered, and sat up straight with a gasp of dismay. "Oh, my gosh! My classes, and the committee's supposed to meet! I've got to call and—"

"Wait, it's okay!" Noah held her back when she would have climbed hastily out of bed. "I called them already."

"You did?"

"Mm-hm. I called Kate about the committee, and I called the Fine Arts Department."

"Well, what did you say? What did they say?"

"I just told them that you were mugged and hurt, and needed a day or two off. Kate will meet with the committee people this afternoon and speak for you."

Leigh nodded her agreement. "What about my classes, though?"

"The department has it all figured out. They canceled the one this morning and got a teaching assistant to fill in this afternoon and tomorrow, and then you have the weekend to recuperate, and that's that."

"That's kind of like getting a vacation when you don't expect it. Thank you for taking care of it." She sipped her coffee and another thought occurred to her. "I guess that was the phone call I dreamed about."

"What?" Noah looked up at her from the foot of the bed, his gaze suddenly sharp and penetrating.

Leigh didn't see why it mattered, but she explained. "The phone call. I dreamed I heard a phone call, but it must have been you talking to Kate or to the department."

Some of the tension seemed to leave him at that. "Yeah. That must have been what you heard." He raised his mug to drain it, and Leigh watched from beneath her lashes, savoring the pure male beauty of him. He lowered the mug, caught her watching him and frowned. She flushed at the knowledge in his eyes and looked quickly away. "Since you have the day off," he said after a moment, "I thought we could go for a walk."

A walk? Leigh stared at his averted profile for a moment. "Uh . . . a walk sounds nice," she said at last, trying to inject some enthusiasm into her·voice.

"It's a nice day for it," Noah said blandly. "It's warm, for February. The high's supposed to be about fifty, and it should be sunny all day."

"It sounds like spring," Leigh offered, and he nodded.

"It will feel like it, after the cold we've had. I thought we'd have a quick lunch here and then go. Will it take you long to get ready?"

"Give me ten minutes," she said, and he left her to dress.

This just wasn't what she had anticipated. Something was wrong this morning; something was missing between them. She had gone to sleep with Noah at her side and had expected to wake with him there, warm and lazy and cuddly. She had read somewhere that many men felt sexy in the morning, but Noah was apparently not among them. She had hoped that his remoteness would be gone, too, but she had evidently been wrong about that, as well; even that perfunctory kiss he'd given her had been as impersonal as a handshake.

Disgruntled, but determined to try to pull him out of his mood, whatever it was, she dressed carefully for the walk he was so interested in taking, rummaging through her closet to dig out a pair of designer jeans he had admired for their fit. It took some effort to pull them on with only one good arm, but she managed to wriggle into them, adding a pretty, eyelet-trimmed mauve sweater and narrow-heeled boots. Her makeup was something of a challenge, for the bruise on her cheekbone had blossomed into a brilliant combination of reds and purples. The final touch was her favorite perfume, a headier scent than the light florals she customarily wore during the day, and after quickly brushing her bright curls, she went to join Noah.

If he noticed anything unusual about her appearance he didn't mention it; he only said, "The bruise is hardly noticeable now. You shouldn't have anyone staring at you."

"Thanks," she said quietly, and walked past him to the

kitchen, where he had sandwiches and chips waiting for them. If that was the way he wanted things, so be it. She couldn't fight his attitude until he told her what the problem was, but she could only pick at her lunch, and the conversation was nonexistent. Her tension grew until she could hardly stand the light touch of his hands as he helped her into her jacket, dealing with the problems of sling and bandage with impassive courtesy. She moved quickly away from him when he released her, waiting with downcast eyes for him to open the door, then stepping outside with a sigh of relief.

It was a gorgeous day for a walk, she had to admit when they walked down the porch steps and into the unseasonably brilliant sunshine. After three weeks of cold, wind and snow they were being given a foretaste of spring. Leigh tried to relax, hoping she might even enjoy herself, but the effort seemed to be in vain.

She looked around her as they walked, trying to interest herself in the beauty of the campus, in the other afternoon strollers, trying to take her mind off the day she had expected to spend with Noah and off the seemingly insoluble problem she would face on Monday, when she would be expected to lead the committee in carrying a picket sign and chanting slogans. She wasn't outstandingly successful at either endeavor, but as she looked at the other women out walking in the sunshine she noticed them looking at Noah, and at her.

It was silly, of course, but she didn't like them looking at him with hungry eyes, and then turning to her with hostility, or jealousy, or frank assessment of her as a rival. She wanted to order them to look at other men, not at Noah. She wanted to have the right to say, "He's mine! You can't look at him that way. You can't have him."

But she didn't yet have that right. He wasn't hers yet; he wasn't her lover yet. She wanted to love him, to make love with him. She had wanted him last night, but her timing had been wrong, and she had wanted him this morning, but for reasons of his own he hadn't wanted her, and now she wanted him so badly it made her tremble. She was aware of him beside her with every nerve in her body.

When he took her hand and tucked it in the crook of his arm, she was conscious of his hard muscles and latent strength. When he took a shortcut across a stream and reached back to help her step across the mossy stones, she watched the bunching and flexing of his muscles outlined by the snug denim of his jeans, and when she sat beside him for a few minutes' rest she could smell the scent of his skin, faintly carried on the fresh, cool air.

She was almost painfully attuned to his presence. Images of him filled her mind; she saw him emerging from the shower, damp skinned and flushed from the heat; saw him concentrating on a recipe for spaghetti sauce, his hair ruffled and a frilly apron tied around his waist, an incongruous contrast to his powerful chest and the thick hair visible in the V of his half-opened shirt. He was so very male, and now that she no longer felt threatened by that maleness, Leigh was tremendously excited by it, by the contrast with her own femininity.

Leigh had heard the phrase "sexual tension" without ever fully understanding what it meant, but now she knew. The air around them seemed to crackle with electricity, to vibrate with thoughts and wishes and desires, unspoken but understood. It was a sweet torture, being so close, yet not close enough. In desperation she forced her mind back to present problems, finding them easier to deal with than this agony of wanting, because that wanting was pointless when something was still wrong between them, very wrong.

"Noah?"

"Hmm?"

"What's wrong? Why did you want to take a walk today?"

He took several steps before he answered. "We need to talk." His reply was no more comforting than his silence had been. Leigh waited to hear what they had to talk about. "You said last night that the committee voted to picket."

"Yes, they did. On Monday."

"Will you be with them?"

"I'm the chairperson. I'll be with them."

"Even though it's an action you disagree with?"

Leigh saw where he was going with his questions, but she answered him calmly. "I made a commitment to the committee, and the fact that I didn't vote with the majority doesn't mean I can walk out now."

"Then you understand how I feel about my position."

"No, I don't think I do, because while I'm working for a cause I believe very strongly in, you're just doing a job, as you put it." They walked half a block in silence. "Will we be arrested when we picket on Monday? I mean, will we go to jail and be fingerprinted and searched and everything?"

Leigh hated to sound so naive and scared about the possibility of arrest, but when all was said and done she *was* both naive about the process and scared to death of it. She couldn't believe Noah would let her go through that, not when he had been so tender and strong and protective the night before, and yet he had made it very clear how highly he valued his professional objectivity.

There was a pause before he answered. "If the injunction is granted, then yes, anyone picketing will be arrested," he said, in a careful, courtroom voice that Leigh found she didn't like at all.

"*If* it's granted? Does that mean it hasn't been granted yet?" And perhaps there was still hope?

"No, it hasn't been granted yet, but if the dean decides he wants to go through with it, we can have one by midmorning Monday." The hope was gone.

"I see," she said quietly, and walked on. "Noah, if the dean decides he wants to do this, will you help him, even though it might mean arresting a lot of people, including me, who are simply trying to do something worthwhile?"

He let his breath out in a long sigh. "Leigh, I agreed to represent the administration in this, and as their representative I'm obligated to act as they instruct me to."

"Even if they want you to do something you don't agree with?"

"Even then."

"But what if you were working for someone who was doing something illegal, or immoral? If you discovered that, what would you do?"

"If I discovered that I was being asked to participate in something illegal, I would quit. I'd have to."

"What about something immoral?"

"That would be the same."

"Well, do you think the committee has a good cause?"

"Excellence in education? Of course it's a good cause."

"Then why are you going to help them put us in jail?" she cried in frustration. "You say you wouldn't do something immoral, and you say we have a good cause, so why are you doing this?"

"You know, Leigh," Noah observed, dryly amused, "you can argue like a lawyer when you want to."

"I'm not sure that's a compliment," she snapped. "And it sounds to me as if you have an awfully flexible moral sense."

"I'll ignore that," he said coldly. "And I'd like you to keep in mind that there's a long time between now and Monday, and a lot can happen. I wouldn't anticipate the worst if I were you."

"That's easy for you to say," she grumbled. "Nobody's going to cart you off to the slammer!" Noah gave a choked bark of laughter, but Leigh didn't share the joke. "It's already Thursday, Noah. How can you say Monday is a long way off?"

"Because it is! And where do you get your terminology, anyway? 'Cart you off to the slammer'?"

"Noah, this isn't funny!" Leigh pulled free of his grasp, really angry now, and stood in the middle of the sidewalk glaring at him.

After a moment he mastered his mirth. "I know it's serious, Leigh, really I do, but you have to admit that your phraseology is funny." Leigh's reply was a wordless glower, and he shrugged. "I'm sorry; I don't mean to trivialize things."

"Good," was her terse reply. "I don't know what's happening, Noah, and I don't like that feeling. We're on opposite sides in this mess, and even though you said it wouldn't, it keeps coming between us. I don't agree with your stand, and you don't agree with what I feel I have to do, and sometimes I wonder why you wanted us to live together in the first place!" She took several quick paces with her head down, staring at the pavement beneath her feet, then sniffed hard. "Sometimes I think I was right all along, Noah. Sometimes I think this just isn't going to work out. This committee issue seems to keep dividing us, and yet it shouldn't. It's not that important in itself, so it must be acting as a lightning rod for some other problem."

One large hand snaked out and caught her uninjured arm, pulling her to an abrupt halt. "What are . . . ?"

". . . blocking the sidewalk!" The irritated mutter from a passerby interrupted him. He pulled her off the pavement onto the winter-flattened grass in front of the Biology Building and tried again.

"What are you saying, Leigh? Don't beat around the bush." His eyes were cold and hard, his anger hurting her, and Leigh was suddenly angry, too.

"I'm saying this whole thing—us—may be a big mistake!" she cried. "I'm saying something is wrong, something we're not admitting to ourselves, because an issue that shouldn't be all-important, like the committee, is becoming that way. I'm saying I was right in the first place when I thought that getting to know you would only open me up to pain!"

"You're overdramatizing things," he said curtly, but Leigh shook her head sadly.

"I'm not, and I'm not imagining things, either. You've been cold and so remote this morning, and even last night, in a way. I thought it was just because you felt guilty that I'd been hurt, but it's more than that, isn't it? I'm not all that badly hurt, so you don't have to feel guilty, Noah, and if you don't want to tell me what's bothering you, you don't have to do that, either!" She stared at him for a long moment, searching for something in his eyes. She found nothing but a chilly blue blankness, hiding anything he might have felt. The anger drained out of her, leaving behind only emptiness. "But, Noah," she went on slowly, "let's not pretend that there's anything here if there isn't."

"All right," he said after a pause. "We won't pretend. You think this is all a mistake, just as you said at first, that the committee business is acting as a lightning rod for a deeper problem."

Leigh held his eyes for a long, chilling moment, saw nothing there to change her answer and nodded once. How could he be so calm, so cold? How could he simply let things come to an end without even a protest? Leigh felt as if she were shattering inside as she waited for him to deny what she'd said, shattering further as he accepted it, as if he had been thinking those same thoughts.

"You may be right," he concluded.

The last fragments of Leigh's soul fell in tinkling, useless shards to the stony ground. She gulped and swallowed hard, wanting to scream.

"I think I want to go home, Noah." Her voice was as steady as she could make it.

"All right, we can—"

"You don't have to come. You can finish your walk," she offered almost desperately, wanting to be alone when she fell apart.

"No, I'll walk with you." The words were spoken with neither warmth nor anger. There was nothing there at all but a sort of abstract courtesy covering the nothingness that had loomed between them all morning. Leigh followed, numb and cold at his side, as Noah turned to walk back toward the house that would soon be her home again, no longer theirs.

It was funny, almost laughable, how calm she was, Leigh thought, how apparently in control, when her world had fallen apart just as she discovered how badly she wanted it.

She glanced over at Noah, but learned nothing. His face was grave, and he walked head down, apparently deep in thought. It hurt her to look at him, and she shifted her gaze to the sidewalk. They were near the main administration building, and Noah paused.

"I have to pick up some papers here. Do you mind if we go in for a few minutes?"

"Mind?" She stopped when he did, then shook her head. "No, I don't mind." Why should she mind? She didn't care about anything anymore.

"It won't take long," he added, and she shrugged.

"I don't have anything to do; you know that."

He let that pass and led her up a flight of wide, limestone steps and into the building. Leigh walked through the halls beside him, paying little attention to where he was taking her until he paused to pull open a tall, ornate door. Leigh read the brass nameplate and stopped short, a little prickle of interest finally piercing the fog of apathy that clouded her brain.

"This is the president's office, Noah."

"I know. This is who I need to see."

"I thought you said you just had to pick up some papers."

"I do, but I need to have a few words with him, too. It won't take long."

As if she cared about time, Leigh thought. It didn't matter; nothing did. Forestalling further argument, though she hadn't intended to offer any, Noah opened the door and ushered Leigh into a large, luxurious outer office. A huge mahogany desk was positioned halfway across the room, and the secretary sitting there smiled at them.

"Good afternoon, Mr. Burke, Miss Michaels. He's waiting to see you."

"Come on, Leigh."

He took her arm and started toward the door to the inner office, but she had frozen at the secretary's use of her name and held back, pulling against him. "What's going on, Noah? Why did she know my name?"

"Because we have an appointment with the president. Now come on!" He was getting annoyed, but no more so than Leigh, who was beginning to feel that she had been manipulated, and she didn't like it. She wasn't going anywhere, or seeing anyone, until she knew the facts.

"Us? You and me? To see the president of the university?" He nodded in reply to her question, and she pulled back harder. "Noah, what's going on here?" Her eyes were trained on him in suspicious scrutiny. "What's going on, Noah?" she repeated.

"You and I"—he ground the words out slowly, with exaggerated patience, as if she were of limited intelligence and might not understand—"are going to see the president of the university; we have an appointment. Now come on." He dragged her irresistibly toward the door, and Leigh was given the choice of fighting uselessly against his greater strength, or going along with as much composure as she could manage. She went, angry, embarrassed and completely confused.

"Good afternoon, Miss Michaels, Mr. Burke." The president, an affable man in his sixties, rose and came around his desk to greet them. Leigh said something conventional as she shook his hand, then dropped gratefully into the chair she was offered. Too much had happened in the last twenty-four hours, and her brain was having trouble processing new input, so she sat quietly and waited to discover the reason for this surprise meeting. She didn't have long to wait.

"Good afternoon, sir," Noah replied. "It's good of you to see us on such short notice."

Short notice? Leigh slanted Noah a questioning glance, but he refused to meet her eyes. Instead, while she listened in growing amazement, he briefly outlined the course the negotiations and confrontations between the committee and the dean had followed since September, emphasizing Leigh's role as the voice of reason and the opponent of such measures as strikes and picketing.

"It's primarily due to her efforts," Noah concluded, "that a strike has been avoided, and she both spoke and voted against the resolution to picket that was approved last evening. I know that the university has a position to maintain, but I feel the time for compromise has arrived, sir, and I hope you agree."

"I do." The president turned to smile at Leigh, who was sitting in thunderstruck silence. "Miss Michaels, I appreciate both your concern for education and your commitment to negotiation as the vehicle by which goals may be accomplished. I'd also like to apologize, belatedly, for Dean Anderson's rigidity. I was remiss in not keeping myself apprised of what was happening, and I regret that this has dragged on so long." He stood again, a document in his hand. "I would like you to be the first to know, Miss Michaels, that a university representative has been appointed to testify before the state legislature, asking that our budget be increased." He held out the document and Leigh took it with fingers that trembled.

Leigh supposed that she said something appropriate, but as she walked out of the building, dazed, the official statement in her hand, she had no idea what those appropriate words had been. The news was still too surprising, the implications so broad that she couldn't easily grasp them.

"Noah," she said after they'd walked half a block, "what just happened?"

"What do you think happened?"

"I'm not really sure," she admitted, "but I think you just managed to arrange an end to all this wrangling and arguing, and that the committee has won."

"You've won." He confirmed her surmise.

She abruptly swerved off the sidewalk and dropped onto a park bench, no longer willing to try to walk and think at the same time. There were simply too many things to consider, to comprehend. She tried to pick a starting place, half-hopeful and half-fearful of the conclusions she was beginning to draw. The bench creaked as Noah sat beside her.

"I've won," she whispered, barely audible. "We've won. The committee's won." She paused. "It's all over at last."

"That's right," he murmured. "You've won."

"No!" Leigh sat upright with a jerk. "That's not right!" She turned to stare at Noah. "That's not right at all! *I* didn't win, Noah; the committee did. But *you* orchestrated it, didn't you? You called the president this morning and set things in motion!''

He shrugged, and as she sat staring at him, Leigh was thinking hard. Some things were beginning to add up, but a lot of others weren't.

"Why?" she asked at last. "Why do this now, when things seem to be falling apart for us anyway? Why do this when you've been so cold to me since last night?"

"The vote was to picket. I didn't want it to go as far as having people arrested, and I especially didn't want to think of your being put through that—it's never pleasant, Leigh—so it was time for me to act."

"But why act on your own? Obviously Dean Anderson wasn't in on this, but you've said over and over again that you would act only on his instructions."

"The vote had been taken. There was no more time to wait for things to resolve themselves." His answer was bland, reasonable and entirely unsatisfying.

"There's more to it than that," she insisted. "You were cold last night, withdrawn, after you had cooked dinner for me and everything, and I can't believe there was no reason for that. I have to know, Noah, what was the reason?" She studied him for a moment, wanting to hope, but afraid. "Was it just guilt, Noah?"

He scowled down at his hands. "Of course I felt guilty!" he snapped, only partly answering her question. "I still feel guilty, and I still feel that I should have kept you safe. I don't care if it doesn't make sense; it's the way I feel!"

Leigh sat very still, surprised by the suppressed violence in him. "You aren't guilty," she said after a moment. "I am, if anyone is. You offered to drive me home, and so did Kate, but I turned you both down."

"Yeah, so why do I disgust myself so much?"

"I don't know the answer to that." It hurt to see him hurting, and she waited silently for him to explain.

"Maybe it's because I know that I've hurt you. I've pushed you in directions you really didn't want to go, pushed you into situations you wanted to avoid. Maybe you would be better off living with your phobias without my prodding at you for my own selfish reasons." He sighed heavily. "You're right about the committee, Leigh. It's never been more than a hook to hang our differences on, though there was always enough substance there to convince us that our feelings were legitimate. And they were, really; it's just that they weren't as important as we made them out to be. What's important is that I forced my way into your life, manipulated my way in, and maybe you would be better off if I had never done that. And maybe you'd be better off if I just quietly faded out of your life now."

"And you?" Leigh whispered. "Would you be better off?"

He looked at her, then away, and swore quietly and vehemently. "No!" He bit the word out as if it hurt him.

"Then why," Leigh asked gently, "do you think it would be better for me?" Noah looked up, his eyes startled, wary, and she reached out to take his hand in hers, turning it over to examine his palm, as if she could read the future there. "Why do you think that would be better for me, Noah? I'm alive now; I wasn't before. I feel things now . . . happiness, sadness; before I only felt fear. You've brought me to life, and yet you think it would be better for me if I were still buried alive?"

Her words had been so quiet that it took an instant for Noah to react. When he did, his reaction was as quiet, as misleadingly calm, as Leigh's questions had been. Slowly, achingly slowly, he reached out to capture her face in both his hands, tipping it up as he slid close beside her on the bench and carefully took her mouth with his. There was no passion in the kiss; that was for another time. This was a promise, tender and sweet and touching, and a little sad, too, because of all the pain they'd shared.

He scared her half to death when he suddenly broke the kiss off, jerked up his wrist to glance at his watch and swore in exasperation.

"Good God, I forgot! Come on, Leigh." He grabbed her wrist and hauled her to her feet. "We have to get moving, or we're going to be late!"

"Noah!" Leigh stumbled along after him, trying to keep up. "What in the world is going on? What are we going to be late for?" There was no immediate answer. *"Noah!"*

"The meeting," he grunted, and darted recklessly across the street in the middle of a block. The irate driver of a red delivery van beeped at them and shouted something Leigh pretended not to hear. "The committee meeting that Kate is chairing, and which is waiting at this very moment for you to arrive and make your announcement."

"Oh." Leigh panted along in his wake. *"That* meeting."

"I set it up this morning after I spoke to the dean and President Rhodes. I thought you'd overheard, when you said you dreamed about phone calls."

"Oh." That answered another of Leigh's questions. "We still have to talk, Noah."

"We·will. After the meeting, all right?"

"After the meeting." It was somewhere between a threat and a promise, and he got her meaning.

Chapter Fifteen

"I can't believe this day!" Leigh looked across the table at Noah, half-smiling and bemused. "I can't believe it, and I can't believe you."

"Me?" He shrugged, his eyes hooded and unreadable in the dim glow of the restaurant's lowered lights. "I didn't do very much."

"You set the wheels in motion, and without that nothing else would have been possible. No wonder I thought I'd dreamed of telephone calls! You must have spent hours on the phone this morning, setting up all those meetings." She looked down at the tabletop for a second, tracing a pattern on the linen cloth with her fingertip. "Why did you do that, Noah?"

"Basically because I disagreed with what I saw Anderson doing."

"What was that?"

"He was using this committee issue as a power play, stonewalling you and dragging it out for his own purposes.

He wasn't making a serious effort to resolve anything, and I thought it was time to bring a higher authority in on this. I asked Anderson to come and meet with the president this afternoon, but he was 'too busy.' I think he had a feeling that he would come out of it on the short end once the president heard both sides of the story. As a matter of fact, I'm pretty sure the president telephoned him before our appointment, and we can surmise the way that conversation went, can't we?"

"I guess so. I kind of feel sorry for Dean Anderson, though. I wouldn't want to get him into trouble."

"You, or we, couldn't get him into trouble," Noah said dryly. "He did that for himself. And don't feel sorry for him, either; he put you through enough in the last months, didn't he?"

"He didn't exactly make life any easier for me," Leigh said slowly, and sighed. "I'm really glad it's over. I'm almost happier that it's over than I am about the fact that we won."

"Enjoy the winning, too," Noah advised her.

"Oh, I will, but I think I'm happiest that this complication is finally removed from our lives." She studied him for a moment as he sipped his drink. "We have to talk about it, Noah."

"I know we do." He looked across at her, his mouth quirking in a wry half smile. "But can you honestly say you know where to start?"

She had to laugh at that, and somehow the admission of their shared helplessness did more to bring them together than anything that had happened that day. Leigh began to relax at last.

"I wish I did! I feel like something momentous has happened, like we've been freed by the conclusion of the committee's work, and yet I feel a little lost."

"Missing that hook to hang your troubles on?"

"Perhaps." She looked gravely across at him. "The committee was what brought us together in the first place, after all, and it's been a thread running through our entire relationship. I don't know whether I miss it or I'm glad to be rid of it."

"At least with that out of the way we can finally take a look at ourselves," he said, "and see what is there."

"Take a look at ourselves." Leigh found that she was excited by that idea; she was also a little afraid, but she had the memory of Noah's kiss to sustain her hope.

"I don't know what we'll find," he said slowly, his face almost grim as he reached out to take her hand. "I'm almost afraid to look too closely at myself, because I have a feeling I won't come out of—"

"Excuse me, sir." It was the waiter, and by the time they had received their entrée and a bottle of wine, and had begun eating, a musical trio in one corner of the dining room had begun to play. Noah looked across at the musicians with a comically dismayed air, then turned to Leigh.

"I think we'd better discuss this somewhere with a little less . . . activity, don't you?" he asked, and she nodded, accepting the futility of further conversation.

She tried to give her excellent Italian meal the attention it deserved, but she knew the effort was futile. There were too many questions still unanswered, too many things left unsaid, and, of course, there was Noah, across the table from her, his knee occasionally brushing hers, his hand touching hers as he poured the wine, each fleeting contact a message, a promise.

The sexual tension she had felt earlier in the day was returning with each sip of the heady, fragrant Chianti they drank, with each flicker of the fat candle on the table between them. Their conversation dwindled to long silences punctuated by comments that seemed idle but covered a wealth of communication carried out with eyes and hands and bodies. Leigh's mouth was dry, her hands cold, and when Noah asked if she wanted any more to eat she could only shake her head in silent denial.

The walk home was a sweet torture, the cool evening air contrasting sharply with their heated bodies, each sensation keenly felt. When Noah took her hand outside the restaurant, Leigh curled her fingers into his with the impression that she was giving him far more than her hand. They walked slowly, prolonging the anticipation, each casual brush of their bodies, each seemingly accidental touch, a promise of more to come.

A block from home Noah pulled her into the shadow of a huge Victorian monstrosity of a house, sliding his arms around her, pulling her into the curve of his body so that she felt herself surrounded, ensnared, mesmerized. In the darkness she couldn't see him, but she could feel his presence, strong and warm and so marvelously, wonderfully male. With a soundless sigh of acquiescence she molded her body to his, laying her head on his shoulder, but he wanted more, nudging her cheek with his mouth so that she turned the fraction needed for their lips to meet.

This was what she had waited for, had been on fire for all this endless day, and at the first touch of his mouth Leigh seemed to melt from within, pressing into the hard bulwark of his body, holding him tightly as their lips teased and tasted, deliberately withholding what they both wanted so badly. Noah's hands moved over her back, sliding over the cool leather of her jacket, rasping over the denim of her snug jeans as he caressed her slim bottom, then moving up again as she squirmed against him in an instinctively seductive motion.

"Come on." His voice was a husky whisper. "Let's go home."

She could barely breathe for the hammering of her heart as they mounted the porch steps. Noah kept an arm around her shoulders, holding her close beside him as he unlocked the door and pushed it open; they slipped inside and closed the door on the rest of the world. Leigh expected Noah to take her in his arms and kiss her, but instead he led her through the darkness to the living room and pushed her gently down on the sofa.

"Noah?" Surprised, frustrated and more than a little

apprehensive, she looked across the dark room at him. "Noah, what is it? What's wrong?"

The heat of anticipation drained from Leigh's body as she watched him, leaving in its place a nameless unease. She could feel the change in him, feel the emotional distance opening up between them as he moved across the room to switch on a lamp. She blinked against the sudden brilliance.

"We have to talk. Now, before anything else, with no interruptions."

Leigh nodded her understanding and leaned back. "I think it's your turn this time, Noah. I've done a lot of talking today, and none of it seems to make much sense in light of recent events. I think it's time for you to explain some things."

He dropped onto the couch, leaving a space between them, and sighed. His first words weren't an explanation, though, but a question. "This afternoon, when we were walking, I saw the way you looked at the women we passed. What were you feeling then, Leigh?"

She looked down at her hands for a moment, then forced herself to meet his eyes as she said, "I think you already know how I felt."

"I think I do, but I need you to tell me. I need to hear you say the words." His eyes were intent on her face, and Leigh looked down again, shrugging.

"I was jealous," she said softly. "I didn't want them to look at you. Is that what you wanted to hear, Noah?"

"It's what my ego wanted to hear," he admitted. "And in a way, in a small, petty sort of way, it even makes me feel good, because it shows you care about me. For so long, you didn't care. . . . I could have had an affair, and it wouldn't have mattered to you at all. Can you imagine how I felt, knowing that?" He frowned at her. "Do you know I actually considered that at one time, as a last, desperate ploy to force you to take an interest in me?"

"You would have had an affair?" she whispered, and he nodded. "Oh, Noah, no!"

"Oh, yes." He looked away, and Leigh had the strange feeling that he didn't want to meet her eyes. "I considered that, hoping to manipulate your feelings for me, such as they were, just as I'd manipulated you so many times before."

"But how did——"

"I'm not proud of myself, Leigh," he continued as if she hadn't spoken. "In fact, when I look at some of the things I did, I'm disgusted . . . repelled. I manipulated you, and sometimes I manipulated events, because I wanted you so badly. I never gave much thought to what you wanted or needed because I was so wrapped up in the fact that I wanted you. That was all that mattered to me. I've been self-centered and conniving, Leigh. I think you ought to know that, just as you ought to know that if the opportunity had presented itself, I probably would have had that affair. Luckily, no opportunity came my way," he added with heavy sarcasm. "But I can hardly take credit for circumstance, can I?"

"Noah, don't say that!" She didn't like to hear him say those things; she didn't want to hear them. "I can't believe you would have had an affair . . . just to . . ."

"Well, why not?" he demanded. "It wouldn't have mattered. . . ."

"Of course it would have!"

"Why?" he barked, and suddenly she was angry with him, furious.

"Why?" She jumped to her feet and stood over him, glaring fiercely. "Because you cared about *me*, that's why! You said you did all those manipulative things because you wanted me! How could you have had some other woman when you wanted me?"

"I would have been having some other woman *because* I wanted you!" He stood as well, his face dark with anger, though whether at her or at himself she didn't know. "It would have been an attempt to make *you* want *me!*"

Leigh glared. "Well, it's a hell of a stupid way to go about it!"

Noah glared back at her for a moment, then gave a harsh bark of laughter. "Don't you think I know that? All I would have been doing was hurting you, and I've hurt you so much." He sighed, his shoulders slumping. "Sometimes it seems that all I've ever done is hurt you."

"Oh, no." Leigh reached for his hand, gripping it tightly. "You've done so much more, Noah. The hurts have been little ones, in comparison. I'm glad you didn't have that affair, though. I wouldn't want to think of you with another woman when . . . when I . . ." She blushed and fell silent.

Noah shifted his hand so that he was holding hers and pulled her gently toward him. "When you what, Leigh?" he asked quietly, his gaze intent upon her face.

"When I want you for myself," she whispered with a broken laugh. "Isn't that stupid? I have no right to say that; I have no right to be possessive when I haven't even been able to give you my love. You don't belong to me, and I have no right to—"

"Do you want to give me your love?" His quiet question interrupted her, and she looked into his eyes, startled.

Slowly, very slowly, she nodded. "Yes, I do. I love you, Noah." He gazed into her eyes for an endless moment, drowning in them, and then, with an exultant laugh, he swept her into his arms, half lifting her off her feet.

"Oh, God, Leigh, I thought I'd never hear you say that," he muttered into her hair. "I've hoped and waited and prayed, but sometimes I thought I'd never hear you say that. . . ." His words were lost against her lips as he kissed her with tender reverence, a solemn declaration of love given and returned. They clung together as time flowed past unheeded, and the kisses began a metamorphosis from tenderness to long-denied passion.

All the frustration Leigh had felt all day came flooding back to overwhelm her, and this time when Noah's lips hardened in a probing demand, parting hers to deepen the kiss, to savor all the sweetness of her mouth, she answered with a passion to equal his, with no intrusive trace of fear or hesitation. Her hands moved restlessly over his shoulders, through his hair, seeking to memorize the feel of him, as her body moved sinuously, enticingly, against his. The evidence of his desire for her was obvious, but in the place of apprehension she felt excitement and a heady sense of her feminine power.

She let herself be molded to him, her hips pressed into his body, her breasts flattened against his chest as she held him, and with a low groan of surrender he lifted her into his arms to carry her to her bedroom. He laid her carefully across the bed, lowering himself to lie braced on his arms above her, then hesitated.

"I don't want you to be frightened, Leigh. Do you want me to put on the light, so that you'll know it's me?"

Leigh shook her head and reached for him. "I'll know it's you. It could never be anyone else."

"Are you absolutely sure," he asked in a husky whisper, "that this is what you want?"

"Yes." Her eyes glowed with certainty. "Oh, yes, I'm sure," she breathed, and he came down to her, enclosing her in his arms.

"If you're afraid at any time, stop me. I don't ever want to frighten you, or hurt you."

"I'm not afraid, Noah. I'm not afraid." She slid her hands up his back and locked them behind his head, her body moving against him, tempting, pleading. "Just love me, please?"

With a stifled growl he gave in, kissing her with a feverish, starving intensity, as if he would never get enough of her lips. Leigh was as hungry as he was, and as the fever grew within her she clung to him, drowning in the magic of his mouth until she had to have more. She twisted her body in his embrace in instinctive invitation, muttering wordless pleas against his lips, and with a last taste of her mouth he half lifted himself away, and his fingers moved to the first of the many tiny buttons closing her sweater.

Slowly, deliberately, pausing to kiss each newly revealed bit of her, he undid the buttons one by one, then pushed the soft cashmere off her breasts, leaving them barely covered by a brief, lacy bra. She heard his breath catch sharply; then he bent his head to brush his lips over the soft upper curves of her breasts, following the edge of the ecru lace until Leigh muttered something incoherent and clutched at his shoulders.

Gently he lifted her into a half-sitting position and slipped her sweater off her shoulders, easing it past the bandage on her arm and laying it aside. "Does your arm hurt?" he whispered, and she shook her head. He bent to kiss the point of her shoulder, trailed his mouth to her collarbone, then to the warm, scented hollow between her breasts. He slipped his fingers under the small clasp that closed her bra and opened it, sliding the satin straps off her shoulders as he found one rosy nipple with his lips, catching it, tugging lightly.

Leigh gasped in surprised pleasure, her head falling back as her body arched instinctively up to his. He shrugged out of his flannel shirt and threw it aside, then lowered her to the mattress, following to cover her body with his, their legs tangling together as their hands moved over each other eagerly.

Noah's hand moved along Leigh's waist, his fingertips slipping beneath the waistband of her jeans, and her flesh contracted at the touch, a shiver of pure excitement washing over her. He opened her belt buckle deftly and slid the zipper down, but the tight jeans defeated his first effort to remove them. He tried again, then softly said, "Damn!"

"You'll have to help me, darling," he whispered in apology. Leigh squirmed out of the offending jeans with his help, and he chuckled softly as he tossed them aside and took her in his arms again. "How did you ever get those on, anyway?"

Leigh hid her face in his neck, kissing the warm skin. "It wasn't easy," she admitted shyly, and felt him shake with laughter. "I wore them 'cause I know you like them."

"Mmm, you are right about that." He stroked a hand

down the long, smooth curve of her back and cupped her bottom, his fingers slipping over the silky fabric of her bikini panties. "I love those jeans, and I love you in those jeans. . . ." He brought his hand around, letting his fingertips slip beneath the narrow elastic and slide over the satin skin of her abdomen. ". . . But I especially love you out of them." His caressing hand moved again, and Leigh gasped helplessly, shuddering with pleasure as he led her into the mysteries of love.

She wanted to make love to him as he was making love to her, to give him as much pleasure as he was giving her, and her first shy caresses were succeeded by a sweet boldness as she felt her own power to please him. She was lost in delight, knowing nothing in the world outside Noah and herself, and when their urgent need could no longer be denied, and he moved to cover her body with his, she could only cling to him while a spiral of tension wound tighter and tighter until it burst in a paroxysm of joy so intense it left her weak.

"I didn't know it could be like that."

Long, ecstatic minutes later Leigh was held warm and safe in Noah's arms, one of his legs lying over hers. She was still shaken by little aftershocks of pleasure that gradually died away as she slid back to earth. "I never dreamed it could be like that."

Noah's arms tensed around her. "I want you to forget everything you knew about love or lovemaking," he muttered harshly into her hair. "I want you to forget everything you thought you knew about men, or marriage. I'd like to wipe out every memory you have of Tony and your marriage to him. I want you to forget all the things he did to you, the pain he caused you. I wish I could erase it as if it never happened!"

"Noah, stop." Leigh laid her fingers across his lips to still the angry words. "It's already forgotten. The past is no more than a bad dream now; it's unreal. This is the reality, here, now, with you."

"Are you sure you can put it in the past?" He brushed back her tumbled hair and kissed her brow briefly. "Are you sure it won't all come back to haunt you again?"

"I'm sure," she whispered. "I'm really sure."

"I don't ever want to hurt you, Leigh."

"You couldn't hurt me, Noah, unless you left me."

"I couldn't leave you," he muttered, his voice choked, his arms holding her almost desperately to him. "You have to know that I could never leave you." They clung together for a moment; then he chuckled deep in his chest. "You said before that I didn't belong to you, but you were wrong. I've belonged to you since that first day in the Commons, and you couldn't get rid of me if you tried."

"Well, I don't intend to try." She kissed his shoulder and then his neck. "You're stuck with me, Noah."

"Good." There was a wealth of satisfaction in the single word. He was silent and still for a few minutes; then he asked, "If I can't get rid of you, will you marry me?"

"Oh!" Leigh gasped softly and began to tremble again. She hadn't expected this, hadn't really had time to think about anything but just how badly she wanted him. This generosity, this forgiveness for her unthinking cruelty, moved her almost more than she could bear. She had to swallow tears before she could give him his answer. "Yes," she said, her voice a husky thread of sound. "Oh, yes, I'll marry you—if you still want me."

"I think you know the answer to that," he growled with a low laugh, breaking the too-taut mood, and proceeded to demonstrate just what he meant, wrapping Leigh in his arms and trapping her beneath him to kiss her breathless. Abruptly he released her and rolled out of bed to walk, naked and unembarrassed, across to the door. "Don't go away," he commanded, and disappeared into the hall.

"Where would I go?" Leigh called after him, her voice low and husky.

"You'd better not go anywhere," he told her as he returned and climbed back into bed with her. "If you did go, though, I'd come after you, and I'd find you, no matter where you went. I want you to be mine, Leigh, legally, officially, in the eyes of the law and the world. I want the world to know I love you, and I want to give this to you." He opened the small velvet box he had brought from his room and took out the engagement ring he had kept for her. "Leigh Michaels, will you take me to be your husband?"

"I will," she replied in a choked whisper, blinking back tears as he slipped the ring on her finger. "I'll be proud to be your wife, Noah."

They gazed into each other's eyes for an endless moment, and Leigh thought she would never forget the way Noah looked, his face and body dimly lit by the glow from the hall, the hard planes and angles highlighted, the shape and feel and scent of him imprinted on her body by his possession, as she knew she was imprinted on his. His eyes gleamed as he gazed at her, but she felt no shyness, only pride that she was pleasing to him, and a desire to please him once more. She reached out to him and slowly, very slowly, they moved together, tightly controlling their eagerness as they returned to each other's arms.

Leigh felt as if she were moving in slow motion, floating with Noah back into a soft nest of quilts and pillows, but as his lips met hers, their dreamlike embrace was rudely interrupted by the telephone's strident ring. They tried to ignore it, but the ringing went on and on.

Leigh sighed heavily. "It's no use, Noah. I'll have to answer it."

"Well, whoever it is, just tell them you're involved with something very important." Noah's hand moved up to cover her breast, cradling the soft globe as she reached to lift the receiver.

"Hello?" Her voice was a husky croak, and Noah began to caress the other breast. "Oh, hi, Kate. . . . No, I don't feel too bad. . . . Yes, wasn't that a great meeting? A good way to end things. No, I won't be in tomorrow; they're having someone take over my classes. Is anything going on?

Well . . ." She slanted a laughing glance at Noah, who ran his thumb across her nipple, drawing an involuntary gasp from her. "There is one little bit of news, but you probably wouldn't be interested in—Okay, okay! Don't yell at me! I'll tell you! The news is—Noah and I are getting married!"

There was a piercing shriek from the telephone, then a rapid babble. "Yes, that's what I said. . . . When?" She turned to Noah for the answer.

"Saturday," he said, and Leigh's eyes widened, but she repeated it calmly for Kate.

"Noah says we're getting married on Saturday. No, I wasn't holding out on you; I didn't know myself until about five minutes ago." She listened to Kate for a few more minutes. "Thank you, Kate. I'll tell Noah you said so. . . . Of course champagne would be nice, but not to-night, okay? I have other plans for tonight. Bye, Kate."

Gently Leigh cradled the receiver, cutting off Kate's unchecked flow of words, then lifted it again to lay it on the nightstand.

"Kate thinks this is the best news she's heard in ten years," she informed Noah, turning into his arms.

"So I gathered." His teeth gleamed in a dry grin.

"Are you serious about getting married on Saturday?" she asked him curiously.

He nodded. "Yes, dead serious."

"But that's only two days away. Can we get married that soon?"

"I'll work it out. It's Valentine's Day, and I want to get married on Valentine's Day."

"You'll work it out?"

"Mm-hm. I'm a lawyer; we're good at working things out."

"I guess I'll take your word for it. I'll have to, won't I?"

"Yes, you will." His hands began to move over her body again, exploring, seeking the spots that made magic for her. "Do you want to talk about it?"

"I don't want to talk anymore," she whispered, then shivered as Noah moved his body over hers, trapping her, making her a willing captive. "Do you?"

"Hm-mm," he murmured against the tender skin of her throat. "I have other plans."

And slowly, tenderly, he began to love her again.

MORE ROMANCE FOR
A SPECIAL WAY TO RELAX

$2.25 each

79 ☐ Hastings	105 ☐ Sinclair	131 ☐ Lee	157 ☐ Taylor
80 ☐ Douglass	106 ☐ John	132 ☐ Dailey	158 ☐ Charles
81 ☐ Thornton	107 ☐ Ross	133 ☐ Douglass	159 ☐ Camp
82 ☐ McKenna	108 ☐ Stephens	134 ☐ Ripy	160 ☐ Wisdom
83 ☐ Major	109 ☐ Beckman	135 ☐ Seger	161 ☐ Stanford
84 ☐ Stephens	110 ☐ Browning	136 ☐ Scott	162 ☐ Roberts
85 ☐ Beckman	111 ☐ Thorne	137 ☐ Parker	163 ☐ Halston
86 ☐ Halston	112 ☐ Belmont	138 ☐ Thornton	164 ☐ Ripy
87 ☐ Dixon	113 ☐ Camp	139 ☐ Halston	165 ☐ Lee
88 ☐ Saxon	114 ☐ Ripy	140 ☐ Sinclair	166 ☐ John
89 ☐ Meriwether	115 ☐ Halston	141 ☐ Saxon	167 ☐ Hurley
90 ☐ Justin	116 ☐ Roberts	142 ☐ Bergen	168 ☐ Thornton
91 ☐ Stanford	117 ☐ Converse	143 ☐ Bright	169 ☐ Beckman
92 ☐ Hamilton	118 ☐ Jackson	144 ☐ Meriwether	170 ☐ Paige
93 ☐ Lacey	119 ☐ Langan	145 ☐ Wallace	171 ☐ Gray
94 ☐ Barrie	120 ☐ Dixon	146 ☐ Thornton	172 ☐ Hamilton
95 ☐ Doyle	121 ☐ Shaw	147 ☐ Dalton	173 ☐ Belmont
96 ☐ Baxter	122 ☐ Walker	148 ☐ Gordon	174 ☐ Dixon
97 ☐ Shaw	123 ☐ Douglass	149 ☐ Claire	175 ☐ Roberts
98 ☐ Hurley	124 ☐ Mikels	150 ☐ Dailey	176 ☐ Walker
99 ☐ Dixon	125 ☐ Cates	151 ☐ Shaw	177 ☐ Howard
100 ☐ Roberts	126 ☐ Wildman	152 ☐ Adams	178 ☐ Bishop
101 ☐ Bergen	127 ☐ Taylor	153 ☐ Sinclair	179 ☐ Meriwether
102 ☐ Wallace	128 ☐ Macomber	154 ☐ Malek	180 ☐ Jackson
103 ☐ Taylor	129 ☐ Rowe	155 ☐ Lacey	181 ☐ Browning
104 ☐ Wallace	130 ☐ Carr	156 ☐ Hastings	182 ☐ Thornton

Silhouette Special Edition

$2.25 each

183 ☐ Sinclair	190 ☐ Wisdom	197 ☐ Lind	204 ☐ Eagle
184 ☐ Daniels	191 ☐ Hardy	198 ☐ Bishop	205 ☐ Browning
185 ☐ Gordon	192 ☐ Taylor	199 ☐ Roberts	206 ☐ Hamilton
186 ☐ Scott	193 ☐ John	200 ☐ Milan	207 ☐ Roszel
187 ☐ Stanford	194 ☐ Jackson	201 ☐ Dalton	208 ☐ Sinclair
188 ☐ Lacey	195 ☐ Griffin	202 ☐ Thornton	209 ☐ Ripy
189 ☐ Ripy	196 ☐ Cates	203 ☐ Parker	210 ☐ Stanford

SILHOUETTE SPECIAL EDITION, Department SE/2
1230 Avenue of the Americas
New York, NY 10020

Please send me the books I have checked above. I am enclosing $_____
(please add 75¢ to cover postage and handling. NYS and NYC residents please
add appropriate sales tax). Send check or money order—no cash or C.O.D.'s
please. Allow six weeks for delivery.

NAME _____

ADDRESS _____

CITY _____ STATE/ZIP _____

Silhouette Special Edition

Coming Next Month

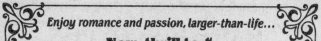